# RESTLESS DEAD

### DAVID J. GATWARD

WEIRDSTONE PUBLISHING

By
David J. Gatward

 Created with Vellum

*To Ems*

**Grimm**: nickname for a dour and forbidding individual, from Old High German grim [meaning] 'stern', 'severe'. From a Germanic personal name, Grima, [meaning] 'mask'.
(*www.ancestory.co.uk*)

It was because the place was just the same
that made your absence seem a savage force,
for under all the gentleness there came
an earthquake tremor: fountain, bird and grass
were shaken by my thinking of your name.

(*Elizabeth Jennings: Absence*)

# CHAPTER ONE

WHEN LATER ASKED WHAT HAD ACTUALLY HAPPENED TO cause the crash, all that retired Army Colonel James Fletcher could remember was the brightest of lights. It had come from ahead of them, he assumed from a car whose driver simply forgot to dip their headlights, blinding both himself and his wife, Helen. Then out of that astonishingly bright light a corner in the road had come up far too fast for Helen to react to, the vehicle had lost its grip, and as a sturdy drystone wall threw itself in their way, James had been rather surprised to find that although not his whole life, but the last few hours of it anyway, had flashed by in front of his eyes. A movie rewound for his enjoyment only.

As Monday evenings went, it had been a very pleasant one indeed, and James had very much enjoyed driving himself and his beautiful wife, Helen, over from their home in the dales, to spend the evening in a restaurant in Kendal with some old friends. It was a nice, simple way to celebrate his seventy-fifth birthday and they had both been looking forward to it for quite a while. He had seen Ruth, his daughter, and her son, Anthony, earlier in the day, and Patricia, his eldest, had promised to call. There was still time. The weather was cool and the roads clear, and the Land Rover Discovery had eaten up the miles with the ease one would expect of a vehicle that was not only brand new, but which had cost just enough to make James' eyes water. But what were investments for, if not for spending? And that old military pension really was fantastic.

On the way over, their conversation had been little more than observations about the countryside, and idle chit chat about what they were going to eat that evening. The restaurant, a wonderful little bistro called The Joshua Tree, was well known for its starter and pudding club, and that's exactly what they were looking forward to—five courses each from a truly delightful selection of sweet and savoury dishes. The wine was awfully good, too. Retirement, for sure, was something that James was really enjoying very much indeed.

Having parked up in town and enjoyed the stroll along to the bistro, James, with Helen on his arm, had entered the Bistro and been welcomed with a huge glass of the best claret he had supped for a long time. And the wine, like the conversation, had flowed easily, with stories dancing around the table, memories being brought to life through laughter and food, which, with every course, seemed to just get more and more delicious. And Helen, bless her, even though she really didn't like driving in the dark, had said that she would drive, so if he fancied getting a little tipsy, then he could.

At the end of the evening, and having said their goodbyes, James had walked Helen back to their vehicle. On the way he'd slipped off a curb, twisting his ankle just a little, and Helen had helped hold him up as he had hobbled for a while.

'We're getting too old for this,' she had laughed. 'Well, you are, that's for sure!'

Fifteen years between them didn't seem too much, not really, James had thought, but she never really let him forget it.

'You're catching up though,' he had replied. 'We're neither of us teenagers, if you hadn't noticed.'

With this particular conversation replaying in his mind, and the air now filled with the screeching of tyres and the scattering of grit, James found himself wondering just why the wall was taking such a long time to smash into the front of the vehicle. Which was when he remembered asking Helen to dance with him in the dark under a streetlamp.

'Absolutely not,' she had said, though he'd noticed the grin threatening to break through her apparent disapproval of such silliness.

'Then I'll dance on my own,' James had said, and after making a bit of a fool of himself, Helen had joined in, and together they had done a little waltz, much to the amusement of some people walking by, heading back to their own homes.

After what seemed like hours, though was clearly mere seconds, the Discovery slammed into the wall and James was aware then of a feeling of weightlessness, as the vehicle felled the wall with the ease of an elephant snapping a sapling. But the weightlessness wasn't something he'd expected and it took James a moment to realise that it was because they hadn't actually stopped moving at all but were now airborne.

Having climbed into the car, James had given Helen a somewhat lengthy talk about how to drive the car, including how to turn on the heated seats.

'I do know how to drive,' she had said. 'And I'm sure heated seats will make all the difference.'

'Yes, but this is your first time driving it,' James had said.

Helen had rolled her eyes at him, then started the engine and rolled them out of their parking space to begin the journey home, leaving the fading lights of Kendal to take the road back over the M6 and on through Sedbergh, then into the final stretch to home. Which was when, at long last, Patricia had called to wish him a happy birthday, and she had been so full of apologies, about always being busy, and there, right in the middle of the conversation with his daughter, was when it had happened.

The night had been black as oil, James had noticed, the stars not just bright but piercing, and it was when he had pointed this out to Helen that he had noticed once again, just how beautiful she was and just how lucky he was to have met her at all.

The weightlessness was now twisting, James noticed, and then things started to throw themselves around the cabin in gay abandon. Some loose change from his pocket stung his cheek, a pen shot past his eyes, and the bottle of wine he'd bought as a take-out from the restaurant hurled itself at the windscreen with such force that it shattered, covering everything in blood-red wine and thin razors of glass the deepest of green.

When the corner had come at them, it had initially seemed far off and gentle, and Helen was certainly having no trouble at all driving the Discovery. Then the cabin had filled with a light as bright as a thousand suns, or so it had seemed, particularly with the night around it being so dark, and James had covered his eyes with his hands, dropping the phone, sending Patricia's voice into the passenger footwell. Helen, on the other hand, had screamed. And the light had stayed there, blinding them both, scorching into their retinas, the driver of whatever car it was that was equipped with such ridiculously bright lights clearly unaware of the impact they were having on James and Helen. Then there the corner was, right in front of them, by which time it was all too late.

The world was a blur and James tried to lock his eyes onto something that made sense, as he gripped the armrest in the door hard enough to leave finger marks. Then they were upside down, he knew that for a fact, because it reminded him of when they had gone on one of those godawful extreme rides at some theme park or other. But the reality of it seemed so bizarre that even though what was happening was clearly catastrophic, he felt surprisingly calm. He even had time to glance over at Helen, whose face was a rictus of shock and horror.

The Discovery slammed into the ground nose first and hard enough to whip the back end up and over to have it land on all four wheels in the middle of a field facing the opposite direction.

James tasted wine and blood, and the ringing in his ears was of sirens and screaming, and the screaming was his own, his twisted, horse vocal cords ripping themselves to shreds as the shock of the moment raked its way out of him and into the night. Then a small orange light in the night waved at him for attention, but he didn't want to take any notice, because of the pain he was in and the ringing in his ears, well, that was enough to be going on with. And he needed to check on Helen as well, didn't he, to make sure that she was okay? That's what mattered most, more than anything, because she was his everything. But the light was insistent, its orange waving developing a little flicker as it grew, then the orange was joined by some red and yellow, forcing James to take notice, and there, to his horror, he saw flames dancing in front of him. And right then, he was back in combat gear, in theatre, in another upturned vehicle, blood everywhere, and he could hear screaming and rounds pinging off the armoured shell of the vehicle.

'Helen? Helen, love, come on! We need to move! The car, it's on fire! We need to get out! We need to get out now!'

Pushing away the memory of bullets and blood and terror, James shook Helen, but she wasn't responding, her head hanging, her chin against her chest, flopping unnaturally, he noticed. She would though, once they were outside and away from the vehicle, he was sure of it. The cold air would do its work and she'd wake up and they'd be happy to be alive.

With a shove, James managed to open his door, and as he ran around to the driver's side, he thought to himself how lucky they were to have been in such a vehicle, that its frame really was extraordinarily strong for them to have survived at all, and how Helen's Citroen 2CV, that idiotic little car which was no more than a metal shed on wheels, but which she loved and looked after and had even given the name, 'Betsy', would have disintegrated on impact.

Helen's door was already open, having popped open when the Discovery had flung itself into the dirt. James reached in for his wife, calling her name, unclipping her seat belt, calling her name once again, dragging her out from beneath the steering wheel, then racing them both away from the vehicle to a safe distance, just in case the fuel tank went. Which it did, just a few seconds later, shattering the night with the wrenching, ripping sound of metal and plastic giving in to the gleeful thrust of ignited fuel.

'We're okay, Love,' James said, holding his wife, the heat from the fire chasing away any cold in the night hiding around the edges of the field. 'I just need to give the police a ring, have them come out. And an ambulance.'

But Helen wasn't responding and there was something horribly floppy about the way she was just lying in his arms now, like a rag doll, a puppet with its strings cut. Then James noticed the blood and before he knew what he was doing he was trying to scoop it up, to sweep it back up into the wounds which covered his wife's body, cuts from which sprouted thick spikes of glass from the smashed bottle of wine.

'You're not dead, you can't be dead, you're not, you're not allowed to be, dear God no, you can't die, you can't! You have to stay! Please!'

James could hear himself screaming, roaring at the world to not take his wife, praying through tears for God to do something, anything, to take him instead, to just let her live, because she was the most wonderful person he had ever met, and the world needed her more than him. But the dark of the night didn't care, the flames licked high, and in that field, James witnessed the sound and the pain of his own breaking heart as he said goodbye to his beautiful, gentle wife.

# CHAPTER TWO

Harry was hunched up on a chair inside the Penny Garth Café in Hawes, at a small square table, a steaming hot mug of tea in his hand and a bacon butty in front of him ready to be devoured. Outside, the day was refusing to accept that it was time for autumn to leave, even though November was settling in and soon enough December would be impatiently knocking at the door.

The morning had started bright, with a sky of deep blue scratched here and there with thin claw marks of cloud. The air had a metallic tang to it which, after being in the dales for a good few months now, Harry recognised as the faint promise of rain. It would come eventually, he had no doubt, as Wensleydale seemed to have its own weather system. A day could begin bright and promise so much, and yet change in a moment, with thick storm fronts sweeping down the valley, or creeping over the fells, as though here was where they felt truly at home.

Harry's mind was about to drift off onto something else that was bothering him, a conversation he'd had not just with

Detective Superintendent Alice Firbank, his DSup from his life down in Bristol, but Detective Superintendent Graham Swift as well, the DSup he was working under while up in the dales. And the subject of it, about his thoughts on turning what was still a temporary position into a full-time one, was playing on his mind more and more. Then a voice pulled him back into the moment and he stared across the table at its owner, through the steam curling itself up from out of the top of his mug.

'What was that?' Harry said.

'I still can't believe it.'

'Well, you need to,' Harry replied, as his younger brother, Ben, reached out for his own butty, clutching it between slim, careful fingers, as though holding something worthy of reverence. 'You've been here a few weeks now, give or take a day or two. And if you don't mind me saying so, you seem quite happy.'

'It's flown though, hasn't it?' Ben said.

'I'm hoping that's a good thing,' Harry said.

'Back in prison,' Ben said, 'the days didn't just drag, they became one, you know? Just one long bloody day. Nothing to do but sit and stare at the walls.'

Harry replaced his mug with his butty and took a bite. He was still managing to keep up with his running, in no small thanks to the relentlessly enthusiastic, focused, and encouraging Police Constable Jenny Blades. But his diet was still a little hit and miss. And how anyone could resist a bacon butty no matter what health regime they were on, he had no idea. He'd heard rumour of meat alternatives using plant-based proteins. Sounded all a little bit too like science fiction, he thought, the kind of food eaten by people crazy or lucky enough, depending on your viewpoint, to scoot off into space and spend a few days on the International Space Station. He doubted it could ever replace real bacon.

'So, tell me what your supervisor was here for, then,' Harry said. 'He was over earlier than usual, I noticed.'

'Don't worry, it wasn't because something was wrong,' Ben explained, waving a hand in the air, as though trying to placate Harry. Not that he needed placating as such, he was just concerned. And had every right to be.

'You've got a year in total of supervised probation to get through,' Harry said. 'So, don't be surprised if I, being your older, and therefore considerably wiser, brother, am rather keen to see that you get to the end of it without any hiccups. There'll be no horseshit nonsense of any type while I'm on watch, of that you can rest assured.'

'I will, and there won't be any,' Ben replied, and Harry saw the ghost of a smile on his face. 'Oh, and its offender manager, not supervisor,' he added.

'Well, la-dee-bloody-dah,' Harry said, shaking his head, then he pointed at his brother with his butty. 'And you're right, there won't be. At all. So, come on then . . .'

Ben raised an eyebrow. 'Come on then, what?'

Harry sighed. 'What did he say? The offender supervisor manager bloke!'

Since Ben had arrived in the dales to move in with him, after being released from prison on probation, it hadn't escaped Harry's notice that Ben had already changed considerably. That was hardly a surprise, and it was difficult to see how somewhere inside the relaxed man in front of him was still the all-too-clear echo of the damaged, terrified one he'd visited in prison. But he had no doubt at all that he was, because the nightmares, though fewer now, were still there, and not a week went by where he wasn't woken by his brother's screams.

'He's pleased with my progress,' Ben said, wiping his mouth free of grease. 'Not much else to say, really.'

'And you're keeping up with your end of things?' Harry asked. 'All that paperwork and whatnot. It's important.'

'You don't need to check up on me so much,' Ben said, his bacon butty now finished. 'But yes, I am.'

'I do and I will,' Harry said. 'The prison service may have someone employed to keep an eye on you, true, but you've an extra pair of eyes on you: mine. So, you'd better accept it.'

'I'm not a teenager.'

'No, you're not,' Harry said. 'But neither are you someone who's had an easy time of it. And I'll be seeing to it that you don't put a step wrong.'

Harry saw then a darkness flicker behind his brother's eyes. And it was because of it that he was laying it on thick. Happy and relaxed though Ben seemed, he knew it wouldn't take much of a push to have him back down where he was.

Ben rose to his feet, draining his mug.

'Work?' Harry asked.

Ben gave a nod. 'I know Mike has to give me time off to see the offender manager, but I don't like to take the piss too much.'

'Or at all,' Harry said. 'And supervisor is a lot easier to say than that offender manager nonsense, don't you think?'

'They don't like the idea of us thinking we're being "supervised,"' Ben said, shooting out air quotes with his fingers around that last word. 'Even though we know we are. Apparently, it's more motivational if we have a manager, and less like still being seen as someone who's been in prison.'

'Whatever floats your boat, I suppose,' Harry said. 'It'll

probably change again in a year or so to something like offender motivator or some such bollocks.'

Ben laughed. It was a sound Harry loved and would never grow tired of.

'Sometimes,' Ben said, 'you talk and act like you're in your mid-sixties, not your mid-forties, you know that, right?'

'Old and wise before my time,' Harry said, stretching and standing up to face Ben.

Ben made to walk to the café door.

'Oi!' Harry said.

Ben stopped. 'Really? Here? Come on, Harry . . .'

'Something else you need to get used to,' Harry said, and he reached out and pulled his younger brother into a hug.

Ben groaned, not so much out of embarrassment as from having his ribcage crushed.

'Right, off you go then,' Harry said, sitting back down to finish his food and drink. 'And I'll see you back home at around six, right?'

Ben nodded and made to leave, but paused, then turned back to face his brother.

'What is it?' Harry asked. 'Something you forgot to tell me that your supervisor, sorry, I mean your manager, mentioned?'

'No, it's not that,' Ben said.

'Then what?'

'You said home,' Ben explained. 'And it's not, is it? I mean, not really.'

'It's not Bristol, no,' Harry said, then his mind was back to that conversation he'd had with Firbank and Swift, and to that decision he was going to have to make sooner rather than later. 'But would it be so bad if it was? Home, I mean.'

Ben shrugged. 'I'll see you later, Harry . . .' but he paused again.

'Are you leaving or what?' Harry asked.

'I am. It's just that, there's the other thing, you know? The thing we don't talk about?'

Harry saw a dark shadow flicker behind his brother's eyes. 'You don't need to worry about him,' he said. 'That's dealt with. It's done. Trust me.'

'You sure, Harry?' Ben said. 'I mean, Dad isn't someone who just backs off, is he?'

'I'm no longer a threat,' Harry said. 'There's plenty of others out there who are, so he's got other things to worry about now. And anyway, I've wasted too much time on him as it is. You're my priority now. You and me, Ben. Family.'

Ben gave an uncertain nod.

'If you say so.'

'I do.'

And Ben was gone.

Harry slumped back down to finish off his food then ordered another mug of tea. He had seen the team first thing that morning, and there wasn't anything urgent to be going on with, so a few extra minutes to himself seemed only fair.

As he waited for his drink, Harry thought over what Ben was on with now, and how much his brother's life had changed. And it only served to emphasise to him how important it was to keep him where they were, in Hawes, and not to head back in Bristol. Yes, it was good to have him living with him, and yes, Ben was working hard to move on from his past, even keeping down a proper job with Mike the mechanic, who had very kindly offered to take Ben on in an apprenticeship role.

The thing was, Harry was becoming increasingly sure

that the bigger part in what was happening was being played out by the place itself, by Wensleydale. He knew that if he said these thoughts out loud they would sound idiotic, and he wasn't one for seeing things where there weren't, or for that matter, attributing anything good to any kind of supposed spiritual force, but to him, there was no denying the fact that Ben was far better off up here, in the dales, than he would ever be back down in Bristol. Here, he was free of all those old influences, the old connections, the old friends. He not only had no choice but to change, he was in a place that pretty much helped him along the way. But still, his brother had a point, Harry thought; this wasn't home. Not yet, anyway. But that could soon change, couldn't it? But there were hoops to jump through first, and Harry had never been much of a fan of that. Which brought him back to that conversation he'd been having with Firbank and Swift. And as for that stuff about their godawful father? He was still wary, and would be so for a long time yet, he was sure, but that wasn't something Harry was worried about anymore.

The mug of tea arrived and Harry took a sip, the blisteringly hot liquid burning his mouth. The café door opened and Harry noticed that the air which gusted in was damp and he saw that the pavement outside was wet.

'Thought I'd find you here.'

Harry looked up into Detective Sergeant Matt Dinsdale's face, which he was attempting to wipe dry with his large hands.

'Raining, then?' Harry asked, as Matt sat down in front of him.

'No,' Matt replied, flicking water from his hands onto the floor. 'I just throw water over myself now and then for fun, and sometimes, if I'm feeling really crazy, I throw myself in the beck. How's Ben?'

'Good,' Harry replied. 'How's the rest of the team?'

'Busy,' Matt said. 'Liz is manning the office, Jen's down dale at something or other. I think a couple of kids have done a runner from school or something, so she's best for that.'

'You didn't fancy having to chase after teenagers, then.' Harry smiled.

'Always good to let the younger ones have a go,' Matt said. 'Doing her a favour I think.'

'Anything else on that RTA?' Harry asked, remembering Matt's update earlier that morning.

Matt shook his head. 'Terrible thing, that,' he said. 'As you know, Gordy is out there this morning, chatting to the family. Don't know what I'd do if I lost Joan.'

'It was headlights caused it, you said?'

'Looks that way.' Matt nodded. 'Halogen bulbs on some of these new cars now are proper bright, like. I've been near blinded by them myself. And if it was a 4x4 with a rack of lights on a roll cage or across the bumper, then it's like someone's switched on the sun.'

'No chance of finding the driver of the other car, I suppose?' Harry asked.

'Can't see how,' Matt said. 'No dashcam on the car, and no cameras or anything else along that road. And I dare say the driver just didn't realise their lights were on full beam and drove on, no idea of what had happened at all.'

'Tyre marks on the road?'

Matt shook his head. 'Like I said, I doubt the other driver even noticed.'

For a moment, the two men sat in silence, until Matt

broke it, saying, 'Mike tells me Ben's doing fine, by the way. And you know why he took him on, don't you?'

Harry gave a nod. 'Did time himself, apparently. No idea what for, mind.'

'Doesn't talk about it, that's why,' Matt said. 'And if he ever wants you to know, he'll tell you himself.'

'It's a good thing he's done,' Harry said, asking then if Matt wanted a mug of tea himself. 'Ben seems to be getting on well enough.'

Matt refused the tea, which surprised Harry immensely. 'And yet,' Matt said, 'using my not inconsiderable powers of deduction, I detect an air of concern.'

'Me too, having just heard you mutter that sentence,' Harry said.

'Well, what is it?' Matt asked.

'It's nothing,' Harry said.

Matt leaned forward. 'You sure about that, Boss?'

Harry wondered then about talking things through with Matt. He was a colleague, yes, but as was the way with the whole of the team, it seemed, he had also become a friend. Which had taken Harry rather by surprise, as he'd never really been one for having friends at all. He'd known plenty of people he could regard as acquaintances, yes, but that was about it. And he'd had good mates in the Paras, but friends? People he could share things with? Never. He was pretty sure that he was the problem himself. It didn't help being the kind of person who generally regarded people as a collective pack of bastards, and who was, in the main, fairly happy and content with his own company.

Matt was still staring at him, expectation in his eyes.

Harry leaned forward, ready to say what was on his

mind, when once again the door to the café opened and there, blocking the wind, was Police Constable Jadyn Okri.

'Let me guess,' Matt said, turning to the PC, 'you've left your lunch money at home.'

'You're a funny man,' Jadyn said.

'I am that,' Matt replied. 'Among other things, but I doubt we've got the time to talk about my dashing good looks, swashbuckling approach to life, and thirst for justice.'

'Well, anyway, it's not that,' Jadyn said, and Harry could see that Matt's reply had only served to confuse Jadyn. 'I mean, that's not why I'm here, though it's funny you should say it, because I did leave my wallet at home and—'

Harry rubbed his eyes wearily. 'Get to the point, Constable. Please.'

'It's Jim,' Jadyn said.

'What is?' Harry asked, he and Matt now alert to whatever it was Jadyn was here to tell them.

'He seemed fine this morning,' Matt said. 'Obviously, I expected him to be a bit hungover, really, seeing as he'd been out with an old mate of his from back at school, so that was a little disappointing. I mean, what's the point of a reunion if you don't have to recover from it?'

'Has Fly run off?' Harry asked, shocked then by how bothered he was at the thought that Jim's dog could be missing, because it was just a dog, and he'd never really been into dogs or pets of any kind. But Fly? Well, Fly was different.

'Well, it's not Jim, as such,' Jadyn said. 'It's his dad. I mean, it's not him either like, except that it is, but it's the sheep mainly, and—'

'Good grief, lad, what's wrong with you?' Matt said, then he slapped a hand down hard on the table. 'Spit it out! Come on!'

'They've had fifty go missing,' Jadyn said. 'Nicked.'

'You what?' Harry said.

'Jim's dad found one of their barns empty this morning,' Jadyn explained. 'He collapsed, probably from the shock of it. Jim's on his way over there now to sort things out, see what's been going on.'

Harry paid up and was out the door so quickly, with Matt and Jadyn at his heels, that it wasn't until he was halfway back along the marketplace that he realised he hadn't even finished his bacon butty.

# CHAPTER THREE

The speed at which Matt raced them out of Hawes and then on and up through Burtersett had Harry hanging on to the handle above the passenger door, the bones of his knuckles threatening to break through his skin. The rain was fairly coming down now, crashing into the windscreen as though the road was lined with people just lobbing buckets of water at them, and the wipers were working full pelt to just keep it clear.

'Nice to see that you're taking the road conditions into consideration,' Harry observed, as they zipped past the old Methodist chapel on their right, then up and round the left-hand bend in the lane, then on towards Jim's farm.

'I know the roads, we're fine,' Matt said, his eyes staring hard through the now-awful weather. 'Anyway, this isn't proper rain, is it? Nowt but a shower!'

An ambulance swept past them going the other direction, spraying them with a thick, grey wave of water, its edges laced with diamonds. Hard to believe the day had started so bright and sunny, Harry thought.

'Well, I'd rather not get to know them too personally,' Harry said.

Matt hung a left, then immediately after, drifted them just a little sideways into the farmyard on their left, past the house Jim had grown up in, which he still shared with his parents.

'Nicely driven, Sarge,' Jadyn said. 'Learn to drive on the bumper cars, did you?'

Harry was up and out of the car in a beat, Matt and Jadyn following close behind, the rain crashing down to ping off the roof of Matt's car like jumping beans, the farmyard an explosion of tiny crowns of dirty water as the drops slammed down into new and rapidly growing puddles.

'Over here, Boss!'

Harry looked over to the house to see Jim at the back door, waving at them through the rain. Fly was at his feet. As Harry jogged over the dog raced to meet him, ignoring Jim's calls for it to stay. Harry dropped to his heels as Fly skidded into him, his teeth bared in what they had all started to refer to as Fly's Happy Face, flipping over onto his back and into a puddle, his tummy to the sky. Harry gave it a rub, then stood up and quickly closed the distance to Jim, Fly at his heels, ducking inside out of the rain.

'So, what have we got, then?' he asked. 'How's your dad? What happened?'

'He's okay,' Jim said. 'He's away to the hospital now, over in Northallerton. You just missed the ambulance.'

'So that was your dad, then?' Harry said.

'Mum's with him,' Jim said. 'He's fine, I'm sure. Tough old sod, he is. Didn't like that we were all making such a fuss. Good luck to them getting him to stay overnight if he needs to.'

Matt and Jadyn were with Harry now and Jim led the three of them into the house. It was the first time Harry had ever been inside, and it, like the rest of the farm he'd seen on the way in, told him that when it came to farming, Jim's parents were the kind of people who liked things just so. Outside in the yard, the tractors and other machinery he had seen were parked away nicely under shelter, the barns and other outbuildings all in good repair. In the small field adjacent to the yard, a haybarn stood, its contents stacked neat and dry. In the house, that same sense of order prevailed and as they walked through the hall and into the kitchen, Harry saw nothing out of place. Even the small number of pictures on the wall, which comprised of either prints of views of the dales, or photographs of Jim at various stages of his life, were, Harry was sure, dead level. He also noticed on the walls, both in the hall and the kitchen, numerous rosettes and certificates, and whatever they were for, they were clearly held onto and regarded with pride.

'Right then, I'll be mother and get the kettle on,' Matt said, striding across the kitchen and over to the sink. 'Because, as we all know, a decent brew solves most of life's problems and helps you think clearly. Jim, get yourself sat down and fill us in on what's been going on.'

'There's cake in the cupboard, just above the toaster,' Jim said. 'Mum made it last week.'

'Homemade cake?' Matt said. 'Seriously? Does she take orders?'

Jim laughed. 'I'll ask,' he said. 'I'm sure she would, for you anyway.'

Harry sat down at the large, worn kitchen table which took up most of the central area of the kitchen. Jadyn joined him.

The room was warm, Harry noticed, and he put this down to the fact that instead of a normal cooker, a huge Aga was standing proud against one wall. Fly was already curled up in a basket in front of it.

'Come on then, Jim,' Harry said. 'Have yourself a seat and tell us exactly what's happened.'

Jim sat down and Harry saw that despite the smile the young PCSO had greeted them with, there was a weariness in his eyes. But there was something else there, too, Harry thought, a steely look which told him that anger was bubbling just beneath the surface. He understood that completely. Dealing with crime when it happened to others was one thing, but when it sneaks through your own front door to do its worst to you and yours? Well, that was something entirely different.

Matt came over with mugs of tea all round and some of Jim's mum's cake, which Harry saw was a sponge covered in light brown icing.

'It's a coffee cake,' Jim said, reaching for a piece himself. 'It's my favourite and absolutely bloody delicious!'

Harry reached for a piece and took a bite and discovered that Jim wasn't lying. 'That's amazing!'

'Mum's a pretty excellent cook,' Jim said with a nod. 'She does this millionaire's shortbread that's so sweet, I swear that after a slice of it, you can feel the sugar at the back of your eyeballs.'

'Details then, Jim,' Harry said. 'And I don't mean about your mum's amazing baking.'

'Oh, I don't know,' said Matt. 'Could be useful.'

'Right,' Jim said, brushing away a few crumbs and ignoring Matt. 'First off, I've no idea what time they came, or anything like that.' He leant forward, his elbows on the table, hands clasped together just in front of his mug. 'I was out last night with Neil.'

'Your old school mate, right?' Harry asked, and Jim gave a nod.

'Neil Hogg, or Hoggy as we call him. Not seen him in a few years. He's been away for a good while, like, so it was good to catch up. Anyway, I was out till closing time, walked back across the fields—there's a nice little footpath from Hawes to Burtersett—and this morning, Dad went out like usual, but not early, which isn't like him. And he wasn't even up when I left for work, so I should've known something was wrong with him then, but he doesn't like a fuss, like I've said, so I didn't think anything of it, and I suppose when he found what had happened, down in the barn—'

Harry held up a hand and said, 'Jim, you're running away with yourself. How's about you slow down a bit?'

'Am I?' Jim asked, lifting his mug then setting it down again without taking a sip. 'Sorry. It's just, you know, I should've noticed, shouldn't I?'

Harry watched Jim look down at his dog, Fly, and pat it on the head. 'Your dad is usually out early then?'

'I don't think he's even been in bed past six in the morning,' Jim said. 'Not once in his life. Thinks he's wasted the best part of the day otherwise. When I was a kid? He would just walk into my room, pull open the curtains, heave open the window to let fresh air in, and that was that!'

'What time does he usually get up, then?' Jadyn asked.

'Five, five-thirty-ish?' Jim said.

'Five-thirty?' Jadyn said. 'Who the hell gets up at five-thirty? Oh, that's right, no one! Is he mad?'

'No, he's a farmer,' Jim said.

'Though the two are quite similar,' Matt said.

'True.' Jim smiled, then explained, 'There's always a job to do, something that needs checking over. The sheep are out all winter, like, not up on the tops, but down in the lower fields, closer to the farm. Dad had them in the barn to give them a check over. They've all been tupped, and his flock is a prize winner, you see, so he's a bit more careful than some I suppose. They're all Swaledales. Beautiful they are. Blackfaces, the lot of them. His pride and joy. Envy of a lot of other farmers up and down dale, that's for sure.'

'Tupped?' Harry asked.

'Tups are the ones who get all the action,' Matt said. 'Quite the life they lead, if you ask me. Must be exhausting though.'

'I know nowt about sheep farming,' Harry said. 'Or any farming for that matter.'

Matt laughed. 'I'm keeping a tally, you know, of how many times you say nowt over the next month.'

'Oh, are you?' Harry said.

'I am,' Matt nodded. 'And if you get to a certain number, we'll know for sure that the dales have really got into your blood.'

'And what's this certain number, then?' Harry asked.

'Oh, well, now that would be telling, like, wouldn't it?'

'Back to you, Jim,' Harry said. 'You were, I think, giving me a very quick lesson in sheep farming. And you said something about other folk envying your dad's flock?'

'The ewes are the females,' Jim explained. 'Tups are the males we don't castrate, instead, keeping them on to breed from. And dad's been working on this flock of his for years now. Proper special, they are. And yes, there are a few out there who wish they had my dad's flock. But most haven't got the passion and drive he has to see it through, to put years into it.'

'So, you don't think someone out there would be jealous enough to come and have one over on your dad by taking them, do you?'

Jim laughed at this as though it was the daftest thing he had ever heard.

'Not a chance!' he said. 'There's a friendly rivalry, yes, but that's all.'

'So, what happens, then, to the ones you castrate?' Harry asked, knowing the answer, but for some reason needing to hear it as well, just to make sure.

'We eat them,' Jim said. 'Well, not only us, as in my mum and dad and me scoffing our way through the flock, but the general public. What did you think lamb was, then?'

'Can't say I've ever given it much thought, if I'm honest,' Harry said. 'Like most people, I'm sure. Anyway, back to your dad finding them gone.'

'Like I said,' Jim continued, 'Dad wasn't up when I left for work. Mum says he was feeling a bit rough and she tried to get him to take it easy, but as soon as he was up he was out. And that was around nine-thirty I think. Proper late for him, that's for sure.'

'And that's when he found them gone?' Matt asked.

'Not right away, no,' Jim said. 'He likes to do things a certain way, so he does his usual walk around. Chickens first, most times, has a little chat with them and a shout at Tom.'

'Tom?' Jadyn asked. 'Who's he when he's at home? Does your dad employ a farm labourer?'

'The cockerel,' Jim said.

Harry laughed hard. 'Your dad named the cockerel Tom?'

'After Tom Jones,' explained Jim, 'on account of him being so bloody loud. Though dad reckons the cockerel would give Tom a run for his money.'

Harry smiled at that.

'After the chickens, he checks the yard,' Jim continued, 'and usually takes a broom with him and a bag, to sweep up a bit, pick up any rubbish that blows off the roads and the fells. You'll be amazed at the crap we find out and about. Then he's away over to the sheep, if we've got them down off the fell. He knows every single one of them. And that's when he found them gone.'

'What did he do?' Harry asked.

'Nowt other than have some kind of funny turn,' Jim said. 'Mum went looking for him, having expected him back, and she found him flat out on the barn floor, like he'd been thumped.'

'The shock must have been pretty bad,' Matt suggested. 'What did the paramedics say?'

'Not much.' Jim shrugged. 'I don't think it was a stroke or anything, but it's still a worry, isn't it? I mean, you think your parents'll live forever, don't you? Then something like this happens, and suddenly there they are, all old and vulnerable and you're in the position of carer.'

Harry noticed a crack in Jim's voice and made a note to himself to keep an eye on him for a while. If he needed time from work to keep an eye on his dad, then as far as Harry was concerned, the team would work around it. He couldn't see any of them complaining, more than likely, the complete opposite.

'Yeah, it was the shock, I think,' Jim said, agreeing with Matt. 'That flock, it's his life and soul, like. They're everything to him.' He paused, took a sip of his tea. 'And now some thieving bastards have come in and—'

Jim's voice crumbled then, the crack Harry had just heard splitting deep in an instant, as the emotion of that morning, of what had happened, finally caught up with him.

Harry reached over and put a hand on Jim's shoulder, giving it just enough of a squeeze to let him know it was okay to be angry and upset and to not know exactly how to deal with it. Tears were fine, too, and Harry wasn't going to have anyone on his team think otherwise. He'd been in situations back in the Paras, where the pressure, the terror, had bubbled up not just out of those fighting with him, but himself. Bottling things up did no one any good.

'Right then, we need to take a look,' Harry said, pushing himself to his feet. Jim made to rise as well, but Harry kept him in his seat with his hand still on the PCSO's shoulder, adding just enough pressure to make his point clear. 'You give yourself a few minutes, Jim,' he said. 'It's the barn I saw just down at the far end of the yard, right?'

'Yeah, that's the one,' Jim said.

Harry glanced over to Matt, who said nothing, and just returned a knowing nod. 'Jadyn?'

The police constable shot to his feet.

'Boss?'

'We'll go and have a little look-see around the place,' Harry said. 'Just need to grab some evidence bags and PPE from the car on the way.'

'I'll go grab all that now,' Jadyn said. 'Keys, Sarge?'

Matt lobbed his keys at Jadyn who snatched them out of the air. 'But don't you go rummaging around in there,' he said. 'My wallet's in the glove compartment, so you just leave that well alone.'

'You really don't trust me, do you?' Jadyn said.

'Not one bit of it,' Matt said, a smile just turning the corner of his mouth. 'Would you?'

'No, probably not.' Jadyn smiled, then left the kitchen and Harry made to follow.

'When will you hear from the hospital?' Harry asked, pausing at the kitchen door.

'Can't say that I know for sure,' Jim replied. 'Mum's not exactly great with texting. She either forgets how to unlock her phone, so you don't hear from her for hours on end, sometimes days, or messages are pinging up at you every five minutes with updates about what she's doing, what she's cooking for tea, how dad is, if there's weather coming in over the top. And she really doesn't understand emojis. Honestly, the number of times I've been sent an angry face after telling her I'm on my way home!'

'Well, as soon as you do, you let us know,' Harry said, then added, 'and if you need to go over, then you just let me know.'

'Oh, that won't be necessary,' Jim said. 'Dad's fine with Mum, I'm sure.'

Harry walked over to stare down at Jim. 'It's not just about whether he's fine,' he said. 'Family comes first. And your mum will need you as much as anything. And you'll need them. Understood?'

'Yes, Boss,' Jim said.

'Good,' Harry replied, then turned and left the kitchen, to follow Jadyn back out into the day.

## CHAPTER FOUR

RUTH STARED ACROSS THE KITCHEN TABLE AT HER OLD dad, desperately trying to think of something to say, her own grief threatening to crush her into a breathless mess. The visit from that police officer, Detective Inspector Haig, a female no less, earlier that morning had helped a little, and both herself and her dad had been impressed by what she'd said, the help and support offered.

'We're not just here to arrest people, you know,' she had said, her softly lilting Scottish accent a brief moment of light and joy in an otherwise dark day. 'We're here to help. And, if you don't mind me saying so, we're actually rather good at it, too.'

Glancing down at the card Detective Inspector Haig had left with them, Ruth then leaned forward to say something to her dad, but the words crumbled to dust and ash in her mouth. She reached a hand over towards her dad's own, which were clenched in front of him, resting it just on top of his thumbs. His skin was cold and taut, and she could feel the awful tension in him, a spring coiled so tight that, if and when it finally broke, she feared it would snap his sanity in two.

'Dad?'

The old man didn't even register her voice, his head down, eyes staring into nothing. At his side was a stick, one he'd cut himself from the woodland outside, to help him get around, what with his leg aching a little from the accident. He'd been checked over and there was, quite amazingly, nothing really wrong with him, except for some bruising and lacerations. Strong old ox, he was.

'Do you fancy a cup of tea?' Ruth asked. 'There's some of that chai stuff you like.'

'No, I'm good, thanks,' her dad replied, but he still didn't look up to face her. 'How's Anthony?'

'Oh, he's fine,' Ruth said, forcing a smile onto her face to make her answer to the question about her son more convincing.

'He's a lovely lad, you know,' James said. 'A gentle soul I think.'

*A bit too gentle*, Ruth thought, but knowing that this was not the time to talk about her son, about the bullying, and how she knew that at some point, the school would be asking questions about all the supposed headaches, the absences. But what was she supposed to do? She couldn't exactly force him to go in, could she? And neither would she. And with what had just happened, well, if Anthony needed time at home, then so be it. She had her dad to deal with as well as her own grief, so everything else would have to take a back seat.

With her legs and backside numb from sitting so long on a hard chair, and the shock of what had happened to her mother still as raw as it was surreal and impossible to take in or accept, Ruth pushed herself to her feet, her muscles aching so much it was almost as though the grief had penetrated every part of her body, squeezed her dad's hands, then walked over to fill the kettle from the sink. Looking through a window, she rested her eyes, weary from tears, on the garden, which stretched out from the back of the house. Woods sat to the right, hiding behind them the stepped falls of Cotter Force. Beyond that, lay the ancient valley of Cotterdale, the slopes of Black Hill Moss rising in a sleepy incline to the sky, with Great Shunner Fell hidden far off and behind, a resting giant of a hill.

Ruth, broken inside in so many ways now, felt a tug of the wildness just beyond the glass and wondered what it would be like to just walk off into it, drenched in her overwhelming sadness. Would the raging torrent of loss be swept away by the deepness of what was out there, the moorlands and becks and the skeletal remains of mines? Or would even that breath-taking wilderness be unable to drown out the wrenching screams inside her head, her heart calling out for her mum to come back, to come home, to tell her it was all just a mistake, a misunderstanding, that it was all okay now?

As the kettle came to a boil, a cry raced up out of her and Ruth jolted forwards, her hands thumping down on the granite worktop her mum had been so happy to have installed, along with the kitchen, barely two years ago now. She raised a hand to her mouth as if it would ever be enough to hold back the anguish that, right there and then, Ruth simply didn't see that there would ever be an escape from. Because how could there be? Her mum was gone and she would never see her again, hear her voice, her laugh, ask her advice, or answer when she called her name. It was as though she had found herself at the bottom of a waterfall, and the weight and the cold of the grief was crashing down into her from above, taking away her breath, drowning her.

'Ruthy . . .'

Ruth wiped her eyes, dug deep to find the shredded remnants of her brave face, and turned to face her dad.

'I can't live without her,' James said. 'I can't. I don't know how. And I . . . I don't want to, Ruthy.'

'None of us do, Dad!' Ruth snapped back, her words curdled by her cry. 'I'm . . . I'm sorry, Dad. I didn't mean . . .'

Ruth had nothing to say that would make her old dad feel any better, nothing to give, no well deep enough inside her from which to draw. But what he had just said, well, that was frightening. She picked up the card left by the police officer.

'There's help,' she said. 'Professional help. Remember? I'll give this number a call later, okay? Might be good for all of us, perhaps.'

'Let's just see,' James said. 'And don't worry, I'm not saying I'm going to do anything stupid, I promise. You know that, don't you?'

Ruth forced a smile. 'Promise me that you won't.'

'I promise,' James said. 'Really, I do.'

Ruth heard the words but wasn't sure that she could see enough conviction in her father's eyes. She would have to keep an eye on him, definitely give the police a call later, just in case. Though part of her wondered if she would ever be done with looking after him. Even with Mum around, that was what she'd done, wasn't it? It was why she was still there. And sometimes it was a little too much. It wasn't even that he needed caring for, just that it was the way things had always been. But then dark thoughts swirled, dragging her into a mean place of cold, where she was free of his demands, even though they really weren't that onerous, and like a stab from a jagged spear, the harshest of thoughts tore through her mind, that this would be easier to deal with if it had been Dad, not Mum.

Pushing the terrible thoughts down as deep as she dared, Ruth held up a mug and asked, 'You sure you don't want one?'

'Go on, then,' James said.

Ruth made two large mugs of tea, half wishing that if she left them to brew for long enough, she would never have to face the reality of what had happened outside of the simple act of making a hot drink.

'Here,' she said, sitting down eventually and passing her dad a mug of tea. 'Biscuit?'

James shook his head and for the next couple of minutes, the two of them just sat there, staring at their drinks, lost to their own emptiness.

'The light, it was so bloody bright,' James said eventually. 'She couldn't see. Neither of us could. It was blinding.'

'It can be like that,' Ruth said. 'The headlights on some cars, they're dangerous.'

'Maybe, though, if I'd been driving . . .'

'No, now don't go down that road,' Ruth said, although inside she was thinking the same. 'What-ifs won't help anyone, will they?'

'It was her first time driving that car, though, wasn't it?' James said.

'It wouldn't have made any difference, Dad,' Ruth said, though she noticed then, as the words fell from her like tasteless scraps of food, that a darkness inside her had her wondering. It was a new vehicle after all. Big, too. Why hadn't her dad been driving? Why had he not just let her have a few drinks instead of himself? She shook her head then, to dislodge the thought, but it didn't work. 'Don't start trying to blame yourself in this,' she continued, hoping her voice would drown out her unhealthy thoughts. 'You can't. It wasn't your fault. At all. It wasn't anyone's fault. It was an accident. A terrible, awful, horrible accident.'

James sipped his tea, Ruth did the same, but she noticed no taste to it, as though the loss of her mum had now tainted everything around her, turned even water to dust and ash. Nothing would be the same ever again, would it? she thought. Colours would never sing to her as they once had, not even the rich and endlessly varied greens of the dales, which had always managed to breathe life into her, even on the darkest of days. But no day had ever been as dark as this.

'Do you think there's an afterlife?'

The question took Ruth by surprise and she choked a little on her drink.

'Pardon?'

'Heaven,' James said. 'You know, some place where we all go to after we die. Do you think there is one, up there, or wherever?'

Ruth stared at her father as he raised his eyes a little as though looking heavenward.

'I really don't know,' she said, a little taken aback to be asked such a deeply personal question about belief and spirituality by a person she'd known to never hold much truck with anything spiritual beyond a good measure of whisky. 'Can't say I've thought about it much, to be honest.'

'But do you think there is?' James asked pressing for an answer. 'Or could be? Do you think your mother's there now, looking down on us?'

Ruth took another sip, to give her time to think of a reply that wouldn't be trite.

'Well, I don't see how we can just end,' she said finally. 'That just doesn't seem right, really. Impossible almost. And I'd like to think that we go on, somehow. It seems only fair, doesn't it? Otherwise, what's the point?'

James nodded, sipped his tea. 'What's the point indeed,' he said.

Silence descended again, but James didn't let it last too long this time. 'I prayed, you know?' he said, his voice quiet and soft. 'After the crash, in the field, holding your mum in my arms, I prayed. I begged for God to help, to save her, to save Helen, and to take me instead, but he didn't.'

'She was gone, Dad,' Ruth said. 'There was nothing anyone could do.'

'Not even God?' James replied. 'Then what's the point of being God if you can't even do what I asked, what I prayed for, with all my heart and soul?'

Ruth shrugged, because she had nothing that she could say that would help and was worried that anything she managed to say would only make things worse. And talking about whether God would kill her dad to save her mum was, she was fairly sure, something that would only make things worse.

'Anyway, I don't think she can be gone, not completely,' James said. 'Because I can feel her, inside me still, in this house, everywhere.'

'Me too,' Ruth said.

'So, you don't think it sounds weird, then?'

'No, not at all,' Ruth said, and she genuinely meant it. 'She loved this house. She poured her heart and soul into turning it into a home, didn't she?'

'I've tried to talk to her,' James continued, his voice quieter now, Ruth noticed, almost conspiratorial. 'Just to ask if she's okay, if she's in pain, or if everything's okay. And I've told her that I love her as well.'

'That's nice, Dad,' Ruth said with a gentle nod and soft smile. 'And I'm sure that if she's out there, somewhere, then she's smiling down on you, on all of us actually, asking us to not be too sad, to remember how wonderful she was, and what a great life she had.'

'It was cut short though, Ruthy,' James said, the words a hammer slamming down on an anvil.

'I know it was,' Ruth replied, her mind whispering, *and it wouldn't have been if you'd been driving, would it, Dad?* And the sound of those dark thoughts frightened her more than a little, because she knew that they were wrong, that it wasn't her dad's fault, but they were so hard to dislodge, like they were strangers who had pushed themselves in through the cracks opened up by the darkness now inside her where her mum had once been.

'I've asked for proof actually,' James said. 'That she's out there. From her, I mean, from Helen.'

At this, Ruth couldn't help keeping the shock from her voice. 'You've what?'

'Because if she is,' James continued, almost as though he hadn't heard Ruth's interruption, 'then she has to be able to show me, don't you think? I mean, I know I've not seen the ghost that supposedly haunts this old house, none of us have, but others have, right? Previous owners? So, why shouldn't I be able to see Helen? Why shouldn't she be able to come and see me, just to let me know it's okay? Does that make sense, Ruthy? Does it? I'm not sure it does. I'm worried I sound mad. But I'm not. I'm sure I'm not.'

No, it doesn't sound mad at all, Ruth thought, it sounded completely insane. Desperate then to say to her dad, 'you're a retired army colonel, the most no-nonsense person I've ever known in my entire life, and here you are, just a few hours after the tragic death of your wife, talking about trying to see her ghost?' But she didn't. It just didn't seem fair. Because she knew that grief did different things to different people and that everyone coped with it and dealt with it in their own way. And perhaps this was Dad's, as surprising as it seemed to her right then. Maybe it was because he felt responsible, to blame even. And that little voice inside her called out then, just loud enough for her to hear, that he was.

'I don't think anything makes sense right now,' Ruth eventually said, doing her best to ignore her internal dialogue. 'And I don't think anything will for a very long time.'

'No, neither do I,' James agreed. 'But do you see what I mean? What I'm saying? I don't want to sound crazy, because I'm not, I'm really not. I just need to know that she's alright, wherever she is. That's all. That's all I want, all I'm asking for right now.'

'What about giving the minister a call?' Ruth suggested, half because she wanted to stop her dad from talking the way he was, but also because it might genuinely help. 'He's already been in touch anyway, after he heard. And he's popping over later, isn't he? So, might be worth talking things through then, maybe?'

'Rawlings, you mean?' James said. 'That young Methodist minister chap? I don't know . . .'

'It might help,' Ruth said. 'Just to have someone else to talk it through with. This kind of stuff is all part of the job for him, I'm sure. He's trained for it. It's what he does for a living.'

'I'm not sure it would help,' James sighed. 'I don't want people to think—'

'Think what?' Ruth said. 'That you're suffering after Mum's death? That you don't know how to deal with it? What's wrong with any of that? It's normal, Dad! I feel it, too. Anyway, we'll need to speak to him . . .' Ruth paused, the next words ones she could hardly bear to mutter. '. . . to sort out . . . the funeral.'

'And you say he's coming out later on today?' James said.

Ruth gave a nod over her mug of tea.

'Perhaps I will, then,' James said. 'It can't do any harm, can it?'

'No,' Ruth said. 'It really can't, Dad.' Then, as she took another sip of tea, she said, 'Pat said that she'll be here as soon as she can tomorrow, once Dan has finished whatever project or contract he's on with right now. Oh, and I'll be heading off later as I'm on night shift over at the care home.'

'They're coming, then?' James said. 'Well, that's something. It'll be good to see them.'

Would it though, Ruth thought, because when had Pat and Dan ever visited unless they wanted something? But she said, 'They are, yes,' recalling the brief phone call she'd had with Pat, declining to say anything further about her somewhat distant older sister.

'They don't need to,' James said. 'But it is nice of them to come.'

'Well, you know what Pat's like,' Ruth said. 'She's not one for taking no for an answer once she's decided to do something.'

'I'll be fine, though,' James said. 'Just need some time, that's all. We all do. And you're next door, aren't you? So, I'm okay, really.'

Yes, I am, Ruth thought, which is where I've always been. But she said, 'You're not okay, Dad. And none of us will be, not unless we lean on each other for a while.'

Tea finished, and with a few jobs to do before she headed off to work that afternoon, Ruth pushed herself to her feet, the aches still there, in every bit of her, inside and out.

'Thanks,' James said. 'And I'm pleased you're here, you know. I know I'm lucky to have you so close, you and Anthony, and I've always appreciated it. And for what it's worth, I don't know what I'd do if you weren't. And I'll always look after you, you know that, don't you? Even when I'm gone. You've done so much.'

'I'd have come over regardless,' Ruth said. 'That, and the fact that Anthony and I live next door is beside the point.'

'Thanks, anyway,' James said, then he added, 'I'll be out in my shed if you want me for anything.'

Ruth wasn't so sure that was a good idea. 'It's a bit cold for that, isn't it, Dad?'

'I'll get the stove going,' James explained. 'Get it all nice and cosy. Just like your mum used to like it when she'd come over and fall asleep in that chair with a book on her lap.'

Ruth left her father to himself in the kitchen and headed on into the house. The place seemed so silent and empty, as though the absence of her mum was enough to make the walls turn even the smallest of sounds into the meanest, coldest of echoes. Then she was outside, having not made the conscious decision to find some fresh air, but glad that she had.

She walked away from the house, heading down the lawn at the front, towards the road. When she turned back to stare up at it, the overly grand dwelling glared back, as though conscious of its broken shell and that Ruth's pain was a mirror to its own.

Ruth's eyes swept left, to where a large gap sat between the main house and what was now a smaller cottage, the one she and her teenage son, Anthony, lived in. Seeing the gap, and the thick shadows which hung inside it like vast blankets of darkness on an invisible washing line, she thought back to what her dad had said, about the ghost that had caused the then owners, many, many years ago now, to have that section pulled down, turning a once-grand place into the two houses it was today. True or not, the tale of death breaking a home quite literally in two, spoke to her in that moment. And as she stared up at that empty, gloom-filled space, her own brokenness came at her in the shape of a million memories of her mother.

Her tears flowed then, even though she was sure she had no more to cry, and she let them fall, wrapping herself up in a blanket of sorrow, wishing, like her father, that the ghost of her mother would come to her and tell her that everything was going to be okay.

# CHAPTER FIVE

Back outside, Harry breathed in the day good and deep. The rain had subsided and the air was now somehow even more alive than ever. He thought back to Bristol, how the air there had its own distinctiveness; a city it was, but London it most definitely wasn't. His memory brought back the air of the place, rich in a way that was filled with scents and tastes designed to make you want to stop and eat. Cafes and bars and restaurants sent out inviting aromas to dance together along the streets, twisting themselves around passers-by, tempting them to stop, to sit, to feast. And rather too often, Harry recalled, he had done exactly that.

Dales' air, though, well that was another thing entirely. Yes, there was a clear and present danger of walking through Hawes marketplace to trip up on thin tendrils of taste drifting from cafes and bakeries. And Harry had succumbed often. However, it was what came blowing off the hills that now had him, and he paused just for a moment to enjoy it, as it whipped around him as cool as the water of a lagoon in deep shade, and heady with scents of grass and fern and herb.

'You alright, Boss?'

Harry saw Jadyn staring at him from over where Matt had parked the car, though 'parked' was probably far too polite a way to describe how the detective sergeant had skidded the thing to a halt in a spray of grit and water.

'And why wouldn't I be?' Harry asked.

'Well, you look . . .' Jadyn began, but then he paused.

'I look what?'

'It's nothing,' Jadyn said, then held up the PPE from the car. 'Shall we go?'

'We will,' Harry said, 'but first, you'll finish what you were going to say.'

'Relaxed,' Jadyn said, suddenly blurting the word out. 'Peaceful, even. And you don't usually look like that. Not ever, if I'm honest, almost like you can't, I mean—'

Harry watched with amusement as Jadyn's eyes grew wide with horror at his own words.

'No, I mean, you look fine,' Jadyn said. 'I didn't mean like the, you know, the scarring was . . . oh, crap . . .'

Harry smiled. 'There's a shovel over there against that wall if you want to try and dig yourself a bigger hole.'

'Sorry, Boss,' Jadyn said, walking over to Harry. 'Didn't mean to sound like such a pillock.'

Harry took the PPE Jadyn had in his hand.

'Can't see that there's anything to apologise for,' Harry said. 'A face like mine could curdle milk, I reckon.'

Jadyn laughed then.

'Yeah, you're not wrong!' he said, then once again the horror came back into his eyes. 'Oh, God, sorry, Boss, I don't know what's wrong with me! My mouth just runs away with itself sometimes, and then my feet catch up and throw themselves in there good and proper. I'm sorry.'

Harry stared at the police constable just long enough, then winked. 'Come on,' he said. 'Let's have a look around.'

As they made to head off, the sound of an approaching car had them pause. Harry turned back to the entrance to see a smart looking metallic blue BMW pull in.

'Who's this, then?' Jadyn said.

The car stilled, fell quiet, and from the driver's side emerged a young man, around the same age as Jim, Harry guessed, dressed smart casual, more town than country, sunglasses on as well, regardless of the fact that summer was all but a distant memory. He had a cigarette lit and in his mouth.

'Is Jim in?' the young man called over, removing the cigarette then dropping it to the ground and grinding it into the dirt.

'And you are?' Harry asked, walking forwards to put himself between this new arrival and Jim's house.

'Hoggy,' the young man said. 'Neil Hogg, Jim's mate. Is he in? He texted earlier, told me what had happened, and I came over as soon as I could.'

It took a moment for Harry to realise who he was talking to.

'Oh, right, you're who he was out with last night, right? Old school friend, yes?'

'That's me,' Neil said, reaching a hand out to Harry as the back door opened and Jim appeared.

'Now then, Hoggy,' Jim said, calling over. 'You didn't have to bother coming over, you know.'

'Yes I did,' Neil replied. 'I know there's nowt I can do, but still, I felt that I'd best come over, just in case.'

Harry watched Neil walk over to Jim and give the PCSO a manly hug, then they both headed into the house. That done, Harry turned back to Jadyn.

'Right, where were we, then?' he asked.

'About to have a look around the farm I think,' Jadyn said.

Harry walked away from the house, on the way stopping to pick up the cigarette stub left by Jim's friend, Neil. It wasn't something he'd usually do, go around cleaning up after others, it had just struck him as a little disrespectful.

Just as Harry had expected on seeing the farm when they'd driven in, and on having been inside the house, the yard and its buildings was a place of careful order. There was clearly a place for everything, and everything was very much in its place.

'So, what do you know about farming, then?' Harry asked as they walked through the yard and down to the barn.

'Not much at all,' Jadyn said. 'Probably less than you.'

'That's saying something.'

'I'm a Bradford lad,' Jadyn said. 'Closest I got as a kid to farming was buying milk.'

'So, why are you here, then?' Harry asked.

'Used to come up here on holiday a lot with my family,' Jadyn said. 'Not one for holidays abroad, my parents, not that they wouldn't like to, it's just a simple case of economics. You know, those kinds of holidays cost a lot of money and they haven't got much to be splashing about. Always liked the place, because it's pretty special, isn't it? So, when the opportunity came up to get placed up here, I took it. Thought I'd broaden my experience, if you know what I mean. I know the city well, like. Up here is different.'

'I'm impressed,' Harry said. 'My experience of new

constables, in which I include myself, is that it's all about being in the city, right in the thick of it.'

'Rural police work has that, too,' Jadyn explained. 'And I needed to get out, you know, see the world a bit?'

Harry smiled to himself then, at the idea that Jadyn thought going to work in the dales qualified as seeing the world. But then, why shouldn't it? In many ways, he would've been hard-pressed to find anywhere more different to Bradford, or any other major town or city for that matter, than the dales.

'This is the barn, then,' Harry said, walking up to a metal gate to look inside. 'Notice anything?'

Jadyn stood beside Harry and peered in.

'No sheep?'

'It's always best to start with the obvious,' Harry smiled. 'And that covers something which should be here, but isn't.'

'What about forensics?' Jadyn asked. 'Shouldn't we be calling them in?'

'That's what we're here to decide,' Harry said. 'Right now, it's hard to say if we need to call in the Scene of Crime team, and I don't want to be dragging them over here if there's bugger all to see. And even if we do, this is hardly going to be high on their priority list, is it, an empty barn and some missing sheep?'

'We called them CSI in Bradford,' Jadyn said. 'The SOC team, I mean.'

'Well, it's the same thing, just a sexier name, that's all,' Harry said. 'And it'll be a while, I think, before it takes over completely.' He opened the gate. 'After you.'

Jadyn walked into the barn and Harry followed, noticing how the air changed from the fresh, crisp outdoor smell, to one richer, deeper, more earthy.

Once inside, Harry paused, Jadyn coming to a stop at his side. The barn, like the farm, was ordered and clean. The floor was covered in straw, with feeding and water troughs dotted about. Around the walls of the barn were dotted wire cages filled with hay. The smell of it in the air grew stronger the further in they walked, mixing with the tang of lanolin from the fleeces of the sheep filling the space beneath the roof overhead.

'So,' Harry asked, rubbing his chin thoughtfully, 'how does someone empty a barn like this of sheep, then? And manage to do it without anyone noticing?'

'No idea,' Jadyn said. 'And how many were there?'

'Jim said fifty,' Harry said. 'So, it's not like someone just decided to pop in and throw a couple into the back of a trailer and sod off, is it?'

'No,' Jadyn agreed. 'This was an organised job. They knew what they were doing. Reminds me of a gang we dealt with in Bradford that could clear a street of its cars in under fifteen minutes. They had all these drivers who were experts at breaking into cars. They'd just choose a street, turn up together early morning, then all break into a car at the same time and drive off without waking a soul. Amazing, really. You can't help but admire something like that. I mean, I'm not condoning it, but you know what I mean, right?'

As Jadyn was talking, Harry knew that what was worrying him the most, and had been from the moment he'd heard just how many sheep had been taken, was that the only way to do it, the only people capable of pulling something like this off at all, was a well-organised gang, and probably one that had done it before. Because if it was organised, then there was every chance that what they were dealing with wasn't just a one-off, but a larger operation, something involving manpower and money and criminal connections that Harry was pretty sure the dales wasn't exactly prepared for.

'Right, you go that way and I'll go round over here,' Harry said, gesturing with a wave of his hand for Jadyn to walk on down the right-hand side of the barn.

'And what am I looking for exactly?' Jadyn asked.

'Anything that shouldn't be there and is, and the opposite of that,' Harry said. 'Anything that should be, but isn't.'

'Knew you'd say that,' Jadyn said.

'Then why ask?'

As Jadyn headed off, Harry took himself in a wide sweep down the left side of the barn, scanning the ground. But all he saw was straw and sheep droppings and tufts of wool. And by the time he met with Jadyn at the far end, the only sign he had that the sheep had been taken was simply that they weren't there anymore. And that wasn't exactly much to go on.

Harry leaned on a gate, staring out across the fields at the back of the barn.

'Looks like they just drove in and took them,' Jadyn said. 'That's ballsy, isn't it? Coming in across the yard like that. Must've been pretty confident that Jim and his mum and dad weren't going to bother them.'

'Hmm,' Harry said.

'What's that mean?' Jadyn asked.

'Either they were confident that they weren't going to be discovered,' Harry said, 'or they weren't actually bothered if they were. And I don't know which I find more worrying.'

'Why?'

Harry turned to face Jadyn.

'Imagine you're a burglar,' Harry said.

'Why?'

'Because I said so,' Harry said. 'Now, say that you're off to rob a huge house, right? Lots of nice stuff inside, jewellery, that kind of thing. And you've sorted out the alarm, so that's not a problem.'

Harry stopped talking and stared at Jadyn.

'Do I need to ask why you've got your eyes closed?'

'You said imagine you're a burglar,' Jadyn said. 'So, I am. Imagining.'

'And you need your eyes closed to do that, do you?'

'I do,' Jadyn said.

Harry took a deep breath, shaking his head.

'Right, so, as I was saying, you're a burglar, you're at this big posh house, so what's going to make you confident about possibly disturbing someone?'

'You mean there's someone in the house?'

'I do,' Harry said.

'And I'm breaking in?'

'You are.'

Harry watched as Jadyn screwed his face up a little, the thoughts of his mind playing themselves out in the lines dancing around his face.

'I'd be armed,' Jadyn said.

'Exactly,' said Harry. 'And you can open your eyes now,' he added.

Jadyn did as Harry instructed.

'But you don't get armed gangs in the dales,' Jadyn said.

'You can get them anywhere,' Harry said. 'If there's easy money to be made, then take it from me, there are people out there willing to do anything to get it.'

'But an armed gang, though,' Jadyn said. 'That's a bit of a leap, isn't it?'

Harry had to agree, but he didn't do so out loud and instead continued to stare out over the fields. They stretched out before them, once again demonstrating in their quiet beauty just how many shades of green there were in the world. The grey drystone walls held fast the pasture, locking the beauty in and refusing to let it go, as they had done for centuries past. Across the pasture, tracks led from the barn and out to other fields, their scars on the ground eventually fading to nothing. Except that wasn't quite true, Harry noticed.

'Jadyn?'

'Boss?'

Harry pointed out across the field.

'Those tracks look different to you at all?'

Jadyn turned to look where Harry was pointing.

'Those ones leading down the hill? Yeah, a bit, I suppose,' he said. 'Fresher, maybe?'

'It's not only that though,' Harry said, and pointed at the ground just in front of where they were standing. 'See all these other tyre marks? They head off, right, to other fields, yes, but those tracks, not only do they look fresh, they just keep on going, don't they? Right on down the hill. But where to, though?'

Jadyn gave a nod. 'You're right,' he said. 'What are you thinking?'

'I don't know quite yet,' Harry said, and before Jadyn could say anymore, Harry was through the gate and following the tracks across the fields and away from the farm.

# CHAPTER SIX

It wasn't that Patricia didn't want or need to visit her father, because she really truly did, more than ever actually. And yes it was absolutely bloody awful that her mum, Helen, had been killed, hugely upsetting actually, because death was, wasn't it? And she was upset, of course, she was, but really she just didn't have the time or the space in her life or her mind to be dealing with it all right now. But what choice did she have? It wasn't that she was being heartless and cold, just pragmatic, practical, and she was right in the middle of putting together the final stages of the launch of her next new business venture, this one as a freelance accountant and consultant, and that was where her energy really needed to be focused. Not in sorting this other thing out, not when she'd worked so hard to get everything else sorted.

Sometimes, life really did send things her way to try her, she thought. Why couldn't it all just go to plan? But, as her husband Dan had pointed out, she could pretty much launch and run the business from anywhere couldn't she, and wasn't that the point, anyway? He had also helped her to realise that the only real reason she needed to visit was because it was her duty to do so, and that would do just fine. Also, they could do with a break, which was a little rich coming from him, she had thought, as he'd never really bonded as such with her parents, but he had a point. Not that what they were driving into now was in any way a holiday as such, but her parents' house really was quite something, and a couple of months in the dales would probably do them both the world of good, wouldn't it? It would also help take her mind off her last venture, which had gone south rapidly, and perhaps this visit would help her solve it. Something certainly needed to.

'At least there's plenty of room at the old place,' Dan said, pulling off the motorway to head on towards their destination, a tractor towing a huge trailer immediately in their way. 'Your dad will appreciate having you around, I'm sure of it. And for this to happen on his birthday, too. Well, it's just awful.'

Patricia wasn't really listening, her laptop out on her lap, and the Wi-Fi dongle immediately losing signal as hills started to rise about them, as though the earth was alive now and swelling up on each side to close in and consume them, the road itself dropping down a steep twisty slope.

'Well, there's no way I'll be able to do any work now until we get there,' she said, shutting her laptop with a huff. 'Not unless I want to end up being travel sick. And as we both know, I don't do well at being sick at all. And I'm tired.'

'The travel sickness tablets not working?' Dan asked.

'They're working fine at the moment,' Patricia snapped back. 'But these roads are just terrible.'

Resting her head in her hand as she leaned on the window, Patricia felt a squeeze at her knee from Dan.

'You've not said much,' Dan said, his eyes on the road. 'About your mum, about what happened, I mean.'

'Well, what's there to say, really?' Patricia replied. 'She's dead, isn't she? And it's absolutely bloody awful and tragic and terrible, yes, but I just don't have the time to be upset, not right now. I really don't. I'll deal with it in my own time, in my own way.'

'Well, perhaps you need to make time?' Dan suggested. 'You'll have to anyway, once we get there. Your dad will need you. So will Ruth. That's why we're going, remember? Well, that and the fact that it'll give us a chance to get to know the place a little better. Think what we could do with it!'

'This was your idea,' Patricia said. 'Not mine. And I'm not sure it's entirely appropriate to be going around measuring up for new curtains quite yet, do you?'

Dan laughed. 'And just how was this my idea, then?'

Patricia shook her head. 'You suggested it.'

'I absolutely did not,' Dan replied. 'Maybe we both sort of suggested it together? How's that sound to you?'

'You said how Dad would need me, and here we are, rushing off up there.'

'I pointed out the obvious,' Dan said. 'That's not the same as saying we should do something. And anyway, you went off in a huff and the next thing I know, you're in the kitchen with your bags packed. But it's a good idea for a lot of reasons.'

'A month away from home, though? What were you thinking? It seems somewhat excessive. You're not usually this keen to go away.'

'It isn't, not really,' Dan said.

'This new business of mine,' Patricia continued, 'it's important, not just because it has to work, but because we've invested in it.'

'Yes, I have,' Dan said, and Patricia caught not just the emphasis but the change from plural to singular, but said nothing. 'And it will all be fine, I'm sure. As to the time, well, that's what I've got between now and the next contract. I can nip back to check on the house as and when. Aren't we better off using this time to help out? You would only be travelling up here every weekend anyway.'

'Not every weekend.' Patricia sighed.

What Dan was saying made sense, though, to visit.

'Let me know if you want me to drive,' Patricia said. 'You've been away the last two days and you got back late last night.'

'You've been busy yourself,' Dan said. 'Just had to tie a few things up. All sorted now. And I'm fine. Have we got any of those boiled sweets in the glove compartment?'

'Ruth is there anyway,' Patricia said, finding the tin of sweets and offering them to Dan. 'I'm sure she's doing fine looking after him.'

'You need to look after each other,' Dan said, popping a sweet into his mouth. 'Because that's what families are supposed to do.'

Patricia went to say something, but Dan hadn't finished.

'And you'll need Ruth and your dad as much as they'll need you,' he said. 'That hard exterior will need to let something through if you're going to deal with this properly and grieve.'

At this, Patricia's eyes widened and she snapped round to stare at Dan.

'Hard exterior?' she said. 'I'm not a cold-hearted bitch, you know!'

'I know that,' said Dan, holding up a hand as though to fend Patricia off, 'but you do have that tough protective layer that you wear so well. And at times like this, you need to take it off. It's good for business, but not necessarily for the rest of your life.'

'Rich coming from the person who's already talking about what to do with the house that isn't even ours yet and may well never be,' Patricia said. 'Anyway, I don't know what you mean. I'm delightful.'

'You know exactly what I mean,' Dan replied, and once again squeezed her leg. 'Just relax a little, that's all I'm asking. Oh, and it's okay to cry, in case you were wondering.'

Patricia shook her head. She couldn't remember the last time she had cried, or the last time that Dan had been so full of empathy, never mind for people who he'd never really found much in common with. And, when she had taken the call from Ruth the night before, and they had spoken about what had happened, she had known that tears were there, somewhere behind her eyes, but that's where she'd made sure they stayed. Because tears were no use, really.

'Going quiet on me isn't proving to me that you've heard a word I've said,' Dan said.

'How long is it until we're there?' Patricia asked, glancing out through the window, the scenery bringing back memories, making her want to close her eyes to it. 'I could do with a nap.'

Dan checked the clock in the dash of the car, a Jaguar F-TYPE, in classic racing green livery. It was a thing of beauty and he really did love it, she knew that, and sometimes suspected that it was a toss-up as to which of them he would rather be inside. 'Twenty minutes,' he said.

'Well, that should give me just enough time to warm up, don't you think?'

The words were jokey, but the sentiment wasn't, and Patricia turned away from Dan to stare out of the window. On the other side of the glass, the day was grey, matching how she felt inside, and the green of the fells and fields seemed to her to be muted rather than vibrant, the low cloud above dousing the landscape in an almost tangibly depressing mood.

As Dan drove on, the car taking the miles with ease, Patricia yawned, but couldn't sleep. She spotted so many barns that she knew would just make the most perfectly wonderful little country escapes. She wondered why people weren't snapping them up for conversion, why their owners weren't taking advantage of what was, to her, a very obvious way to make some quick, easy money. Dan had done a few himself and that's what he had been on with this last while, sorting out another deal or whatever, not that he ever told her the details, but that was for the best, because it was really rather dull.

She saw another barn, just wallowing in decrepitude, and in it, she saw the seed of what had sent her away from the dales in the first place all those years ago. It was the lack of vision that the people had, at least that's how she saw it. They were all just so damned happy to simply stay where they were, instead of heading out into the world, to venture beyond the invisible boundaries they seemed to think existed around the dales. She'd never understood it. Never would. Or why her younger sister liked it.

'When was it you moved here?' Dan asked, as the road

cut its way along a valley bottom, their progress observed only by the occasional field of sheep. 'I can't quite remember.'

'I was thirteen,' Patricia said. 'Dad was still in the army, but he wanted to have some roots, so he bought the house with various investments and whatnot.'

'He was still away, then?'

'He managed to secure a permanent placement over in Catterick, a training position, I think it was,' Patricia said.

'Well, that must have been nice,' said Dan. 'After all that moving around.'

'I guess,' said Patricia. 'For him and Mum, anyway. And Ruth.'

'Not you, then?'

Patricia shook her head. 'It's hard to make friends at thirteen,' she said. 'I never really settled. Couldn't wait to leave. And I was never really as close to our parents as Ruth, you know how it is.'

'Is that why you don't come back that often, then?'

'I'm busy, you know that,' Patricia said.

'Indeed, I do,' said Dan, then pointed ahead. 'Looks like we're here, then. How's that warming up coming along?'

'Ha ha,' Patricia said as Dan slowed down then pulled left off the road and rolled them up the track to the rear of the house.

They passed the smaller house first.

'How long has Ruth lived here now?' Dan asked, eventually bringing the car to a stop.

'Too long if you ask me,' Patricia said. 'Why on earth she doesn't want to get away from the place, I'll never understand.'

'Perhaps she likes it,' Dan suggested.

'Yes, I'm sure that she does,' Patricia replied, unclipping

her seatbelt. 'The low rent and beautiful surroundings must be difficult things to consider leaving behind. Always in Daddy's good books, the favourite.'

'That's not so fair now, is it?' Dan said, opening his door. 'The divorce was rough, regardless of how many years ago it was, and she's basically brought Anthony up on her own. And I'm pretty sure that she pays a fair rent to your dad.'

'Oh, you're pretty sure, are you?' Patricia said. 'And what are you basing that presumption on?'

Dan was out of the car now and swept the door closed behind him. Patricia did the same, though she heaved the door shut with considerably more force. Then a voice caught her attention and there, walking towards her, she saw Ruth.

'Dear God, what is she wearing,' Patricia muttered to herself, but she saw that Dan had heard by the look he shot her way.

'Ruth,' Patricia said, breaking away from the stare her husband was giving her, with a disarmingly bright smile. 'How are you? How's Dad?'

Then Ruth burst into tears and fell into her arms and Patricia, despite everything Dan and she had talked about on the journey over, immediately wished that she was anywhere else but here. But home was where she had to be, for now.

# CHAPTER SEVEN

'So, sheep rustling is actually a thing, then?'

Ben's question sat in front of Harry as he reached over to take a good helping of the tomato pasta he'd made for dinner. It was now a couple of days since he had been out on Jim's farm and forensics hadn't turned up much of use other than to confirm that yes, indeed, sheep had been stolen, most likely by a well-organised gang, the members of which parked up on the road below the farm, drove up through the fields, did the deed, then shoved off before anyone was the wiser. If the sheep were, as he suspected, intended for the meat black market, then he just couldn't see that there was much that could be done to recover them. It was not an outcome that he was happy with at all. And he knew that the impact on Jim's parents would be dramatic. Jim himself was also beating himself up about it, sure that if he hadn't been out, then he'd have been back home and would have heard something. Harry had pointed out that with an organised gang, Jim and his mum and dad were very lucky that they hadn't heard anything and gone to investigate. Because likely as not, the gang would have dealt with them swiftly and violently.

'Harry?'

Ben's voice stabbed at Harry's thoughts.

'Yes? What?'

'Sheep rustling?' Ben said.

'What about it?' Harry answered, staring down at his plate which was piled perhaps a little too high, but he was hungry, so he wasn't about to put any back.

'You okay?' Ben asked. 'You drifted off there for a moment.'

'Yes, I'm fine,' Harry said, forcing himself to look alert.

'Then what do they do with the sheep?' Ben asked. 'Once they've nicked them, I mean. They can't be worth that much, can they? I mean, a sheep is just a sheep. It's not like a car or jewellery or money, is it?'

Harry took a gulp from a glass of water at his side. 'Nick fifty of them and sell their meat on the black market? Yeah, they're worth a fair bit,' Harry said. 'Happens all over the country.'

'Don't they have to be killed in a proper place, though?' Ben asked. 'You know, an abattoir or something?'

'Can't see the kinds of people who think it's fine to steal sheep being too fussed about the ins and outs of killing them,' Harry said. 'Which is half the problem with illegal meat. No traceability. Could've been killed in some rotten old shed for all anyone who ends up eating it knows.'

'But fifty sheep, though,' said Ben. 'Surely that's not easy to do?'

'You'd be surprised just how easy it is to do and to get away with a lot of things,' Harry said. 'How's the pasta?'

'Fine,' Ben said. 'But you do know it's possible to cook things other than pasta, don't you?'

'I do,' Harry said.

'And I don't mean a pie in the oven or whatever. I mean proper cooking.'

Harry rested his fork on his plate and stared over at his brother. 'So, let's get this right then,' he said. 'My younger brother, who's currently on probation after a stretch in prison, and has thus not exactly been munching on restaurant-quality food, is now deciding to tell me to vary the menu a little?'

Ben leant back in his chair. 'I'm just saying that I think we could mix it up a bit. And I like cooking. Love it, actually.'

'Do you now?'

'I do.' Ben nodded. 'It won't be anything too fancy, but how about tomorrow evening I cook something?'

'Like what, exactly?' Harry asked, then watched as Ben paraded before him a face of deep thought and consideration, as he shuffled through the obviously extensive collection of recipes he held in his head.

'How does spaghetti bolognese sound?' Ben said.

Harry laughed. 'And that's your idea of mixing it up, is it? Mince and pasta, instead of what we're eating right now?'

'I worked in the kitchens, inside I mean,' Ben said. 'I know the recipe. It's easy.'

'But that would be a recipe for a few hundred blokes,' Harry said. 'There's only two of us.'

'I'll adjust the amounts. What do you say?'

Harry shrugged. 'Sounds good to me. So long as you promise that there'll be none of that grated cheese nonsense on top.'

'Still don't like it, then?'

Harry paused at this, because here was another way that the dales had changed him. He hadn't exactly fallen in love with cheese, and he wasn't about to start investing in a weekly cheese board. But the whole cheese and cake thing? Well, that was something that he'd moved on from reacting to with abject horror, through just about being able to stomach it, to almost appreciating the bizarre combination.

Harry was about to try and vocalise his ongoing love-hate relationship with cheese, when his phone rang.

'Grimm,' he answered.

'Boss, it's Dinsdale,' came Matt's voice from the other end of the line. 'Busy?'

'Depends,' Harry said.

'On what?'

'On whether what you're about to ask me to do involves me getting no sleep and then spending tomorrow drinking so much coffee that I end up being able to literally hear time.'

'We've had a call in from over at Black Moss House,' Matt said.

'That supposed to mean something to me?' Harry asked.

'Belongs to James Fletcher,' Matt said.

The name jogged Harry's memory.

'The accident?'

'That's the one,' Matt said. 'I don't think he's doing so well, if I'm honest.'

'So, why the call?'

There was a pause at the end of the line.

'Matt?' Harry said.

'He's called in, saying that there's someone in the garden,' Matt said.

'An intruder?' Harry said. 'So, why do you need me? Isn't Liz available?'

'She's over Aysgarth way,' Matt said. 'Some idiots messing around down at the falls or something. And Jim's with his mum and dad still.'

'You're still not telling me everything, are you?' Harry pressed, putting his cutlery down.

'It's the intruder, you see,' said Matt. 'James thinks . . .'

'Thinks what?'

Harry heard Matt suck in a deep breath.

'He thinks he saw his wife, or someone who looked like her, anyway.'

'But she's dead!' Harry said.

'Exactly.'


HALF AN HOUR LATER, Harry was driving up the track to the back of Black Moss House. He'd been looking forward to an evening of doing very little indeed, perhaps a game of cards with Ben, some TV, then an early night. Life, it was clear, had other plans, as it always seemed to. He also had that other thing to think on as well, the whole moving-up-north-for-good thing, and time was running short on that, and he really needed to discuss it with Detective Superintendent Firbank, and Swift as well, but there was still time. Not much, but enough. The job application didn't have to be in for a couple of days, and that was plenty long enough.

'Sorry about this, Boss,' Matt said, greeting Harry as he climbed out of his car.

'Not your fault,' Harry said. 'Can't see us being out here too long anyway, can you?'

'Shouldn't think so,' Matt agreed. 'I just thought it best we come out, if only to reassure James, see how he is, like.'

'How many days is it now since the accident?' Harry

asked as they walked over to the main door, hearing the concern in Matt's voice.

'That was Monday evening,' Matt said and knocked at the door. 'Three nights, then.'

'And he, this Mr Fletcher, I mean, he thinks that he saw his wife in the garden?'

Matt said, 'Well, someone who looked like his wife at any rate, like I said. Which is why I thought it best we both come over. I know we would, anyway, seeing as it's an intruder he's reported, but if he's thinking it's his wife, then it'll give us a chance to check he's okay, that kind of thing. Dealing with what happened to his wife, well, I've seen what it can do to folk.'

Harry glanced over at Matt, a quizzical look on his face. 'Isn't that going a bit further than what the police are supposed to do?' he asked.

'My view,' Matt said, 'is that there's quite the difference between what we're supposed to do and what we should do. Don't think there's ever anything wrong in us going that little bit further now and again.'

'Neither do I,' Harry agreed as the door opened and a striking face, all angles and narrow eyes, stared back, hair black as oil hanging down onto her shoulders.

'So, he called you then, did he? I tried to dissuade him, but he really wouldn't listen.'

'I'm Detective Sergeant Dinsdale,' Matt said, introducing himself to the woman in front of them. 'This is Detective Chief Inspector Grimm. Usually, one of our PCSOs would be out to see you, but you know how it is in the dales; everyone mucks in!'

The woman was obviously listening to Matt but was staring at Harry.

'Can we come in, please?' Harry asked, keen to avoid a conversation about the scarring on his face. It didn't bother him, it was just a little tedious having to explain it every time someone asked about it.

'Yes, of course,' the woman said, then held out a hand. 'I'm Patricia Hurst, James' daughter. I'm sorry, but I'm sure this is a complete waste of your time.'

'No such thing,' Harry said, attempting a smile. 'Well, there is, but I doubt this is it.'

Patricia stepped back into the house, gesturing to Harry for him and Matt to follow her inside.

'As I said, I tried to persuade him not to call you,' Patricia said. 'He's really not been himself at all since the accident. Which I know is hardly a surprise, is it? But still, calling the police? It's just not necessary, is it? You have other things to be dealing with, not the hallucinations of a grieving old man who's probably had rather too much to drink.'

'I heard that, Pat,' said another voice, as an older man now approached them from down the hall, stepping through patches of light splashed across the walls and floor from various lamps, as though using them as stepping stones. He was leaning on a stick, too, Harry noticed.

'Mr Fletcher?' Harry said.

The man reached out a hand and Harry reciprocated, shaking it firmly. 'James, please,' he said. 'It's kind of you to come out. And I'm not drunk, and I know what I saw. I'm not making it up.'

Harry said, 'First of all, I, and Detective Sergeant Dinsdale here, would like to offer you our deepest condolences. What happened, well, it was really terrible. And if there's anything we can do to help, you let us know.'

'Thank you,' James said. 'Yes, it's been an awful week so

far, I must say. I should have been the one driving, you know. It's terrible, really.'

'Well, perhaps it's best if we can sit down and have a chat somewhere?' Harry said. 'Detective Sergeant Dinsdale here will go for a walk around the property while we do, just in case whoever it is that you saw is still out there.'

'Well, that's not likely, is it?' Patricia said, her voice barely audible.

'Right, I'll be back in a few minutes,' Matt said and headed back out into the night.

'A chat then,' James said. 'I'll put the kettle on.'

'No, I'll do that, Dad,' Patricia said. 'Why don't you go through to the lounge? It's much more comfortable through there.'

'If you insist,' James said.

'I do,' Patricia replied, then turned on her heels.

'She means well,' said James, leading Harry deeper into the house. 'But she can be a little spiky, if you know what I mean.'

In the lounge, Harry waited for James to sit before he did so himself, then gave the man some time to gather himself. It didn't strike him as entirely sensitive to start questioning straight away, not after what had happened earlier in the week. However, as the silence in the room grew, Harry decided it was probably best to at least break the ice and get some form of conversation going. And from that, hopefully, Mr Fletcher would tell him what he had seen that had caused him to call the police.

Harry said, 'I understand you're a retired colonel.'

'Army through and through,' James said. 'Saw a lot of changes, out in theatre a few times, ended up running the whole training of new recruits thing. Yourself?'

'Paras,' Harry said. 'Good times.'

'They were that.' James smiled.

'Nice place you've got here,' Harry said, gazing at the room they were now sitting in. In many ways, it was much like any other lounge, with sofas and a fireplace and cupboards, with photos and paintings decorating the walls, but it was the window that drew Harry's attention. It was the largest he'd ever seen outside of a stately home. Split into three clear sections, the glazing stretched up to the high ceiling, providing, he was sure, a quite spectacular view of the countryside beyond on a clear day.

'We were very lucky to be able to afford it,' James said. 'Helen, she loved it here. The garden was hers, really. I didn't have much to do with it. Though I've got into growing vegetables now that I'm retired, which is rather fun. Flowers, though? All that pretty stuff? I haven't a clue.'

'I grow a bit of my own, too,' Matt said, coming into the room to join them.

'Find anything?' Harry asked, knowing what Matt's answer was going to be.

'Well, if there was someone out there, then they've shoved off,' Matt said. 'I had a good look around, like, and I noticed that there's a footpath runs out back, am I right? Not on your land, but across the fields?'

'That's true,' James said. 'And the Pennine Way is out there, too.'

'Could've been a hiker,' Matt suggested. 'Out on a night walk or something.'

Harry looked at James and saw that there was no response to what Matt had said.

Matt sat down next to Harry. 'The garden's wonderful, Mr Fletcher. Would love to see it during the day. Always struck me as a waste of a garden to not use it to grow some-thing you could eat.'

At this, Harry saw James sparkle just a little.

'Gives you a great excuse to have a shed as well, doesn't it?' James said. 'I never really saw the attraction, probably because I was always too busy, but when I got one, I sort of fell in love with it.'

'It's the smells I love,' Matt said. 'That mix of compost and fresh air and oil for the mower, that kind of thing.'

'I've a little stove in mine,' James said.

'A stove? I'm jealous!' Matt said.

Harry could see that Matt very much was. He was begin-ning to wonder if the only reason they had been called out at all was so that Mr Fletcher could talk to Matt about gardening and sheds.

'Gets really cosy,' James said. 'Lovely place for a nap! Helen loved it in there, too, you know. Had her own chair. I think her book is still there, the one she was reading before . . .'

'So, this intruder, then,' Harry said, keen to keep James focussed.

James was about to answer when the door to the lounge opened and Patricia walked in carrying a tray with a teapot, cups, and a plate of biscuits. Placing it down on a coffee table, she proceeded to pour.

'I'll let you add your own milk and sugar,' she said. 'People can be so particular about how they take it, can't they?'

As Harry leaned over to add milk to his tea, a little nervous about handling the dainty and clearly very fragile and expensive tea set, he became aware of another presence behind him. He turned round to see another man standing in the doorway. He was probably around five foot ten, Harry guessed, and had the narrow bearing of a man with either a ferocious metabolism or a stressful life. Perhaps both.

'Daniel Hurst,' the man said, introducing himself with a broad smile. 'Patricia's husband. Call me Dan, though. Kind of you to come out. Though, like Patricia, I don't think it was really necessary.'

'Not kind at all,' Harry said. 'A report of an intruder has to be taken seriously.'

'Even an imaginary one?' Patricia said, standing up.

Harry didn't need any of his detective experience to sense the unease in the room.

'I didn't imagine it,' James said. 'I saw her, out there on the lawn! Why won't anyone believe me?'

'Because it sounds crazy, that's why!' Patricia said. 'And to phone the police . . . What were you thinking?'

Harry stood up, if only to draw attention to something else other than the argument that was clearly brewing.

'So, Mr Fletcher,' he said, 'James . . . Perhaps you could tell us what it was, exactly, that you saw?'

At this, James stared hard at Patricia, then eased back into his seat.

'It was my wife, Detective,' James said, turning his attention back to Harry. 'I'm sure of it. And there's nothing anyone one can do or say to convince me otherwise.'

## CHAPTER EIGHT

'Probably best if you start from the beginning,' Harry said.

'You're not seriously going to listen to this, are you?' Patricia huffed. 'He's tired, he's upset, we all are, but this, what he said he saw, it's not real, is it? And we shouldn't be encouraging it either.'

'Your dad says he saw something,' Dan said, stepping round to his wife, and Harry heard just the faintest of tension in the man's voice. 'Whatever it was, we have to give him a chance to explain, don't we?'

'Well, I'm not going to stand around and listen to it!' Patricia said, then with a sharp turn, whipped away from her husband's side and strode out of the room.'

'Apologies about that,' Dan said.

'Don't be,' Harry said. 'I understand that this has been a pretty terrible week for the whole family. So, it's fine, I promise you.'

'If you don't mind, I'll go and see how she is,' Dan said.

Harry gave a nod and watched the man leave. Then he

rested his gaze back on James. 'So, in your own time, if that's okay. There's no rush here. You just tell us what you saw and we'll see what we've got.'

James Fletcher stood up, then walked over to the large bay windows, staring out into the thick darkness beyond.

'I know that everyone thinks I'm mad,' he said, 'and I understand that, but I'm telling you, it was Helen.'

'Where, exactly?' Harry asked.

'Probably easier if I show you,' James said. 'Come on.'

James led Harry and Matt back out of the lounge, down the hall, and to the door at the back of the house, grabbing a torch from a shelf to the left of the door. He tried it and the beam which came out was little more than the death throes of whatever battery was powering it.

'Use mine,' said a voice from down the hall and Harry saw Dan looking over at them. 'It's pitch black out there. I brought my own with us because I've experienced using James' torches before, and they're always a little bit, shall we say, temperamental.'

'There's nothing wrong with any of them!' James said, lifting up the one he was holding. 'And this one has done me well for years!'

'Exactly.' Dan smiled. 'It's ancient. Anyway, be careful. We don't want to have to call an ambulance next, do we?'

James replaced his torch and grabbed Dan's, switching it on as they stepped outside. The light flared out, bright and clear, and as James cast it around in front of him, Harry watched the beam cut through the dark up onto the fells beyond the garden.

'My shed's over there,' James said, bringing the beam over to shine on a cabin, which to Harry looked more like somewhere you'd spend a week or two on holiday, rather than a place in which to do a bit of gardening.

'This is certainly a bit grander than mine, I have to say,' Matt said, as they entered the cabin.

Inside, the space was laid out in a very ordered fashion, with bespoke shelving and a workbench, a small stove in the corner, an armchair on which rested a book, and Harry remembered then what James had said earlier about Helen. Along one wall hung the most beautifully maintained garden tools Harry had ever seen. Which wasn't saying much, seeing as he'd never actually owned any himself.

'I was in my chair,' James said, walking over to stand beside it. 'I was reading and a movement caught my eye, out of that window there.'

Harry glanced at the window but couldn't see anything through it, the night seemingly growing darker by the minute.

'And what did you do?' Matt asked.

'I'm an inquisitive old bugger,' James said, 'so I had a look.'

'Could it have been your daughter or her husband?' Harry asked.

James shook his head. 'No, I don't think so.'

Harry nodded at this but thought he might check himself. 'You're sure?' he asked.

'Pat and Dan, they wouldn't come down here,' James said. 'They've no need. And Ruth and Anthony are over in the cottage.'

'Ruth and Anthony?' Harry queried.

'My youngest daughter and her son,' James explained. 'They live in the small house next door. You'll have seen it as you came up the lane.'

'So, you went to the window and saw something,' Matt said, attempting to keep James focused on what he had called them out for.

'And there was nothing there,' James said. 'So, I went outside, just to make sure. We're right out in the country here. And I know there's the main road at the bottom of the front garden, but round here, we're pretty exposed. It's just wilderness, isn't it? And anyone could just walk in off the fells if they really wanted to.'

Harry said, 'And that's when you saw . . .'

'I know, it sounds crazy,' James said, shaking his head. 'But it was her, my wife, I'm sure of it. It's not like she's someone I wouldn't recognise, is it?'

'Did you see her face?' Harry asked.

James paused, then said, 'No. I just saw her going over towards the house. Well, not the house exactly, but the bit in the middle, between the two.'

'Can you describe who you saw exactly?' Matt asked. 'What they were wearing?'

As James started to answer, Harry gave a nod to Matt to continue and turned and headed back outside. Behind him, he could feel the presence of the hills, as though their ancient silence was something ringing inside his head. He turned to stare at them, able to make them out only as a thicker darkness than that which sat above in the sky. It was lonely out here, he thought, and he wondered how he would cope if he'd seen an intruder. Throw in a recent bereavement and he fully understood why James Fletcher had been so bothered by it. It was obvious that what he had seen hadn't been his wife, though there was clearly no convincing the man otherwise. But that didn't matter, Harry thought. Something had spooked him, the man was adamant he had seen a figure in the garden, and if all their presence did was reassure him, then that was a job well done.

Harry looked over towards the house, his eyes tracing the building's lines along to where they were cut off so abruptly by the space between it and the smaller cottage by its side. Leaving James in the more than capable hands of his detective sergeant, he took a stroll over to have a look for himself.

Between the larger main house and the smaller cottage, Harry found the darkness of the night to be, if at all possible, even thicker, and he wished that he had brought a torch with him. He pulled his phone out, flicked through to the light, and switched it on, but the faint beam did little if anything to cut through the blackness that seemed so thick now that it was as though he was wading through it.

The walls of the two buildings loomed over him and Harry felt then, for the most fleeting of moments, that he was being watched. Quashing this unease immediately, remembering numerous other times back in the Paras, when the dark had played tricks on his mind in considerably more frightening conditions, Harry forced a laugh, but it came up out of him like a thing broken and afraid. Just what the hell was wrong with him? he thought.

The space between the buildings wasn't simply a flat area of ground, as Harry had expected it to be, but a sunken garden, as though there had once been a cellar between the buildings perhaps, though that did strike him as a little odd. There was a small flight of stone steps leading down into a courtyard of flagstones populated by potted plants. It was an odd space, Harry thought, and only added to the eerie feel of the place, and he couldn't escape the sense of unease tracing its thin, cold fingers of bone down his spine.

'Boss?'

Matt's voice had Harry stop and he turned to see his detective sergeant at the top of the stone steps, accompanied by James Fletcher, approaching him, the beam from the torch cutting a bright stencil of light out on the ground.

'So, this person you say you saw, they went down here, then,' Harry said, walking back up to meet Matt and James. 'Between the houses? Bit dangerous isn't it?'

'There are lights,' James said. 'Solar ones, but they're not very good if there's not been that much sun.'

'Perhaps you should think about replacing them,' Harry suggested.

'I followed her,' James said, 'down to where you were a moment ago, then out the other side, but when I got to the lawn, she was gone.'

'And how far away from this person were you when you chased after them?' Harry asked.

'She was just entering this bit here, the cut-through between the houses, when I came out of my shed,' James said.

Harry walked back down into the sunken garden, then out the other side until he was at the front of the house. Lights splayed out across the lawn from the windows, and above, he caught the faintest glimpse of the moon as it peeked out from behind a thick cloud, only to disappear again immediately after, as though trying to stay out of sight.

Matt and James joined Harry.

'It's a lovely place, Mr Fletcher,' Harry said, facing the house now, then he pointed at the cottage, which lay to their left. 'That looks to me like it used to be attached, to the main house, I mean.'

'It was,' James said. 'The sunken garden was a bit of the old cellar I think. Runs the length of the larger house, still.'

'Strange thing to do then, knock down the bit in the middle.'

'It was a long time ago,' James said.

For a moment, the three men stood staring up at the house. Then James stepped forward and turned to face Harry and Matt.

'I appreciate you coming out,' he said. 'I know it sounds crazy, but all I can tell you is what I saw. And I'm not one for lying or misleading people.'

'And I've a good description of the person you saw, now,' Matt said.

Harry was about to ask if there was anyone else that James thought the intruder could be, but decided it was best to just leave things as they were, for now. 'Well, we'll be leaving now,' he said. 'And, like I said when we arrived, we really are sorry for your loss. It's a terrible thing that happened, Mr Fletcher. And I think it's good that you have family close by at a time like this.'

'Yes, family is everything, really, isn't it?' James said.

A few minutes later, with their farewells said to James, and having quickly checked with Patricia and her husband that they had not been out in the garden when James said he had seen the woman, Harry was sat in the car, waiting for Matt. Chasing ghosts was certainly something he had never had to do before as part of his job, and it was another surprise that Wensleydale had obviously decided to lay on for him. He couldn't help but feel for James, and Harry had no doubt that the poor man was just suffering terribly from the loss of his wife, his mind desperate to see her in every shadow, every movement of a leaf or branch.

Matt climbed into the car.

'Nothing to report,' Matt said, having just popped

around to the cottage to check if James' other daughter had seen anything strange or out of the ordinary. 'In fact, me turning up at the door was the first that Ruth had heard about it.'

'Really?' Harry said. 'I would've thought Patricia would've let her know. Seems a little strange.'

Matt clipped himself in and started the car. 'Well, with what's happened, I reckon we can forgive them a little strangeness, don't you, Boss?'

'Agreed,' Harry said and glanced at his watch. 'Looks like I'm going to be back just in time to go straight to bed.'

As Matt eased the car quietly down the drive, back to the main road, he asked, 'So, what do you think he actually saw, then?'

'Well, it wasn't his wife, was it, that's for sure,' Harry said. 'Could've been anything. Grief and stress, they can really play on your mind, make it think and see things it shouldn't, or that aren't actually there.'

Matt went to say something, then stopped himself, instead focusing on the road ahead as he pulled out to head back to Hawes.

'What?' Harry asked.

'Oh, nowt, really,' Matt said.

'You sure about that?'

'Yes, I am,' Matt said, but as they headed back, the detective sergeant was strangely quiet, and Harry was left to wonder what would bother the man enough to keep quiet about it.

# CHAPTER NINE

It was Saturday evening, only five days since her mum had been killed, and Ruth was at the door of her dad's house, with Patricia and Dan, staring into the face of a woman standing on the doorstep who was all smiles, flowing scarves, and bangles. Her black hair shone with an almost iridescent blue.

None of them had time for this, what with the funeral to be getting on with, which was proving to be one of the most upsetting things she'd ever had to do in her whole life. The time had both flown and dragged, which sounded impossible, she knew, but that was really the only way to explain it. The minutes and hours and days had dragged by, as though being pulled through tar, they'd had visits from the police, the minister, well-wishers, and then there had been that odd episode with Dad saying he'd seen Mum. And yet, here they were, at the weekend, and it felt then as though the time had raced past, as though the death of her mum was already so long ago. And what they were dealing with now, this new arrival, well, it was, in almost every possible way, Ruth thought, just too bloody much to be going on with.

'I don't believe this at all,' Patricia said, and Ruth found herself agreeing with her sister for once. 'He called you? I mean, he actually called you and asked you to come over here, but didn't tell us, his family?'

'Yes,' the woman said, and held out her business card. Ruth saw that the image on it, behind the woman's name, was of a dreamcatcher. 'He rang yesterday and asked if I could come over. I don't usually do weekend visits, but he was very insistent. I can come some other time, if that suits you better? But perhaps, if I could just chat with James, your father, first?'

'I'm sure he was insistent,' Ruth said. 'He can be quite persuasive. But I just don't think this is all that sensible.'

'Not sensible?' Patricia said. 'It's absolutely bloody ridiculous is what it is! And to not even tell us? It's not on, it really isn't. We're all grieving, and he does this? Honestly, I'm lost for words.'

'Well, there's no point going off on one about it, is there?' Ruth said, taking a swipe at her sister. At first, she'd appreciated their visit, but it hadn't taken long for the novelty to wear off.

'I'm just saying what I see,' Patricia snapped back. 'Whatever is going on with him, he needs help, yes, professional help, actually. And this most certainly isn't that!'

Ruth took the woman's business card and stared at it. Not at her name, because right now that wasn't important. It was her supposed profession that was bothering her, bothering them all.

Dan said, 'I think Patricia has a point, Ruth. This does seem a little off. We all know that your dad's going through it, but this, well, I can't see how it's going to do him any good at all, can you? It's not healthy.'

Ruth said nothing to Dan. Like her father, she'd never really found him that easy to get on with, as though there was always something going on behind the words he was saying.

'You're a medium, then,' Ruth said.

'Yes,' the woman nodded, then held out her hand. 'Beverly Sanford.'

Ruth ignored the hand. 'And what is that exactly? A medium, I mean?'

'I'll tell you what it is,' Patricia said, interrupting. 'It's criminal, that's what!'

'Patricia, you need to calm down,' Dan said, and Ruth was sure that the voice was just a little condescending, though she wasn't sure that the tone was actually aimed at his wife.

'It's preying on people's grief,' Patricia continued. 'A con, hocus pocus nonsense! You should be arrested, you know! They used to burn people like you and I'm beginning to see why!'

'Perhaps I should go,' Beverly said and turned to leave.

'No,' Ruth said, then looked at Patricia, and taking a deep breath, said, 'I think Dad's out in his shed. If not, he'll be in his study.'

'Well, I'm not getting him,' Patricia said. 'I'm having nothing to do with any of this! And if this is the sign of things to come, then we will be heading back home, that's for sure!'

Ruth watched as her sister stormed off, not exactly unhappy to see her go. 'Dan?'

'I'll get him,' Dan said.

Ruth turned back to Beverly, noticing how her age was a little difficult to place, with young eyes set in a warm face that wore laughter lines with pride. If she had to guess, she would've put her at around her mid-thirties, but it was hard to say for sure. 'So, mediumship, then,' she said.

'Are you sure?' Beverly said. 'I can go. Honestly, the last thing I want to do is cause any trouble. That's not what I'm about, it's not why I do what I do. Never has been either.'

Ruth managed a smile. 'Probably best that you come in, I think.'

Beverly hesitated and Ruth saw a flicker of something in the woman's eyes.

'Something wrong?'

The smile which slipped onto Beverly's face wasn't very convincing.

'No,' Beverly said. 'Well, it's just, this house, you know? Black Moss? I've heard about it before.'

'Well, whatever you've heard, can I just ask that we get this done as quickly as possible, please?'

Beverly gave a short nod. 'Of course.'

In the lounge, Ruth offered Beverly a drink.

'No, I avoid alcohol if I'm doing this,' she said. 'Prefer to keep my wits about me as it were. Safer that way.'

'Safer?' Ruth repeated, sitting down. 'Surely it's hardly dangerous? And by *doing this*, what do you actually mean?'

Beverly sat down opposite Ruth. 'No, it's not dangerous, just so long as I stay in control. Have you seen programmes on TV where people go ghost hunting?'

Ruth laughed. 'What, all that walking around a creepy house in the dark stuff, lots of screaming, someone pretending they can talk to ghosts and make tables move, that kind of thing?'

'Yes, exactly that,' Beverly said. 'What I do, well, it isn't anything like that at all. And I hope that's reassuring.'

'So, what is it, then?' Ruth asked, not really reassured at all.

'Like I said, I'm a medium, which means that I sort of act like an intermediary between our world, which is the world of the living, and the world we then move to after death.'

'You mean Heaven?'

'I mean the spirit world,' Beverly said. 'You could call it Heaven, I suppose, but I think it's more complicated than that.'

'How?'

Beverly leaned back. 'Honestly, I don't really know,' she said. 'Which probably isn't what you want to hear.'

'Not really, no,' Ruth said.

'My view is that humanity has been searching for answers about what lies beyond death for all of time,' Beverly explained. 'Religion, spirituality, whatever you want to call it, it's all about trying to find that answer. I don't think we have and I don't think we ever will, either. Just got to keep on searching, I guess.'

'And you can talk to the dead? I mean, that's what you do, isn't it? You go into a trance or something, or have a spiritual guide, is that right?'

Beverly's smile was warm and genuine Ruth thought.

'I do and I don't,' she said. 'By which I mean, I don't sit here and have conversations with ghosts. Though I think that would be pretty awesome, don't you?'

'So, what do you do, then?' Ruth asked. 'If you communicate with the dead, but you also don't talk to them, then how does it work?'

'I sense things,' Beverly said. 'Sometimes I see faces, hear voices or words. I can smell things sometimes, then maybe I'll get a picture of something, a person or a place. It's never the same.'

'And you do this, why?' Ruth asked. She was intrigued now. Not because she thought there was anything in what the woman did, but because she couldn't help but warm to her. She was certainly dressed the part, yes, but she also struck Ruth as genuine.

'Good question,' Beverly answered. 'It's certainly not because I want to, or because I make money from it.'

Ruth was surprised by this and was about to ask what Beverly meant, when in walked her dad.

'Mr Fletcher?' Beverly said, standing up.

'Thank you so much for coming,' James said, walking over to clasp Beverly's outstretched hand. 'Honestly, this isn't something I would usually do.'

'And why would it be?' Beverly said. 'All you need to know is that if I can help, then I will.'

Dan came in then.

'Do you need me or . . .?'

'No, we're fine, I think,' James said.

Ruth stood up.

'You can stay if you want,' Beverly said to both Dan and Ruth. 'It may help anyway, to have someone else here, another member of the family.'

Ruth hesitated. 'Oh, well, I'm not sure, I mean . . .'

'I'd prefer it if you did, Ruthy,' James said, looking over to his daughter.

Ruth saw the beckoning smile, the weariness in his eyes. 'Okay, Dad,' she said, 'but are you sure about this? I mean, why are you doing it?'

Ruth saw thoughts come together behind her father's eyes as he worked out how to answer her.

'It's a lot of things really,' James said. 'I miss her, we all do, but it's more than that.'

'You mean what happened, when you think you saw her, Mum I mean, don't you?' Ruth said.

'I do, yes,' James said. 'And there's something about this house, too,' he continued. 'Like she's still here.'

'They're memories, Dad,' Ruth said. 'And that's okay. You don't need this. Remember what that police officer said? There's loads of support out there. Professional.'

James reached out and gently held Ruth's hand. 'I do, Ruthy. I really do. But this? I need it, too. Please . . .'

Ruth, despite her own misgivings, gave a nod, and with that settled, Beverly asked James if there was anywhere in particular in the house, the garden, where Helen would have often been found.

'You mean a favourite place of hers?' James asked. 'Well, there's the tree out back. The old oak. She loved that.'

'And in the house?'

James pointed across the room to a chair beneath one of the bay windows. 'There,' he said. 'She'd curl up and read and I'd have to come and wake her. I swear she was part cat!'

Beverly walked over to the chair. There was nothing special about it, Ruth thought, just an armchair worn by years of use, the original tartan fabric faded and patchy.

'Do you mind if I sit in it?' Beverly asked.

'Of course, go ahead,' James said.

'I ask, because this is a special place,' Beverly said. 'And I don't want to do anything to get in the way of your memories. So please, do tell me if there's something I'm doing that doesn't feel right.'

Beverly sat down and Ruth watched the woman as she leant into the chair, closing her eyes. And there she stayed for a few moments, still and quiet, her breath slow and steady. When she sat forwards, it was quicker than Ruth had expected and she jumped back.

'Can you give me a moment, please?' she said. 'Alone?'

'Oh, right, yes, of course,' Ruth said.

Dan didn't move. 'Are you sure, Ruth? We don't know her at all.'

'You can search me afterwards if you don't trust me,' Beverly said.

'Come on, out,' James said, proceeding to shoo his daughter and son-in-law out of the room like small children. 'How long do you need?'

'Five minutes, if that,' Beverly said. 'I'll come out when I'm done.'

Out in the hall, Ruth stood somewhat awkwardly between Dan and her father. She had nothing to say and yet also so much, but she couldn't find the words, her voice held fast in her throat as though caught like fishing hooks in a tree.

The lounge door opened and Beverly walked out. 'You mentioned a tree?'

'Yes, it's out the back,' James said. 'Do you want to see that as well?'

'Show me,' Beverly said.

'If you don't need me . . .' Dan said, excusing himself.

Outside, Ruth followed her father and the medium he had invited into their house, across the back garden, and on towards a huge oak tree. The day was a bright one, though cold, and Ruth half wondered if it was the threat of snow she could sense just at the edges of the wind.

'It's a beautiful tree,' Beverly said, staring up into the branches, where darkness hung from them like ribbons, as though ripped away from a night retreating over the horizon.

'She'd sit over there,' James said, pointing at the bottom of the thick trunk.

'Reading again?' Beverly asked.

James nodded.

'Did she have a favourite book or author perhaps?'

'Actually, she did,' James said. 'She loved Alan Garner. Kid's books, I know, but there you go. She was a big kid herself, really. She loved this place because she thought it was sort of magical, at least that's what she said. And the stories about it, you know? She loved those, too.'

Ruth, keen to hurry things on, particularly with her dad rambling a little, said, 'Is any of this relevant? I'm sure my dad's tired, so . . .'

'Weirdstone of Brisingamen, Elidor,' Beverly said, as though reading titles from a library. 'She had good taste, then. He's a superb writer.'

'You know him?' Ruth asked.

'Everyone should know him,' Beverly said. 'Would it be possible to maybe take one of her books?'

At this, Ruth looked to her father. She couldn't think of a reason as to why Beverly would want to take anything from them at all, other than money, she thought. And how much was this going to cost anyway? Not that money was a problem, but still, she would like to know.

'Do you mean home?' James asked.

'Yes,' Beverly said. 'You see, this first bit, well, it's a bit like a consultation I suppose. You get to meet me and I, you, we have a chat, I see what the situation is, get a feel for what's happened or is happening. Then, if I can, I take away what I've learned and felt and experienced, along with something that belongs to, or was used by, or was important to the person you want to contact. Then, I come back at a mutually agreed time, and we can see if we can make contact.'

'Oh, right,' James said. 'So, this isn't it, then?'

'No,' Beverly said, shaking her head. 'Not all of it, anyway. I always do two visits, more if required.'

'And there's a cost, I assume?' Ruth said, preparing herself for the charlatan to reveal her true colours at last.

'Cost? Of course, there isn't,' Beverly said, and Ruth heard just the faintest note of both irritation and hurt in the woman's voice, as though to suggest such a thing was to deeply wound her. 'Like I explained earlier, I don't do this because I want to. And I certainly don't do it to make money! I do it because I have to. I've no choice in the matter.'

At this, Ruth wasn't sure what to say, and as she followed the woman and her dad back to the house, where James found a book for Beverly, she remained quiet.

'So, when would suit you for me to come back?' Beverly asked. 'Evenings are best really, but it doesn't have to be.'

'No, evenings are good,' James said, 'Aren't they, Ruthy?'

Ruth had said, 'Yes, fine, not a problem at all,' before she'd even had a chance to think.

'Then how about you decide when would best suit, then give me a call?'

A few minutes later, and having been given one of the books Helen loved to read, Beverly was gone and Ruth was alone with her dad once more.

'You're sure about this?' she asked. 'I mean, it does seem a little bit, well, not really you, if you know what I mean, Dad. And I don't mean that to sound bad or anything. It's just, well, you've never been one for church or anything spiritual, have you?'

James smiled and Ruth saw within it the need the man

had to be allowed to do what he was doing, to at least search for some answers in his pain.

'Yes, I'm sure,' he said, and that, very clearly, was that.

Back next door, in the cottage, Ruth called up to her son Anthony. There was no answer, so she called again. Still nothing. Probably on that computer of his, she thought, plugged into an imaginary world, and she headed upstairs to check in on him.

Outside Anthony's bedroom door, Ruth leaned in but could hear nothing, though he was probably wearing his earphones, because he knew full well that the sound of all that violence wasn't what she wanted to hear echoing around the house.

Knocking at the door, Ruth waited a moment, then pushed on through.

'Hi, Love,' she said, 'just thought I'd pop in to see if you wanted anything?'

Except her words fell into dead air and darkness and Ruth was staring at an empty room. Anthony was gone. Again.

Ruth closed the door and headed back downstairs. In the kitchen, which was night-dark and quiet, she opened her fridge and allowed the glow from inside to flood out across the floor. She pulled out a new bottle of Pinot Grigio and a moment later had a large glass of the stuff in her hand. She then headed through to the lounge, sat down on the sofa, scooching up into it and under a blanket, before flicking on the television.

As she sipped the wine, Ruth stared at the screen, not really aware of what was on, not really caring. Her mind felt so pummelled by the week's events, that taking in any more information right now was impossible. And to add to it all, she had Anthony's disappearing act to deal with once again, just like earlier in the week, when the police had been around. She knew where he went, knew he was safe, that it was his way of escaping, getting a little bit of peace, but it was still a worry. And even more so now, with Pat and Dan around, because Pat was the kind of person to ask questions, then jump to conclusions. But he would be back later, like he always was, slinking in through the silence, taking himself to his room, and tomorrow they wouldn't talk about it, but they would hug, and that would be enough. Soon though, Ruth thought, it wouldn't be, would it? And they'd have to deal with it.

So, with what was left of the day to herself, and doing her best to not worry about everything all at once, Ruth opened the book that she'd taken from where her dad had pulled the one he had given to Beverly and started to read.

# CHAPTER TEN

HARRY KNEW THAT REALLY, WITH IT BEING A SUNDAY and all, he should have been taking the time off, not least because the force owed him probably a fair few months' worth over the years. But with Ben pulling in some overtime down at the garage, he'd had the choice of sitting on his own watching snooker—which had been very tempting indeed— or heading through Hawes to see how things were down at the community office.

He knew that Jadyn was on duty. Matt, too, if his memory served him right. And it would be good to have a natter if nothing else. And the company of other people was a good way to avoid thinking about that thing Firbank and Swift were now starting to pester him about. He'd promised he would call Firbank at some point in the following week with a decision, not that the decision was in any way a finality. He would still have an interview to go through, and there would be other people up for the same role, and really, did he want the hassle? He knew that the answer was yes, because it wasn't just about him anymore, but he still needed just a little longer to think it over.

Walking down through the marketplace, Harry was pleased to be just out for a stroll. Rain had managed to gate crash every day over the past week, but today was bright and cool, so considerably more pleasant. Rain in the dales had the capacity to come down not so much like stair rods, as he had been informed, but drill bits, with the power to give you a headache if you were daft enough to stay out in it for too long.

Outside the office, Harry found Jadyn updating a community noticeboard with various bits of information and advice on staying safe, reporting crime, and somewhat incongruously, a cake sale for charity.

'Any word from Jim?' Harry asked. Since the theft, Harry had given Jim the time and space to make sure things were okay back home with his dad and the farm. Whenever he had managed to catch up with Jim, Harry had sensed the brooding anger the lad clearly felt about what had happened and about how little any of them had been able to do to bring back his dad's flock. And the worst of it was, Harry had a feeling that they'd never be able to, either. But he'd never say that.

'Just had a message from him, actually,' Jadyn said, a smile in his voice.

'And what did it say?'

Jadyn lifted his phone up for Harry to see the screen.

'That's a picture of a cat,' Harry said. 'A cat wearing a face mask over its mouth.'

'It's Bane Cat,' Jadyn laughed. 'You know, as in Batman? And it's a video, not a picture. Want to see? It's properly funny, like!'

'Bane Cat?' Harry said. 'Who or what is Bane Cat?'

Harry watched Jadyn's face twist itself in confusion.

'Well,' Jadyn said, 'you know the Dark Knight trilogy, right?'

'No, can't say that I do,' Harry said.

'It's Batman, like I said.'

'Yes, I've heard of Batman,' Harry said. 'But that's not Batman, is it? It's a cat. A cat in a muzzle.'

'No, it's Bane Cat,' Jadyn said, and Harry noticed, much to his well-hidden amusement, that Jadyn had started to talk a little slower now, as though he was trying to explain something to someone who was either very, very young, or very, very old. 'You see, in the third film in the Dark Knight trilogy, there's this dude called Bane, played by Tom Hardy, and he wears this mask to give him constant pain relief for some trauma or something. Anyway, he talks in this very—'

Harry held up a hand to stop Jadyn from talking.

'I think it's only right to tell you now, Constable, that I'm not really listening to anything you're saying. In fact, I think I'd stopped listening when you said "*it's Bane Cat.*"'

'So, you don't want to watch the video of Bane Cat, then?' Jadyn asked. 'It's proper funny, like!'

'Not really, no,' Harry said, and made his way back into the building, and over to the kettle, Jadyn following on behind. 'Don't suppose we've got any more on what happened out at the farm? Any surprising little titbits of information from forensics?'

'No,' Jadyn said, putting away his phone. 'We haven't.'

'Can't say I'm surprised,' Harry said with a heavy sigh. 'Wasn't really much for them back when it happened, was there? Not that it's any consolation for Jim and his parents.'

'That's for sure,' said another voice, joining in the conversation, as Matt walked in through the main door.

'Well now, that's a rare thing,' Harry said, staring at the detective sergeant.

'Is there?' Matt asked, looking behind himself. 'What?'

'You, walking through that door, not carrying a paper bag full of pastries, cakes, and pies.'

Matt laughed and sat down opposite his boss, then reached into a jacket pocket.

'You didn't . . .' Harry said.

Matt pulled his hand back out to reveal a paper bag.

'Brownies.' He winked. 'Nice and gooey. Get the kettle on, Constable!'

Jadyn was over at the kettle in a heartbeat, grabbing three mugs from the cupboard.

'You didn't even know I was coming in,' Harry said, shaking his head in fake dismay.

'And who's to say that there's enough here for either of you, anyway, eh?' Matt asked.

Leaving Jadyn to make the tea, Harry said, 'Wish we had more to go on with what happened over at Jim's farm. Can't help feeling we missed something, but I can't see what. There was nothing there to find and that's all we've got, isn't it? Nothing.'

'You're not the only one,' Matt sighed.

Harry was silent for a moment, thoughtful. Then he said, 'We've not even done a board for it, that's how little we have.'

Jadyn whipped around from squeezing tea bags. 'You want me to do a board, Boss? I can, it's not a problem at all. Happy to, in fact. And it might help, right?'

Before Harry could say anything, the police constable was at the board, wiping it clean of some old notes from a previous meeting, and had a red pen poised and ready.

'That's not exactly what I was saying,' said Harry. 'I'm not even sure it'll do much good.'

'It might,' Matt said, then looked to Jadyn. 'Get our heads together on it? Why not? Brews first though, eh?'

Jadyn grabbed the tea, then was back at the board. Harry watched as the young police constable went to write something, then paused, the end of the pen stuck in his mouth like a lollypop.

'Something wrong, Officer Okri?' Harry asked. 'This isn't an art class and we're not expecting you to create a masterpiece, I assure you.'

'Just wondering what to call it,' Jadyn said. 'I mean, is it Jim's Farm, or Metcalf Farm? Or do I put Sheep Rustling? No, wait, what about, The Sheep Rustlers?'

'You can't call it that!' Matt said, shaking his head. 'You're not writing a Western starring Clint Eastwood, are you, lad?'

'What about Jim's Case?' Jadyn asked.

Harry rubbed his eyes, not tired exactly, but just on the edge of weary. 'Put whatever you want,' he said, 'but do it quickly, so we can get on!'

Jadyn waited a moment, then wrote 'Sheep Theft' on the board.

'There now, that wasn't so complicated, was it?' said Harry.

'Details then,' said Matt, watching as Jadyn started to take notes. 'We've got fifty sheep gone from the farm.'

'Taken at some point either very late Monday night or very early Tuesday morning,' Harry added. 'Because they wouldn't have risked being spotted. Jim's parents were in bed, Jim was out having a few beers.'

'And they came up through the fields from the main road

at the bottom of the hill,' Jadyn said, and Harry heard excitement in the young officer's voice. He was clearly enjoying himself. And it was nice to see, as well. Not that Jadyn was ever anything other than happy and enthusiastic, it seemed. In many ways, Harry thought, he was rather similar to Jim's dog, Fly, though not as furry, and he didn't lick you when he was happy or wanted attention. And he was pretty sure that he wouldn't drop to the floor to roll onto his back and ask for a tummy rub either.

'We cordoned off the layby down there,' Matt said. 'Forensics had a look, if you remember, to see if they could get anything, you know, tyre marks and whatnot. There's some up by the barn, too, like, and they're a match. The tracks in the field connect both scenes, but unless we find the vehicles, it's sod all use to anyone.'

'Anything else?' Harry asked. 'Because *whatnot* isn't of much use to anyone, is it?'

'A few cigarette butts,' Jadyn said. 'Though the DNA hasn't come up with any matches.'

'If we catch them, that could come in useful,' Harry said, taking a stingingly hot sip of his tea.

'Apparently, they're posh cigarettes though,' Jadyn added. 'So, that's something, isn't it?'

'Posh?' Harry said, raising an eyebrow. 'How do you mean? Since when has any cigarette been posh?'

'They're French,' Jadyn said. 'Gauloises.'

'Well, you don't find those in your average newsagent,' Matt said.

'No, you don't,' Harry agreed. 'So, they're either from a specialist tobacconist, bought online, or brought back from a holiday.'

'Wait, there's such a thing as a specialist tobacconist?' Jadyn asked.

'There's a cracking little one in Bristol,' Harry said. 'Like travelling back in time.'

'Didn't know you smoked,' Matt said.

'I don't,' Harry replied. 'But a cigar at Christmas is nice now and again, right?'

'What about damage to property?' Matt asked.

'Nothing,' Harry said, 'other than a cut padlock. Whoever they were, they did the job as clean as they could. They knew where they were going to hit, and when. Drove up through the fields, reversed up to the back of the barn, loaded up the sheep, and were gone. They weren't there to rip gates off.'

'You'd think someone would've spotted them though,' Jadyn said, 'and called it in.'

'Not necessarily,' Harry said. 'Really, what would they have seen to report? A truck being loaded up with sheep? This is Wensleydale, remember. That kind of thing happens every day of the week as far as I can tell. I mean, Hawes is a place where farmers walk their flock through the centre of town!'

It didn't happen much, but when Harry had first seen it, he'd been more than a little surprised. The tourists had loved it, the locals barely noticing it at all. He'd half wondered if it was something for a television show, but seeing no cameras and the fact that everyone seemed to regard it as entirely normal had told him otherwise.

'What about down at the roadside?' Jadyn suggested. 'Must've been a fair few people and vehicles involved.'

'And anyone driving by would have just seen people going

about farming business,' Matt said. 'Farmers work odd hours. Bit like us in that, really. And that bit of road, you wouldn't see much anyway. The layby is on a bend, there's trees all around it; you'd not see much even if you were looking.'

'So, what will they do with the sheep, then?' Jadyn asked, stepping away from the board to have a look at his notes.

'Black market meat, at a guess,' Harry said, the sadness and disgust in his voice impossible to disguise, because they'd all heard what Jim had said about his dad's flock, and the thought of all those years of work just ending up in some dodgy Friday night kebabs was more than a little hard to take. But it wasn't just the cheap places that took the cheap meat, was it? 'It's easy money and there's always someone out there who'll buy it. Back down in Bristol, I had to deal with a few places that were selling the stuff. Not your dodgy late-night takeaways either. Well, a few were, but there were high-end places, too. Restaurants with high rents, tight margins. You'd be surprised.'

'No, I wouldn't,' Matt said. 'Which is a shame, really, isn't it? And that flock, seeing as it's Jim's dad's, they won't be just your average, everyday normal sheep either. It's a prize flock. You remember all those rosettes and certificates on the walls in the kitchen? Takes years of work and breeding, does that. It's just a waste.'

Harry thought back to when they'd visited the farm, remembering the rosettes. It only served to make him feel even worse about their seeming helplessness at what had happened.

'Insurance will cover it, thought, right?' Jadyn asked. 'That's what it's for, isn't it?'

'The cost of it to Jim's parents isn't just in the value of the sheep,' Matt said. 'Though that won't exactly be inconsiderable. Like I said, it takes years to breed a good flock. It's Jim's dad's life's work. And you can't just replace that.'

'Didn't really think of it like that,' Jadyn said.

Harry stared at the board. 'You've got the details of the sheep, right?'

Matt said, 'Yes, got the lot.'

'And you've shared it around other areas, because the people who did this, they might not be local, but I doubt they've travelled too far. If this was done in the night, then my educated guess is that they'd want to be back home before daybreak.'

'So, say a couple of hours' journey time, right?' Matt suggested.

'Three at the most,' Harry said. 'You never know, we might hear something. And if forensics come in with anything new, share that, too. Auction mart is open on Tuesday, right?'

'It is,' Matt said.

'Then maybe I'll see if Gordy can come over and join us for a walk around. My face on its own is a little obvious, but Gordy would blend in well, wouldn't she?'

'Nice idea. Here,' Matt said, holding out the paper bag he'd pulled from his pocket, little spots of grease marking its surface.

Harry reached over and removed a brownie.

'Just so you know,' Matt said, 'the funeral for Helen Fletcher? It's a week tomorrow. James Fletcher called in yesterday to let us know. I don't really know why, but it was clearly something he wanted to do, so there we are.'

Harry thought about that for a moment, then said, 'Maybe it's his way of letting us know he's okay.'

'Could be,' Matt said.

'Actually,' Jadyn said, 'about that . . .'

'About what?' Harry asked.

'Mr Fletcher.'

'What about him?'

Jadyn was quiet for a moment then, and Harry noticed, looking a little awkward.

'Well, whatever it is, spit it out,' Harry said. 'Unless that look means you need the loo, in which case, you don't need to ask for permission or put your hand in the air or even wait till break time.'

'No, it's not that,' Jadyn said. 'It's about the house.'

'What about it?' Harry asked.

'You don't know then?'

'Know what?' Harry said, trying his best to not sound too exasperated.

He saw Jadyn's eyes flick over at Matt then back to him.

'It's about the ghost,' Jadyn said.

Harry almost choked on the brownie he'd just swallowed. 'Ghost?'

'Yeah, it's haunted,' Matt said, and Harry heard not a single note of sarcasm in his voice. 'I thought everyone knew?'

The room fell silent, all eyes now on Matt.

'I guess not, then,' Matt said.

'I'm assuming this isn't where you tell me you've been moonlighting as a paranormal investigator,' said Harry, having just about recovered. He remembered then how, as they'd left Black Moss on Thursday, after visiting James, Matt had seemed like he was going to say something, and then waved it off as nothing. Had this been it? Harry thought.

Jadyn said, 'Now that would be awesome! Chasing

ghosts and stuff? Brilliant!'

Harry looked across at the constable, his stare and a shake of his head enough to quieten him down.

'So, what's this ghost, then?' Harry asked, turning his attention to Matt. 'Because I can see you want to tell me, and that if I don't let you, then you either just blurt it out anyway, or hold it in just long enough to give yourself an aneurism.'

'I don't know many of the details,' Matt said, 'but from what I understand, the reason the house is the way it is, well, that's all down to the ghost.'

'By that, I'm assuming you mean why it's missing that bit in the middle,' Harry said, 'and not that the Munsters have moved in, has too many bats, or that people heard strange howls and screams in the middle of the night?'

'Who are the Munsters?' Jadyn asked.

Matt and Harry ignored Jadyn.

'Oh, there's nowt wrong with it as such,' Matt said. 'Just that massive missing section, that's all.'

'And what about it?' Harry asked.

'It was knocked down because it was too haunted.'

At this, Harry roared with laughter. 'Come off it!' he said. 'You're having a laugh! Someone knocked down part of a house because of a ghost? You're surely not going to sit there and tell me you believe that, are you?'

As he waited for Matt to answer, Harry continued to chuckle, amazed that he was having a conversation about ghosts with two members of his team on a Sunday afternoon. And to think he was missing the snooker for this!

With Matt now quiet, Harry said, 'And just out of interest, at what point does a house become too haunted? Is one ghost fine, two bearable, but three or more simply not on?'

Jadyn was sitting down now and leaning forward, his

eyes focused on Matt. 'So, this ghost then,' he said. 'What was it? What did it do? Has anyone ever seen it? Have you seen it? I bet you have, haven't you? I can see it your eyes! What was it like? I'd love to see a ghost! That would be epic!'

Harry shushed Jadyn's rapid-fire questions with a stare.

'What I know is this,' Matt said, and Harry noticed how the detective sergeant dropped his voice and leaned forward, resting one of his huge hands down on a nearby table. 'The ghost itself is that of a headless woman.'

'No way!' Jadyn said, eyes wide. 'That's amazing!'

'It's bollocks is what it is,' Harry said. 'Complete and utter bollocks.'

'I don't know when it happened exactly,' Matt continued, 'but it was in the eighteen hundreds I think. You know, the nineteenth century?'

'I do know when the eighteen hundreds was,' Harry said. 'And no, not because that's how old I am,' he added, having guessed that the look in Jadyn's eye was enough evidence that such a suggestion was very close to tripping off his tongue.

'The hauntings got really, really bad in some of the rooms,' Matt explained. 'Most of the house was okay, like, but in this one section, it was awful. Really, properly bad. The woman, well, was seen everywhere, and the disturbances just became too much for the people who lived there.'

'So, what happened?' Jadyn asked. 'Did someone get possessed?'

'Brilliant!' Harry said. 'The Wensleydale version of The Exorcist! Let me guess, they called in a priest who then went mad, or threw himself out of a window, is that right?'

'You've not seen The Exorcist, have you?' Matt said, looking to Harry.

'No, I haven't,' Harry replied. 'But I'd guess that it's just as daft as this yarn you're spinning right now.'

'Anyway,' Matt continued, turning back to Jadyn, 'the owners eventually decided that enough was enough. So, in the end, they decided that the only solution was to tear down the haunted rooms, and that's why the house looks the way it does now.'

'Yeah, I've seen it,' Jadyn said. 'It looks well creepy, like, doesn't it?'

'But,' said Matt, 'they do say . . .'

He trailed off and Harry watched as Jadyn leaned even closer.

'What do they say?' Jadyn asked. 'What?'

'Well,' Matt said, 'sometimes when the moon is full, and when the sky is particularly clear, if you stand in the place where the old rooms once were, where me and the DCI here walked just a couple of nights ago now, you'll see . . .'

'See what?' Jadyn said. 'What will I see?'

The room was silent, Jadyn and Harry now both leaning in to hear Matt finish his story.

'You really want to know?' Matt asked.

'Of course, I want to know!' Jadyn said. 'This is brilliant! What will I see?'

Without warning, Matt brought down his huge hand in a mighty slap on the top of the table at his side. The sound cracked the silence in two with the sound of a scaffold plank snapping in half, and although Harry flinched, it was nothing compared with what happened to Jadyn, who leapt into the air, knocked his chair over, then stumbled backwards to land on the floor on his backside.

'You evil sod!' Jadyn said, pushing himself back up to his feet.

By the time he was there, Matt was wiping tears from his eyes and Harry couldn't help but laugh himself.

'You walked right into that,' Harry said. 'Well told, Detective Sergeant. Well told, indeed.'

'It's true, mind,' said Matt, still chuckling. 'That really is the reason why the house was split in two. A group of para-normal investigators went up there a few years back, said they recorded lots of evidence. And the folk who were at the house before the colonel, they refused to go out at night into the section between the main house and the cottage.'

'But you were there on Thursday,' Jadyn said. 'What was it like? Could you sense anything? Was it really creepy?'

Harry thought back to when he had taken that short stroll between the houses. He remembered the thick dark-ness and the almost oppressive atmosphere of the place. But how could it be anything else, he thought, with those walls looming overhead, and the night having been as black as pitch?

Harry decided to not answer Jadyn's question, checked the time and saw that the end of the day was gathering pace. 'Well,' he said, rising to his feet, 'fun and exciting though this is, I'm not entirely sure tracking down and arresting ghosts is in my remit as a DCI.'

'Heading back home, Boss?' Matt asked.

At the door to the office, Harry paused and turned back to look at his team. 'I'll be giving Jim a ring in a bit. I'll let you know how he is, how his dad is.'

'And I'll tell everyone else, no bother,' Matt said.

With nothing left to say, Harry walked out into the damp, late afternoon air, the only thought on his mind being what he and Ben were going to have for dinner. And that alone was enough to crease his damaged face with a smile.

# CHAPTER ELEVEN

Tuesday was always busy in Hawes, what with it being market day, and Detective Inspector Gordanian Haig was very happy indeed to be there. She didn't get up dale as often as she would like to, but when she did, this was absolutely her favourite time of the week to do so. And thanks to a call from Harry late on Sunday afternoon, she'd headed over.

'So, nothing from forensics, then?'

'Sod all, actually,' Harry had said, and she'd heard the frustration in his voice. 'Posh cigarettes and some tyre tracks. Not exactly much to be going on with, is it? And although I know that there's every chance those poor animals have been shipped off to some disused warehouse somewhere to be killed and cut up and shipped off to who knows where, I don't want to be giving up on it.'

'That's not really in your nature now, is it?'

'No, it isn't,' Harry had said. 'And this is closer to home as well, with it being Jim's family's farm.'

Gordy had things to be getting on with, but part of being

in the police force was learning to juggle. So, she'd said, 'And you're phoning me because you have a plan?'

'A plan is a grand term for this.' Harry had sighed. 'But my view is that if a gang has been over here and done this, then it's likely that they've done so because they've been keeping an eye on what goes on around here, seen it as easy pickings, and swooped in. And that, Detective Inspector, pisses me right off.'

'A lot of things seem to do that,' Gordy had said, a laugh curling the edges of her words.

'We've already been around to the farms,' Harry had explained, 'just to show our faces, that kind of thing. But I'm thinking the auction mart is where I'd be, if I was this gang, if you know what I mean.'

'I do,' Gordy had agreed. 'You think they're recceing stock there, do you?'

'Not just stock, but farmers,' Harry had said. 'No point turning up to try and nick a couple of truck-loads of animals, if the farm is difficult to get to, actually has some kind of security in place, dogs or what have you–'

'Or geese.'

'What?'

'Geese,' Gordy had said. 'Better than guard dogs, I promise you. My grandma worked a croft, just a couple of acres, and she always had geese. Angry wee bastards, they are. Hate people with a passion.'

'Anyway,' Harry had continued, 'I'm thinking it might be clever, like, if we had you and me and some Uniforms up there, just mooching about. The Uniforms might put them on edge if they're there, the gang I mean, and my face is well known, so that'll get folk talking. You'll just be in plain clothes, you're not as obvious, and you can observe from afar, can't you? You can also be a bit nosy, ask questions, get a feel for what's going on, that kind of thing.'

'You're making it sound really sexy,' Gordy had said. 'Very Starsky and Hutch.'

'Am I?'

'No, not really.' Gordy had laughed. 'More like All Creatures Great and Small crossed with Columbo.' Then she'd reminded him about the book she'd lent him.

'I've finished it,' Harry had said, and Gordy had heard the surprise in his voice. 'Good, too, it was. Bit far-fetched, but that's the point of fiction, isn't it? Tell a tall tale. He could certainly spin a yarn, Charlie Baker, couldn't he?'

'And his sales will go crazy now, after what's happened.'

And on that note, they'd finished the conversation, agreeing that Gordy would be over to the auction mart come Tuesday and take some of the team with her, at the same time pondering over the last case they'd dealt with, over in Coverdale, and the murder of the author, Charlie Baker.

So, here she was, and having parked up in the market-place, Gordy stepped out into crowds, the hustle and bustle already chasing its way through market stalls alive with activity and chatter and the delicious smells of street food. There was always a buzz to the place, Gordy thought, even on those days when the weather was positively apocalyptic, and it seemed to somehow not only bubble and spit with the modern-day, but also to echo of days long past. Markets were an ancient thing, and in Hawes, she figured little had changed over the years. It hardly needed to, either. Add to it the buying and selling of livestock going on at the other end of the town, which was where she would soon be heading, and the rich vibrancy of the place seemed to just reach out and grab you.

The day was clear and cold, Gordy noticed, hunching her shoulders up a little against a sharp breeze. However, having grown up in the Highlands of Scotland, a chilly November day in the Yorkshire Dales wasn't exactly something that had ever really bothered her. Try walking through Glencoe, when it's blowing a hooley, she thought, particularly when the rain is cutting across in sheets thick enough to fell trees. And that was just the summer! Winters were something else entirely, the landscape bedecked in a veil of thick snow, beautiful and dangerous, calling out to the hearts of climbers and walkers. Each year, the winters up there would take a few more of lives, and yet still the adventurous would return. And Gordy would too, and soon, because she missed it, and always would. Though what work she'd find that way she had no idea. She'd been in the force a long time now, and as she'd just pipped past fifty, there was the temptation just to stay and see it through. But also, she couldn't help wondering if there was more to life. Not that she didn't like her job, hell, she loved it, but she'd never really been able to escape the haunting echo of home in her heart, and still she would find herself waking in the morning to the distant tune of a dream spent wandering through Glencoe.

But now was not the time for such thoughts, so Gordy pushed them away and made her way over to the community office, smiling with affection at how this hub of local activity housed the police presence alongside a library and a post office. It wasn't something she would say openly, but part of her believed that this was a much better way for the police to be seen, particularly in areas like this, where communities were small and rural life was a very distinct thing, separate and unique to that in more urban areas. Such notions brought back again her thoughts of the Highlands, and what she would do if she moved back, but she ignored them, and pushed her way into the rooms used by Detective Chief Inspector Harry Grimm and the rest of the team. The first thing to meet her was a torpedo of fur.

'Well, hello there, Fly!' Gordy said, dropping to her knees to give the dog a rub. He flipped over onto his back, his teeth bared. 'Holding the fort again, I see, keeping everything running tickety-boo!'

'He's not in charge, but he certainly seems to think he is,' Jim said. 'Honestly, he's more the team's dog than mine now, I'm sure of it.'

'Not a bad thing,' Gordy said, and hearing laughter looked up from Fly to see the other PCSO, Liz Coates, standing over at the kettle.

'You're early,' Liz said. 'I'm just getting a brew on. Fancy one?'

Gordy rose to her feet, Fly slinking along after her, the sheen of his coat almost metallic.

'No, I'm good,' she said. 'How's everything here?'

'Busy, with it being market day, like,' Liz said. 'Jadyn's out doing a walk around. And I don't know if anyone else has noticed this, but I swear, every Tuesday, he turns up with his uniform all properly smart, doesn't he? It's a shame it doesn't come with lots of brass buttons, because he'd be all over those with a tin of Brasso and a rag!'

Gordy had indeed noticed this and smiled. 'He's keen,' she said. 'Don't knock it.'

'And that's why we love him,' Liz said.

'What about everyone else?' Gordy asked.

'Harry's out for a coffee,' Liz said. 'Won't be long, as he's looking forward to heading up to the mart. He still tries to insist that tea isn't his new favourite drink, but we don't believe him, do we, Jim?'

'Not a bit of it,' Jim said, shaking his head.

'And Matt's over at that little camp of protesters, just on the edge of town.'

'Protesters?' Gordy asked, casting a hook out into her memory, but unable to catch anything related to that word.

'Richard Anderson's place,' Liz said. 'You know, that businessman who walks around like he's the king of the dales or something, all because he's got a few bob in his pocket and found out that a distant relative of his came from Yorkshire!'

'He's what Matt would describe as a complete wassack,' Jim said.

'He's all puffed-up chest and handshakes and smiles,' Liz said. 'Carries this big, brown leather file with him every-where, just to make himself look important, I'm sure.'

'Oh, right, that,' Gordy said, still unsure.

'They've been camped out on his land since spring,' Jim explained, clearly picking up on her lack of recall, Gordy noticed, bless him. 'He's somehow managed to get planning permission to build on this lovely bit of land, and those protesters don't think he should. And most of the locals would be agreeing with them, too, as it happens.'

'And Matt's headed out there, because?' Gordy asked.

'Anderson's told them that he's not going to build there now and wants them to leave. Unsurprisingly, they don't think his word is a strong enough bond.'

'Matt the diplomat,' Gordy said. 'Well, probably more sensible than sending Grimm!'

As Liz and Jim laughed, the office door opened and in walked Police Constable Jenny Blades.

'Right then, who's not going out?'

'Jim and me are due to head up to the auction mart with the DI, here, and Grimm when he gets back.' Liz said. 'Why, is something up?'

'Not sure really,' Jen said. 'Mr Fletcher over at Black Moss House has reported another intruder.'

'What, again?' Jim said. 'Seriously? Harry and Matt were over there last Thursday for the same thing. He was convinced that he'd seen his wife.'

'How did he sound?' Gordy asked, her ears picking up on this, remembering the contact she'd had with Mr Fletcher and his family after the awful crash that had claimed Mr Fletcher's wife, Helen, and what she'd then heard about Harry and Matt's call-out the previous week.

'I think it was his daughter called it in this time,' Jen said. 'But something's not right, is it? Can't be.'

'No, you're right, it's not,' Gordy said. 'Can you tell them I'll call them later, and pop in before the day's out? Just to see if they need anything.'

'Will do,' Jen said, then glanced over at Liz and Jim. 'So, you two both have something to be going on with. Which means I'll be heading out there on my own, then.'

'It'll be nowt anyway,' Jim said. 'Just sounds like the poor old bloke's not dealing well with the loss of his wife. And who can blame him? Right horrible, that.'

'I think it best if PCSO Coates goes with you,' Gordy said. 'I'm sure I can persuade Constable Okri to step in instead.'

'Neil's joining us as well,' Jim said.

'Neil?' Gordy asked.

'My old mate,' Jim explained. 'The one I was out with Monday night, like. He wants to help seeing as I was out with him when it happened.'

'We don't know when it actually happened,' Liz said.

'I know,' Jim said, 'but I didn't get back till late, did I? And I think Neil just feels a bit guilty. Anyway, an extra pair of eyes can only help, right? He's meeting us up there.'

Liz turned back to Jen and asked, 'So, you driving?'

'Of course!' Jen grinned.

Gordy put a hand on Liz's shoulder as she prepared to leave. 'I've seen Detective Constable Blades drive,' she said. 'I've even survived being a passenger with her a few times. You sure you're ready for this?'

Liz laughed. 'I'm never anything else! Come on, then, Jen, let's go and see if Mr Fletcher's seen another ghost.'

As Liz and Jen left, Gordy looked over at Jim and asked how his dad was doing.

'He's back home and under Mum's watchful eye,' Jim said. 'Which means it was probably more relaxing for him in hospital, the poor bloke. Mum's lovely, but she doesn't half mither around given the chance, if you know what I mean. It can be a bit much to take sometimes, but it's what he needs, so he'll just have to get used to it.'

Gordy laughed. 'A very watchful eye, then.'

'You could say that,' Jim said, as the office door opened and in walked Police Constable Jadyn Okri.

'Speak of the devil,' Gordy said.

'And he shall appear,' Jadyn finished, and Gordy heard excitement in his voice. 'So, are you a Batman fan, then? Amazing! Because old Grimm hasn't a clue.'

'Batman?' Gordy said, glancing over to Jim.

'Don't look at me,' Jim said, holding up his hands. 'I just work here.'

'Constable Okri,' Gordy said, turning back to Jadyn, 'I must say that you're looking particularly sharp today.'

She watched as the young police constable visibly swelled with pride.

'Thank you, Ma'am,' he said. 'Important to give the right impression I think.'

'It is,' Gordy smiled. 'So, are you busy today? Lots to do?'

Jadyn shook his head. 'There's always bits and bobs to do, yes, but if there's something you need me on, then I'll be all over it!'

Gordy laughed. 'Where do you get your enthusiasm from?'

'My dad,' Jadyn said. 'He's unbearable. The kind of man who gets excited about finding a packet of prawn cocktail crisps in the cupboard.'

'That's a very specific reference,' Jim said.

'My dad's a very specific kind of man,' Jadyn replied.

Gordy said, 'PCSO Metcalf here is going to accompany me to the auction mart. And I was wondering if you would like to come along?'

'You think that's where your dad's sheep are?' Jadyn asked, looking at Jim. 'Is that it? Are we going to make an arrest?'

'Bugger all chance of that, I reckon.' Jim sighed.

'But there's always a chance we'll hear or see something,' Gordy said. 'I had a chat with DCI Grimm, and he thinks a bit of police presence wouldn't go amiss. I'm more than inclined to agree. And sometimes, that's more than enough to spook someone into doing or saying something they shouldn't, acting out of character, that kind of thing.'

'Like at airports, you mean,' Jadyn said.

'How's that then?' Jim asked, clearly as baffled by the constable's change of subject as Gordy herself.

'You see, I've a mate whose dad works at Nottingham

International,' Jadyn explained, though Gordy wished that he wasn't, but she wasn't about to step in and quash the lad's enthusiasm for sharing information. 'When folk are queuing up and going through customs, and they pick people out at random to do a spot search, it's not always because they think that person is actually carrying in something dodgy.'

'Why do they do it, then?' Jim asked.

'They're doing it to spook anyone in the queue who is,' Jadyn said. 'So, while they're searching, they're looking along for changes in behaviour, anything that might give someone away as not being quite right. Clever stuff, really. Psychological.'

Gordy managed to hold in her chuckle as Jadyn tapped the side of his head to emphasise the word.

'So, you going to join us, then?' Gordy asked.

'What about the office?' Jadyn asked.

'Matt will be back soon enough,' Jim said.

'Then yes,' Jadyn said, and Gordy loved to see the excited glint in his eyes. 'Are we going now?'

'Unless there's something else you have to do first?' Gordy said.

'Nope, not a thing!' Jadyn said, and before Gordy could say anything else, the police constable was at the door.

# CHAPTER TWELVE

OUTSIDE THE COMMUNITY CENTRE, AND AS GORDY, JIM, and Fly chased after Jadyn, Jen reversed to point the car up towards the primary school at the end of town. 'I don't think there's anywhere I don't know the way to around here,' she said, pulling out onto the road. 'Could pretty much navigate blindfolded.'

'You and me both,' Liz said. 'Sometimes, I think the roads and lanes are more like my DNA than my actual DNA.'

Jen laughed as she headed them out of Hawes and past the petrol station to follow the main road out. If they kept on, past their destination, it would eventually lead them to Sedbergh and on towards the Lake District. Liz hadn't been out that way for a good while but had a mind to head over soon. The dales had its fells, and it was where her heart belonged, but the lakes ached with another kind of beauty. Jen knew it for the ultra-marathons and other races she would often head over to take part in, but for Liz, the roads and lanes were the best in the world for anyone on a motor-bike, and they drew bikers from all over. The pubs were good, too, particularly the Golden Rule in Ambleside, a pub set in its own time, stoically refusing to bow to fashion or trend.

The journey to Black Moss House wasn't a long one, only a few miles really, but it wasn't any less enjoyable for that. The road weaved itself between lush pastures, enclosed by drystone walls, and Liz wondered just how old the road really was, how many folk had made their way along it, transporting livestock, their families, between hill and fell and dale.

The morning's rain had eased again, though the clouds were still heavy and grey, threatening more to come. Puddles lay on the tarmac, their still, metallic surfaces like holes to another world.

Arriving in Appersett, the village between Hawes and their destination, Jen eased off the accelerator.

'Ex-boyfriend of mine lives here,' she said, then pointed at a house on their left. 'There, actually. At least he used to. Moved away.'

'He liked you that much, then?'

Jen laughed.

'Lots of folk do,' Liz said. 'Job, was it?'

'He worked at the creamery for a while,' Jen said. 'But then who hasn't at some point, right? I had a job there for a while, but the smell, I just couldn't handle it. Worse than cigarette smoke for getting into your clothes, your hair, on your skin. Anyway, as I was saying, he used to talk about Black Moss House.'

'Everyone talks about Black Moss House.' Liz laughed. 'It's a weird place, isn't it?'

Jen took them over the bridge and out of Appersett, the road following the River Ure on their left, the water rushing on in a tumble of white and grey, like wool tossed into a ravine.

'Just another mile or so,' she said. 'You ever been? To the house, I mean?'

'Never,' Liz said. 'It's just one of those places you know about because you've driven past it so often. And there's nowhere else looks quite like it, is there?'

As she was speaking, the house came into view, just up on their right, the deep grey stone of its walls just visible between some sparse woodland, which grew thicker the further back it stretched up the hill.

'There it is, then,' Jen said. 'It's certainly impressive.'

As they drove past, Liz ducked down a little to get a better view of the house through the windscreen. It was an imposing building, sat at the top of a large sloping lawn, the centre of it bowed out and flanked by two wings. Off to its left was a large gap, then another smaller house, which stood there as though shunned by its larger sibling.

'Doesn't exactly look cosy though, does it?' Liz said, as Jen drove on past the house to then turn right and into a lane, which would lead them back to it.

'Must be worth a fair bit,' Jen said, as she rolled the car to a stop in the parking area at the back of the house. 'So, who is it we're seeing, then?'

Liz was about to say, when a man emerged from a large door in the rear of the house. He was tall, Jen noted, and walked not just with purpose, but with bearing, his shoulders pulled back and his chin out, a stick at his side that seemed to be no hindrance at all to his speed.

'He's a retired colonel,' Liz said, unclipping her seatbelt.

'That would explain why he's marching towards us, then,' Jen said.

Outside the car, the damp chill of the air sweeping in off the fell danced around them, Liz and Jen made their way over to meet the man who had put in the call.

'Thank you for coming out,' the man said. 'Look, I'm sorry, I shouldn't have had my daughter call you.'

Liz stepped forwards and introduced herself. 'And this is Police Constable Blades,' she said. 'You must be James Fletcher, yes?'

She knew he was in his mid-seventies, but Liz couldn't help noticing that he was fit for his age, his face showing little in the way of the chubbiness she had noticed with some who hit retirement and then relaxed perhaps a little too much. But his eyes, now they were tired, she thought, seeing the grey shadows beneath them, like dark dunes swept up by a cold sea.

'It's very kind of you to come out,' James said. 'I'll be honest, I'm feeling a bit daft now, having got you over, but best to be sure, isn't it? I mean, you never know, do you? It's why I insisted Patricia call you.'

Liz caught the raised eyebrow from Jen. 'Can we go inside, please, Mr Fletcher?' she said. 'Then you can tell us exactly what it is that you saw. Okay?'

James gave a nod, and there was sorrow in it, Liz thought, and as he moved away she saw him do his best to stifle a yawn. He was limping a little as well.

'Would you like some tea?' James asked as they neared the house. 'I can do a coffee as well, if you prefer.'

'Tea would be grand,' Jen said. 'But don't go putting yourself out.'

Entering the house, Liz was immediately greeted by the smell of burning wood. The day was cold, so she could understand why a fire was lit, but the smell itself seemed to be part of the fabric of the house, an aroma not just of today but of numerous yesterdays and numerous fires all set against the cold.

'We'll go to my study this time, I think,' Mr Fletcher said, marching on down a high-ceilinged hall, and along past a large staircase. 'It was outside last time, you see, when I saw her, that is. That's why I took those other two officers out there, to my shed. But this time, I was in my study when I saw her. So I can show you better from in there I think. It's comfy, too.'

'Is there anyone else here with you?' Jen asked. 'In the house I mean?'

James said, 'It was lovely when the girls were children, and to be honest it is a little too big now, just for me and Helen.'

'We were so sorry to hear about your wife,' Liz said. 'Really terrible. You have our sympathies.'

'That's very kind,' James said.

'So, you're alone here, now,' Jen said, getting back to what she had just asked because James' answer hadn't really been one at all.

'Yes and no,' James said. 'I've got Ruthy, my youngest, she's in the little house next door, with Anthony.'

'Husband?'

'God, no!' James said. 'That man will never set foot here ever again, of that you can be assured!'

'Oh, I'm sorry,' Jen said.

'Don't be,' James replied. 'He was an utter bastard. And he's never given a penny towards his son. But to be honest, Ruthy wouldn't want it anyway. Anthony is their son. He's turned into a lovely young man. Suffers from headaches though. He's home today, I believe. Can hardly believe that he's sixteen! Where does the time go? And there's Patricia, my eldest, she's come up to stay with her husband. She's the one who called you for me. Though she wasn't exactly happy about it.'

'That's kind,' Liz said.

'They're going to be here for a whole month! It's the longest I'll have seen her for years, since she left for university, actually.'

James Fletcher led Liz and Jen into the study and Liz was surprised to find that it wasn't as grand as she had initially expected it to be. There was a simple desk facing a window, which gave a view out of the rear of the house to the fields and fells beyond, a few well-stocked bookshelves, and a couple of armchairs flanking a burning fire. What Liz noticed most of all, however, was the number of photographs of a dark-haired woman, not just on the walls, but on the mantlepiece, the desk, and a small coffee table. It was more than clear that this was Helen.

'She was out there,' James said, standing around the other side of the desk and pointing out through the window. 'Just over there, do you see? Under that tree. The large oak.'

'Do you mind if we take a few details first, please?' Liz said, taking out her personal notebook.

'I gave those other police officers my details,' James said.

'I know,' said Liz, 'but if I can just confirm a few details and then we can go through what happened?'

Jen turned back to the door. 'Tell you what, Mr Fletcher, if you stay here and have a chat with PCSO Coates, I'll go and have a walk around, have a check on the place. How does that sound?'

'Yes, I think that would be a very good idea,' he said, then looked over to Liz. 'Don't you?'

'Very much so,' Liz said, her smile wide and bright, hoping in some small way to reassure James that they were doing, and would do, everything that they could to help.

'Anyway, like I said, she was out there,' James said, as Jen made to leave, pointing once again out through the window, this time with his stick. 'That tree over there, you see it, yes? Beautiful, isn't it? So have a look there, as it's probably the best place to start.'

Jen nodded and made to leave the study, but as she stepped through the door, she turned and said, 'There's a public right of way across the grounds, isn't there? I remember Detective Sergeant Dinsdale mentioning it.'

'There is, yes,' James replied.

'And have you ever before seen anyone end up on your property from that path at all? Perhaps they've decided to take a short cut, or maybe knocked on your door to use the toilet or something?'

'No, never, at least not that I can recall,' James said.

'Well, I'll go and have a look around, then,' Jen said. 'I'll take a look over by the footpath as well, just to see if I notice anything.' And then she was gone.

# CHAPTER THIRTEEN

'Perhaps we should take a seat?' Liz said, gesturing to the two chairs by the fire.

James hesitated and Liz saw his eyes darting across to the tree. One minute he seemed to be calm, the next jumpy. He was clearly under a lot of strain, she thought, but that was no surprise really, after what had happened.

'Please,' Liz said. 'If you can just go through what happened, I think that would be really helpful.'

James turned from the window and came over to sit down on one of the chairs by the fire. Liz did the same, the heat from the flames resting on her like a warm, toasty blanket. Give me a blanket, she thought, and I could stay right here for hours.

To break the awkwardness that was in the room with them, Liz said, 'The photos, this is your wife, Helen, yes?'

'They are,' Mr Fletcher said, and Liz saw a crack in the military front the man wore like armour. 'Beautiful, isn't she? I still can't believe she's gone. I keep expecting to hear her voice or see her in the house. I've even called her a couple of times, you know? Picked up the phone just to have a chat, only to remember then that she's gone.'

'I really am so sorry about what happened,' Liz said, hearing James' voice falter.

'You have no need to be sorry,' James said. 'It was hardly your fault now, was it?'

James, Liz then noticed, had somehow managed to acquire a glass of what looked like whisky, on his journey from the windows to the seat, and was swilling the amber liquid around and staring into the fire.

'She really was quite wonderful,' James said. 'Life made more sense with her in it, I'm sure of that.'

Liz said, 'First, and like I said before, can I just confirm your details?'

James did as requested and although Liz already had the information he had given her, she did it to relax him more than anything else, and to let him know that this was a statement she was taking, that she was treating whatever he was about to say, very seriously.

'So, Mr Fletcher,' Liz asked, 'what exactly is it that you saw?'

James' mouth went tight and Liz watched as the man twisted around in his chair to look out the window. 'First, call me James, please,' he said. 'I was at the window. My daughter, Ruth, well she had just popped in to say that she was heading into town to do a bit of shopping. Then, a few minutes after she had gone, I was just staring out across the lawn, when under the tree, there she was! I looked up again, and she'd gone, but I'm so sure that I saw her. She must have gone to hide in the trees. I mean, can you imagine it? Seeing her? Just there, right in front of my eyes? I sound mad, I know I do.'

'So, it was a woman?' Liz asked. 'You're sure about that?'

'I may be old, but I'm not blind,' James said, and Liz for the first time heard the faintest of hints of the man's humour just behind what he was saying.

'And you recognised her, you said?' Liz asked. It was clear that James was distressed, so if he had seen someone, and if there was a connection between this and the sighting the previous week that Harry and Matt had dealt with, then they would have to investigate further for sure.

James hesitated at this, before he said, 'She was too far away for me to see her clearly.'

'And what was she wearing?'

'I'm not really sure,' James said. 'It's quite hard to picture it now. It's not long ago, I know, but it was all rather quick.'

'It just helps us to draw a picture of the intruder,' Liz explained.

'It wasn't a dress or anything like that,' James said then. 'But then Helen wasn't one for wearing fancy things, you know. She was a bit more practical. Jeans was her thing.'

'So this person was in jeans, then?' Liz said.

'I think so, yes,' James said. 'That's all I could tell really. It was hard to see clearly through the rain anyway.'

'Can you tell us anything else about who you saw?' Liz asked. 'What she looked like at all? Any small detail?'

'Long dark hair,' Mr Fletcher said. 'It's a family thing I think. Pat, Ruth, they both have it. Even Anthony! But then he's into all that loud heavy metal music, isn't he, so he has it all long and seems to hide behind it a bit. Plays guitar, you know? And he's very good, too. Or so I've been told! It's not really my thing, but I don't tell him that.'

Liz allowed James to ramble, but in her mind had already latched onto what he'd said about his daughters and his grandson, and the photos around them of his wife, Helen. Because if they all looked so similar, then there was every chance that it had been one of them outside, and James was probably just spooked by it, thanks to his clearly heightened state of anxiety. But that didn't matter, Liz thought. If they could just get to the bottom of it, come up with an answer, then perhaps he would be able to relax a little. He certainly looked like he needed to. And they couldn't just keep coming out to check things over based on James seeing things that weren't there.

'And what time was this?'

James checked his watch.

'About an hour ago now, I think,' he said.

'And you said that this woman was standing under that tree,' Liz confirmed.

'Maybe not standing,' James said, 'but that's where I saw her, and then she was gone.'

'Did you see where she went after that?'

Mr Fletcher lifted his glass and took a hefty hit of the drink it held, wincing a little as the liquid filled his mouth.

'Back into the shadows,' he said, the whisky swallowed. 'She was there, right over there! I bloody well saw her! And then she wasn't! And I want to, you know? I really want to see her! It's awful. I can't bear it. That's why I need to know where she is, that's she's okay.'

Liz wasn't sure what James was now talking about, and was searching for something else to say when Jen came back into the room.

'Anything?' Liz asked.

Jen looked thoughtful for a moment then shook her head. 'If there was someone there, then they could easily have slipped off back into the woods behind. Nothing on the footpath either. But it's hard to tell, really. And the ground isn't wet or soggy enough to show footprints,' Jen continued. 'It actually looks fairly dry under the branches.'

'Mr Fletcher,' Liz said, 'I wonder if it would be possible to speak to the rest of the family? Are they around at all?'

'They didn't see her though,' James replied. 'It was me. And they all think I've gone a bit loopy anyway, don't you see? And I can hardly blame them.'

'We just need to confirm where they were, that's all,' Liz said.

'Yes, I can see that,' James said. 'I'm just so sure that I saw her, you know? But then she's everywhere, even now, she's here in this room with us! I'm sure of it!'

Liz shivered and decided it was best to not think too hard as to why.

'If you could give me their numbers,' Liz said.

'No need,' James replied. 'Ruthy will be back soon, I'm sure, and as I said, she lives next door in the little cottage. Anthony is up in his room with one of his headaches, poor lad. Patricia is here with her husband, Dan, but I think they're avoiding me right now because of this, what I think I saw. They've come over, you know, to stay for a while. Which is very kind, don't you think? Oh, I've told you that already, haven't I? Everyone is just so worried, which I do understand, but it's not necessary, it really isn't. Shall I go and get them now?'

James, Liz knew now, had a habit of rambling on a bit, though she wondered if it was mainly a coping mechanism.

'That would be very helpful,' Liz said. 'Then what we'll do after is we'll knock on a few doors. There aren't exactly many properties out this way and someone might have seen something, you never know. We'll also check your security, have a look around the house to make sure everything's okay here. We'll also give you the number for the Hawes office, so if you see anything else, you can contact us directly and immediately.'

'Actually, I've got that somewhere,' James said. 'I was just in a bit of a panic and Patricia had to call for me and I forgot to give it to her.'

Just then, the door to the study opened. Liz and Jen turned to find themselves facing a pale-faced woman with long hair dark with tired eyes and car keys in her hand. Liz did a double-take.

'Forgot to give who what?' the woman asked. 'And why are the police here? Dad? What's happened? Is Anthony alright? What's going on?'

Liz looked at the woman, then at the numerous photos on the walls of James' study, remembering what he had said about the family similarity, but seeing it in the flesh was striking to the point of being uncanny.

'It's nothing, Ruthy,' James said, approaching the woman. 'Don't go getting yourself all worked up.'

Liz approached the new arrival. 'I'm PCSO Coates. You're Ruth, yes? Your father called us over. He believes he saw someone outside the house.'

'What did you see, Dad?' the woman asked, pushing past Liz. 'You know this isn't right, don't you? It can't be what you think it is! It just can't be!'

'A woman,' Jen said. 'He saw a woman, outside the house.'

At this, the new arrival turned to gaze out through the window. She raised a hand and pointed.

'Under that tree?' she asked, her voice heavy and sad. 'That one just over there on the right, yes? I'm right, aren't I?'

'How did you know?' Liz asked.

The woman turned back around, looked at her dad with sadness in her eyes. 'Because,' she said, 'it was Mum's favourite place, wasn't it, Dad?'

And at this, Liz heard the faintest of cries, and she turned to see James holding his head in his hands, and sobbing.

## CHAPTER FOURTEEN

JIM WAS PLEASED TO BE DOING SOMETHING, ANYTHING at all actually, that might have a chance of snaring the people who had taken his dad's sheep. It was a week to the day now and what they had was, in the simplest of terms, bugger all. Back home, his dad was trying to put a brave face on it, had been sorting out insurance and the rest, but it wasn't just the money that was the issue. It was so much more than that. Those animals weren't just pound signs and never had been because that wasn't what farming was about. If it was, the world would be full of rich farmers and everyone would want to be one. It wasn't and they didn't.

Farming, as Jim knew all too well himself, was in the blood. It was a compunction, a passion, something primitive, deep inside you which was impossible to escape. And to be able to do it in a place like Wensleydale? There really was nothing better. Which, in many ways, made his decision to be a PCSO all the stranger, didn't it? But he'd wanted to at least try something else, and being a PCSO meant that he was useful, didn't it? Which, in many ways, made what had happened sting even more, because he hadn't been able to prevent what had happened on his own property.

'So, what's the plan?' Jadyn asked, as Gordy and Harry led the way, with Jim and Jadyn just a step or two behind. They had just passed the ropemakers and were now heading up the hill towards the auction mart, which was a few minutes away yet.

'There's no plan, as such,' Gordy said.

Harry said, 'Probably best if we keep that to ourselves though, eh? Wouldn't want to come off as unprofessional.'

Jim laughed as Gordy continued, ignoring Harry's interruption. 'We want you two to be very visible. We've got details of the flock, and Jim, you're well known up at the mart anyway, so you've a better chance than any of us of finding out if anyone's seen or heard anything. And folk will be asking after your dad, no doubt, so go with that, see what happens.'

'And he's doing okay, is he?' Harry asked.

'He is,' Jim said. 'He's good at keeping busy, and just out of range of Mum.'

Jadyn said, 'But haven't we done all this already? We've all been out and around the farms since it happened. So, what are we hoping we'll find here?'

'Just keep your eyes open,' Harry said. 'Yes, we've been out, and that's good, but that doesn't mean we're done, now, does it? Not in the slightest, actually. Seeing us up at the mart, well that'll certainly reassure people that we're around for a start, because I'm pretty sure that one flock being taken is more than enough to get the whole dale worried. Am I right, Jim?'

'You are that,' Jim said. 'And I know that they shouldn't

be, but I'm pretty sure there's a few out there now who've taken to late-night walks around their fields with a gun. They'll say they're out lamping, after a few rabbits, but they're not. They're scared. And who can blame them?'

'And while we're up there,' Gordy said, turning an eye to Jadyn, 'use this as an opportunity to find out more about farming. Because let's face it, you're not exactly clued up on it, and it's kind of the main thing in Wensleydale.'

'I know more than our DCI does,' Jadyn said.

'Watch it,' Harry said. 'I know what a tup and ewe is now, don't I? Before you know it, I'll be telling you what breeds they are and whatever else you need to know about sheep. Which I'm sure is a lot.'

A few minutes later, they made to cross over the road, when a shout pulled them up short. Jim turned around to see a man coming out of a garden gate to meet them.

'Hello, Reverend,' Jim said.

'Good to see you, Jim,' the man replied, then he looked over at Harry. 'We've met,' he said, 'but I've a feeling we've both been too busy to make it more than that.' He held out his hand. 'I'm Mike Rawlings, the Methodist Minister.'

Harry shook the man's hand. 'Most vicars I know are old and grey,' he said.

'Well, I'm not a vicar for a start,' Mike smiled.

'And where's your dog collar?'

'On the dog,' Mike replied. 'Can't stand the thing. I wear it for official stuff, and if folk want me to, but generally I leave it at home.'

'Is there something we can help you with?' Jim asked.

'You off to the mart?' Mike asked. 'I'll be heading over myself, later. Highlight of my week. Make sure I never miss it.'

'We are,' Jim said.

'After what happened, we're just going to show a bit of police presence, that kind of thing,' Harry said.

'That'll reassure folk, I'm sure,' Mike said. 'After what happened with your dad's flock, Jim, people are jumpy.'

Harry leaned in. 'Don't suppose you've heard anything about what happened?'

Mike shook his head. 'Sorry, no. But if I do hear something, I'll let you know straight away. But it's not that I was coming over for. It's about James Fletcher.'

'Liz and Jen are over there now,' Jim said. 'What's wrong?'

Mike quickly told them about a number of phone calls he'd had with James since the crash. 'I visited right away, and obviously, there was the trauma they were dealing with, but since then, these calls? Something's not right.'

'You mean how he's seeing his wife around the place?' Harry said.

'I know he called you out last week, and he's done it again?'

'Just this morning,' Jim said.

Mike fell quiet.

Harry asked, 'Something bothering you, Rev?'

'James is, or was, a sensible man,' Mike said. 'He wouldn't be reporting stuff, calling you, if he wasn't seeing something. I'm doing my best to keep him focused, to think things through, but this? Well, I just think there's more to it, that's all.'

'You want us to take it seriously, is that what you're saying?' Gordy asked.

'I do,' Mike said. 'What happened, it was awful, and James is really going through it. But this worries me. I know

I'm being vague, and really, I had no idea what I was going to say to you when I saw you, but I thought I'd best just mention it anyway.'

Harry handed Mike his card.

'Call me if you need to,' he said. 'And it's good to know we've not just got another pair of eyes on the mart here and what happened at Jim's place, but over at the Fletcher's too. Much appreciated.'

Mike stepped back. 'Well, I'll let you get on. I'm actually thinking of buying myself a few pet lambs next year, Jim, so I'll need your advice on that.'

'Pet lambs?' Harry said. 'Who the hell keeps a lamb as a pet?'

'No one does,' Jim laughed. 'It's the lambs that are spare, like, where we have triplets and the mum can only look after two, or the mum dies during the birth or just rejects her lambs. If we can't get another ewe to take them, then they get sold.'

'I knew that,' Jadyn said, with a knowing nod.

'You're a terrible liar,' said Harry. 'Anyway, thanks Mike, and good to meet you.'

'I'll give you a call,' Mike said, holding up Harry's card. 'Go for a pint some time. If you're going to stay around, then I'm sure I can give you a good insight into the local community.'

'Of course, he's staying!' Gordy smiled. 'I don't think any of us can imagine the place without him now.'

As they turned to cover the final few steps over to the mart, Harry called out, 'Look, you go on and I'll catch up. I've a phone call to make.'

'Well, don't be long,' Gordy said.

As they walked off, Jim glanced back at his boss and

couldn't help but hope that Gordy was right and that Harry was going to be staying around. It wasn't just that they needed him, but that despite his gruff nature and occasional short temper, they liked him. And that, Jim thought, was worth more than gold.

# CHAPTER FIFTEEN

LIZ WAS NOW SITTING IN A RATHER OLD-FASHIONED farmhouse-style kitchen and nursing a large mug of steaming hot tea. Jen was busy doing a sweep of the house to check windows and the like, and to make sure that the house was as secure as it could be. They had both been rather surprised to discover that such a large and impressive house had no high-end security system installed. Indeed, when they had asked to check it, James had laughed at them, said something about how no security system in the world could be a match for his years of military training, and then taken Jen off for a guided tour.

'I'm sorry about my dad,' Ruth said, sitting down opposite Liz. 'He takes a lot of getting used to. By which I mean, never. I mean, he's absolutely lovely, but right now, I don't know what's going on with him at all.'

Liz kept her response non-committal. 'I'm really sorry about your mum,' she said. 'Must be very hard for you.'

Ruth nodded and Liz saw the pain in the woman's eyes and the effort she was having to put into not breaking down.

She was also still struck by how similar she looked to her mum.

'It was a shock for us all,' she said. 'Mum was a wonderful woman.'

'She looked very happy in the photos,' Liz said.

Ruth just smiled but said nothing more.

'You live with your son, next door,' Liz said.

'Yes,' Ruth replied.

'How old?'

'Sixteen,' Ruth said, then pulled out her phone and flicked the screen round to Liz. 'There he is.'

Liz glanced at the screen to see a pale-faced boy smiling through long black hair. He was wearing a Black Sabbath T-shirt. But what Liz noticed most of all was, once again, that striking family resemblance.

'I like his style,' Liz said. 'Good taste in music.'

'Yes.' Ruth nodded. 'He's a good lad.'

Liz heard something in Ruth's voice, something hidden, but wasn't exactly sure what. 'And he's at school, yes?' she asked.

Another nod, though with more hesitation.

'And he's getting on alright, is he?'

'On and off,' Ruth said. 'But then who's really ever truly happy at school? Like most teenager boys I think he'd rather be listening to music and playing Call of Duty.'

Liz took a sip of her tea wondering not only about what Ruth was hiding behind her words but also if it was relevant. And she was getting hungry now as well, but no biscuits were on offer, so she'd have to ignore that till they were back in Hawes.

'When we were back in the study,' Liz began, not really knowing quite how to approach what had happened after Ruth had entered the room. 'You seemed to suggest that—'

'That my dad is seeing things?' Ruth said, finishing off what Liz was going to ask. 'Of course, he is! You saw the whisky glass in his hand, right? It's only a week since we lost Mum and he's not dealing with it well. Not that he will admit that, of course. No, not Dad. That would be . . .' She paused, staring off into the corner of the room for a moment, as though searching for what to say next. 'He's just a bit stubborn,' she finally said. 'But this whole thing with seeing an intruder that he thinks is Mum? It's really not like him at all. I don't understand any of it.'

Liz sat back in her chair. 'Has this happened a lot then, since the accident?' she asked. 'You know, your dad seeing your mum?'

Liz watched as Ruth searched for what to say next, casting her eyes around the room as though trying to find the words behind the pictures on the wall.

'He's been talking about some strange stuff,' Ruth said eventually, and Liz could tell that she was struggling with the words. 'No, this sounds insane, it doesn't matter.'

'Actually, it does,' Liz said. 'Your dad is clearly in a bad place, you all are, I know, but if he's seeing things and then calling us? We need to be aware of it. This is the second time now that we've come out, and we can't just keep doing so if there's nothing here. That doesn't mean we can't help, though, it's just a case of resources really.'

'I know,' Ruth said.

'It sounds cruel,' Liz continued, 'but it's not. In fact, we're here right now because we're concerned and we need to make sure that things are okay, that he's safe, I suppose.'

'Safe?'

'People suffering trauma can react in different ways,' Liz said. 'Wander off, disappear, behave really out of character. We don't want him to come to any harm.'

'No, I get that,' Ruth said. 'I really do, and it's appreciated, and I promise you won't get any more calls. I can't allow this to happen again. It's not on.'

'You said that he's been talking about something strange or odd?' Liz asked. 'How do you mean?'

'A few days ago he started asking me about the afterlife,' Ruth said. 'Death, and if we exist beyond it. I didn't think much of it, but he kept coming back to it, saying that he wanted to see Mum again, that he even speaks to her.'

'Well, I suppose that's understandable,' Liz said. 'Just needs a bit of reassurance.'

'Yes, but it's gone a bit further than that,' Ruth said. 'He wants proof. He wants to know where she is and that she's okay. It's because he blames himself, says he should have been driving.'

'Perhaps it's all part of how he's dealing with it,' Liz suggested, wondering now where the conversation was going, because wherever that was, none of what they were talking about now was what she had been expecting. A cup of tea and a bit of a listening ear, sure, but this? Well, it did sound a little bit out there. 'Why does he say he should have been driving?'

'It was his birthday and Mum drove so he could have a drink, but she really doesn't like driving at night, never has.'

'Why?'

Ruth shook her head. 'Honestly, I always thought she was making it up, but she always said she couldn't see very well at night, like her eyes just didn't focus properly or something.'

'Well, that's a thing, you know,' Liz said. 'Some people do suffer from night blindness. There's a posh name for it but I can't remember what it is.'

'Well, there was nothing wrong with her eyes, nothing serious anyway, but she was always a bit clumsy, walking into stuff in the evening, shutting doors on herself.'

'No way.'

'Honestly, it's true,' Ruth said, her voice momentarily lighter. 'Even shut her head in a car door once! How is that even possible?'

Ruth laughed then and Liz thought how perhaps this happy memory, however brief, might help the woman a little.

'She even bought those night vision glasses,' Ruth said. 'You know, those massive, daft yellow things? Can't see that they do anything other than make you look like a massive insect with these huge alien eyes staring out. She lost them anyway.'

'So, this poor night vision was something that she had for years, then?'

'I guess,' Ruth said. 'Maybe it was something, maybe it wasn't, but she didn't like driving at night, and if you were in the car with her when she was, and another car was coming the other way, she would always slow down, veer off a little away from it. It was never dangerous, just odd, like she'd just got used to being a bit scared of it all, driving in the dark, I mean.'

'But she still did it?'

'Only on special occasions,' Ruth said. 'Like Dad's birthday. So, in some ways he's probably right, you know? That she would be alive if he'd been driving. God, I feel awful thinking that. And now, with what Dad's on about, it's all just a bit too much.'

Liz let Ruth sit quietly for a moment, before gently prodding her again. 'You were saying how your dad was talking about death.'

'So, at the weekend,' Ruth said, raising her hands then as though talking to a crowd, 'this woman turned up at the door. Beverly Sanford, she's called.'

'Can't say that I've heard of her.'

'She's from up Sedbergh way,' Ruth said. 'Anyway, turns out that Dad had given her a call and asked her to come over.'

'Is she an old friend?' Liz asked.

Ruth shook her head. 'No, she's a spiritualist or psychic medium or whatever it was she called herself.'

'A what?'

'Someone who can talk to the dead.'

Liz had her mug of tea halfway to her mouth and that's where it remained for a moment before she placed it back down on the table. When she next spoke she had to work hard to keep her voice measured, to make sure she didn't sound like she was dismissing what Ruth had just told her.

'And your father, he believes in this, does he?'

'Well, he never used to!' Ruth said. 'Mum used to like going to church a bit now and again, but it wasn't Dad's thing, not unless it was something he could attach some military significance to. Remembrance Sunday is always a good excuse for him to get his uniform out. Takes that very seriously.'

Liz wasn't quite sure now what to do with what they were talking about. But she would keep Ruth occupied until Jen returned.

'And what happened?'

'She was actually very nice,' Ruth said. 'Not that Patricia

was having anything to do with it. But then, I don't really know why she and Dan are here at all, to be honest.'

'And why's that?' Liz asked.

'She hardly ever visits,' Ruth said. 'And she's not the best when it comes to dealing with emotional stuff. And now, here she is, well, here both of them are, and they're staying for two months! It's not like they even asked, they just phoned, told us that was what was happening, and here we are!'

Liz sensed a little family tension.

'It's good to have family around though,' she said.

'Is it?' Ruth replied. 'They're just worried Dad's going to shuffle off this mortal coil and leave me more than them, that's all. You've seen the place! It's worth a packet.'

This was now turning into a conversation that Liz really didn't want to be getting pulled in to. So she said, 'And you live next door, right? Looks lovely.'

'It is,' Ruth said. 'Mum and Dad used to rent it out as a holiday home, but me and Anthony, we've lived there for years, since Anthony's dad buggered off actually. I could move, but it's so nice here.'

For a moment, both women sat in silence. Liz didn't really have much else to say, and she was silently hoping that Ruth was done. It had probably done her the world of good, Liz thought, to just get a few things off her chest. It wasn't exactly in the job description, but she couldn't help feel that this was a good deed done.

'Do you think it's something you ever get over?' Ruth asked, finishing her tea. 'Something like this? I don't see how it's possible. I really don't.'

'If it's hard, then there's support out there,' Liz said. 'But I think it's probably not so much a case of getting over something, as it is a mix of acceptance and working out ways to live with it.'

'Likes scars, you mean,' Ruth said.

'Yes, I suppose I do,' Liz replied.

'I'd like to think that's possible,' Ruth said. 'But for Dad, I'm just not so sure. Mum died in his arms, you know?'

'That's awful,' Liz said.

'After the crash, he pulled her from the wreckage, just a split second before it burst into flames, apparently. And then she died while he was holding her. I can't see him getting over that, can you? I don't see how it's possible. No wonder he's always talking about it, about her, about wanting to see her again.'

'I'm really sorry,' Liz said and reached out a hand for Ruth's. Then, as their hands touched, Ruth shuddered and a sob broke from her so heartfelt and full of pain and exhaustion that it was all Liz could do to remain in her seat.

Liz said, 'It's a hugely traumatic experience. You need to be kind to yourself, to let yourself grieve. Look, there are support counsellors . . .'

'I know,' Ruth said. 'But there's only so much, you know?'

'What about your dad?'

At this, Ruth laughed. 'Dad? Counselling? Can you imagine? No, he's dealing with it in his own weird way, I think, by refusing all the sensible help, and instead, seeing things and trying to talk to ghosts!'

'About that,' Liz said. 'There really is every possibility that he did see someone outside. We can't just assume he was seeing things, regardless of the circumstances and the death of your mother.'

'I know,' Ruth said, 'but I can't see it, can you? Why

would anyone want to come out here and look at the house? There's no reason to it! No reason at all!'

'Perhaps not,' Liz said, 'but we still have to take it seriously and treat it as we would any other report of an intruder. That's why we're here. But what we've seen today, what you've told us, perhaps we can all keep an eye on him for a while?'

'You have a job to do,' Ruth said, 'and if doing that in any way helps Dad realise he needs some help, then all the better, if you ask me.'

A noise from the kitchen door interrupted the conversation.

'Anthony!' Ruth said, as Liz turned to see a pale, teenage boy walk into the room. He was wearing a faded green army surplus jacket over a black Motley Crue hoodie, black jeans, and black lace-up boots. 'What are you doing here?'

The boy stood there for a moment, staring at nothing.

Liz said, 'Didn't you say he was at school?'

'Yes,' Ruth said, 'and he is, just not today. Migraine, isn't that right, Anthony?'

'Yes,' the boy said with a faint nod, though Liz thought with the height on him calling him a boy was pushing it because he was getting into young man territory now. She noticed scratches on the backs of his hands. They weren't bleeding, but they looked fresh, like he'd caught them on a rose bush.

'I saw the police car outside,' Anthony said.

'Look,' Ruth said, 'let's get you home, shall we? If your head is still bad then getting up and walking around isn't going to do it any good, is it?'

'Why are the police here?' Anthony asked.

Liz rose to her feet. 'I'm PCSO Coates,' she said, then

looked at Ruth, who gave a quick nod. 'Can I just ask if you saw or heard anything strange around the house today at all, perhaps outside in the garden?'

'Strange how?' Anthony asked. 'What do you mean? What's happened?'

'Nothing has happened,' Ruth said. 'It's just that your grandad thought he saw someone outside the house earlier, that's all.'

'Really?' Anthony asked. 'Where? Who?'

'It was round at the back of the house,' Liz said. 'Have you seen anything?'

'Nothing,' Anthony said, and Liz caught him flick a glance at his mum. 'I've been off, with a migraine.'

'And you didn't hear or see anything?'

'Nothing,' Anthony said.

'You're sure?' Liz pressed.

'Totally,' Anthony said. 'I've been out for the count. And I've had my curtains closed the whole time. Darkness helps with the headaches a little.'

Ruth looked over at Liz. 'I think I'd better get him back home, if that's okay?'

'You do that,' Liz replied. 'I'll go and see if I can find your dad and Constable Blades.'

Following Ruth and Anthony out of the kitchen, Liz made her way back into the main body of the house.

'Thanks for your time, Ruth,' she said. 'And nice to meet you, too, Anthony.' But as she went to leave them, she asked, 'Those scratches on your hands, Anthony. They look fresh.'

Liz watched Anthony turn his hands over and stare at them.

'There's a bush outside,' he said. 'I must've brushed past it when I came over. Didn't even notice it.'

'Yes, I suppose that would be it,' Liz said.

'It could be the ghost,' Anthony said then. 'What Grandad saw, I mean.'

Liz caught the roll-of-the-eyes from Ruth as the boy's mother tried to hurry him on.

'Less of that, young man!' she said. 'Honestly, far too vivid an imagination!'

'I've not seen it myself,' Anthony continued, his mother trying to shove him along the hall, 'but that's why the house has that bit missing, you know, in the middle?'

'Right, that's it, enough!' Ruth said, her voice louder now, firm and commanding. 'Into bed, or I'll drive you to school this instant!'

Before Liz could ask Anthony anything more about it, he was bustled off along the hall, his mother shooing him with her hands.

'Ah, there you are!'

Liz turned to see Jen and Mr Fletcher approaching.

'All checked, then?' she asked.

All the windows are secure,' Jen said. 'I've checked all the locks, doors, and windows in every room. I've advised he get a proper security system installed, but he's not exactly keen.'

'All utterly unnecessary,' Mr Fletcher said. 'But thank you anyway. Did you have a nice chat with Ruthy?'

'I did, and I met your grandson,' Liz said. 'He mentioned something about the house . . .'

Liz paused then, thought about what Ruth's son had said, about what the family had gone through, about Mr Fletcher's not entirely stable state of mind at that moment, and decided to say nothing more.

'Mentioned what?' James said. 'What did he say?'

'Oh, it was nothing,' Liz said, and she shone a bright smile at the man. 'We've got everything I think, Mr Fletcher. So, we had best be off. If we do find anything out about who you saw, then we will obviously be in touch.'

'And if you see anything at all, you know where we are,' Jen added.

James walked them to the back door, then waved goodbye as they wandered over to the car.

'Well, that was fun,' Jen said, as Liz shut the passenger door. 'Not a happy house, is it?'

Liz shook her head. 'No surprise, really, with what's happened.'

'Yeah, it's pretty much the worst thing ever,' Jen said.

Jen turned the car around and headed them back down the track leading to the main road, ready to turn left and back on towards Hawes. 'I think we all know, though, that there was no intruder,' she said. 'He's obviously just tired, dealing with something truly horrible, and just not coping well.'

As they waited at the road for a sudden flurry of traffic to pass, Liz glanced back up to the house, her eyes drawn to the dark space between the main dwelling and the smaller one off to its left.

'It is an odd place, isn't it?' she said. 'What with that gap in the middle.'

'You know why that's there, don't you?' Jen asked, the traffic finally clear, accelerating them out onto the road. 'Why it was knocked down?'

'So, it used to be one big house, then?' Liz asked.

'I'm not sure when it happened, like,' Jen explained. 'And for all I know it's not even true, but remember when I said about my boyfriend in Appersett? It was him that told me.'

'Told you what?' Liz asked, remembering what Anthony had said.

At this, Jen became quiet, then took a long, deep breath.

'Come on, then,' Liz said. 'Tell me! What did this boyfriend tell you? Did something happen at the house? What?'

Jen changed gear then slowly turned her head to stare at Liz.

'It's haunted,' she said. 'And the ghost is why the rooms in the middle were demolished.'

# CHAPTER SIXTEEN

When the funeral came around, just over a week after the accident, darkness, James realised, was the only word which could even come close to describing how he'd felt since his beautiful Helen had been taken so suddenly, and so terribly, from him. And it was how he felt right now, as he leaned on his stick, his leg still aching from the accident, and watched her coffin be lowered into the ground. Grammatically, such a description wasn't entirely correct, he knew that, and he smiled to himself, thinking of how it would have annoyed his wife for him to describe his feelings in such a way.

'You can't say you feel like darkness!' she would have said, her voice a sweet mix of affection and irritation. 'It just doesn't make sense! Darkness isn't a feeling, is it?'

Well, it was, James thought, very much so, in fact. And it was all around him now, a blanket of darkness so thick, so suffocating, that it was all he could do to not fall into the ground with her and on into oblivion. It mattered not that the cemetery, which sat at the Bainbridge end of Hawes, was easily one of the most picturesque in the world, the deep green hulk of Wether Fell laying far up and beyond them in quiet slumber, tucked up tightly under its own blanket of meadow, moorland, and field. The beauty of the place, James knew, would now be forever marred by his loss, as bright and clear as a splash of blood on freshly washed linen hung on a line to dry in the sun.

'James?'

James heard the voice but didn't respond. His eyes were lost to the grave.

'Mr Fletcher?'

James took his eyes away from the casket containing the remains of his heart and soul and turned to the owner of the voice, aware now that he was still wearing the smile from the memory of Helen's voice, an unwelcome visitor on his face. He would give anything to hear it again. Absolutely anything. God, how he wished he could.

Mr Michael Rawlings, the Methodist Minister, was staring at James with concerned eyes, his rarely worn dog collar a band of white noosed around his throat. He was a man James didn't really know that well, having only been in touch with him since Helen's death. But he had visited him and said all the right things, and not in a churchy way either, James remembered, and he'd appreciated that. He had thought about telling him about the visit from the medium, what she'd said, and that she was coming back to the house, but had decided against it in the end.

'You said you wanted to say something, James. We talked about it last week when I came over?'

'What?'

'Some words, remember?' Mr Rawlings said. 'About Helen? But don't feel like you have to. That's absolutely fine as well. And I mean that. Everyone would understand. And we can come back another day if you want, just you and I, have another little private ceremony together.'

For a moment, James' mind was blank, and he just stared back at the minister. Then a cold wind snapped its way through those gathered with him around the grave, a whipcrack of ice against skin, and he remembered.

'Good God, yes, sorry,' he said, fumbling in his pockets. 'Yes, it's here. I wrote something down, I'm sure I did . . .'

His jacket pockets were empty. His trouser pockets, too.

'I'm sorry,' James apologised once again. 'It's here, I know it is . . .'

He searched again, willing the notes he had written down to be there. Because that's where they were, they had to be, it was where he had put them, and he wasn't one for misplacing things, not ever.

'Shitting hell!' James hissed, his searching growing more frantic. 'Where the hell are they? Where, damn it?'

A hand rested on his arm.

'James, it's fine, honestly,' the minister said. 'I'm sure Helen—'

'It bloody well isn't fine at all!' James snapped back, working hard to control his emotions, but failing terribly. 'I put it here! In my pocket! I swear that I did! Right bloody here! Words about Helen, yes, I remember. Could probably say it off by heart, you know? But I don't want to, I don't want to make a mistake, that wouldn't be right . . .'

James was very aware now of the eyes on him from the small gathering of family and friends. Not that he cared right then. And he pulled his pocket inside out.

'I put it here! Right here, didn't I? I did! So, where in damnation is it?'

'Dad?'

James stopped searching.

'Dad!'

James looked up to see Ruth, his youngest daughter, staring up at him. Dear God, she looked like her mum, he thought. It was almost uncanny. Helen had always been a bright thing, hadn't she, and here she was, shining out through the face of her beautiful daughter, a shimmering thing of gossamer caught in a sunbeam. No, a bee's wing, that was it, like in the song, James thought. But in the end, it wasn't wind that had taken her away, was it? And Ruth's face, usually so warm, so vibrant, well now there was no warmth to it, was there? James thought, as she stared at him now with eyes as hard and dead, and yet as beautiful as a Da Vinci statue carved in marble.

Behind Ruth, James saw Patricia and her husband, Dan, and Ruth's teenage son, Anthony. His family, he thought, and all of them hurting. Behind them, he saw other faces, of friends, relatives who were little more than names on Christmas cards. And then there was a face he took a moment to register, because he didn't immediately have a name to place with it, but the scars he remembered, and that was enough. That the police had turned up to the funeral, well, that said a lot, he thought. And what was the name of that new one, now? Grimm, yes, that was it. And there he was, with two more from his team. It was very good of them to be here at all, wasn't it?

'Dad!'

The shout was a slap at a window, and James jolted out of his rambling thoughts.

'Yes?'

Ruth held out a hand. 'I saw them fall from your pocket, while you were searching.'

James looked down at his daughter's pale hand and saw his notes. He snatched them back, didn't mean to, but also didn't feel quite in the mood to apologise.

Ruth took a long, slow breath and James knew that she understood, that she wasn't hurt by his behaviour.

James turned from his daughter and moved to stand at the foot of Helen's grave. To his side, Ruth walked back to stand with the rest of the family.

'Right then,' James said, clearing his throat, unfolding the notes to read. 'Best I get this done so we can all get home before the rain comes in, eh?'

James cast a look around the small gathering, unable to fully grasp the reality of it, that he was there, that any of them were, and Helen wasn't.

Mr Rawlings, the minister, coughed.

'Right, yes,' James said, realising he had fallen silent for a little too long. 'I suppose I should just get on with it, shouldn't I? Helen was never one for hanging about, was she?' He laughed at the memory, imagining his wife chivvying him along, but his laugh cracked and broke apart, crumbling to dust around him.

James unfolded the notes Ruth had handed him, brushing off a bit of dirt and grass, then stared at the words. At first, they were clear and he opened his mouth to start reading, but then all he could see was the grave, and the words turned to tasteless mush in his mouth, because the grave was the end, and Helen was down there, except she wasn't, because she couldn't be, could she? Whatever it was that was down there, it wasn't Helen, she was gone, and he wanted her back, to hear her voice, to hold her and laugh with her and fall asleep with her and, dear God, the pain of it!

James' cry caught in his throat. He looked up at the people in front of him, at his daughters, his family, his friends, all of them waiting for him to say something, to somehow sum up what they were all thinking, what they were all feeling, to condense their grief into . . . into what? James thought. How could he? It was impossible, all of it! He just couldn't!

James rubbed his thumb over his notes, tried to read the words again, but there was water on the paper now, and the words started to smear because he was crying, and that was all he could do, just cry and weep and let the agony of this moment flow out of him until there was nothing left.

A cough brought James back into the now and he wiped his eyes with the collar of his jacket, sniffed hard enough to burn the back of his throat. With another glance at those gathered around Helen's grave, he folded up his notes and slipped them back into his pocket out of sight.

'I can't . . .' James said, his voice breaking on the pain ripping him apart inside. 'I just can't do this. It's wrong, all of it . . .'

James turned on his heels, whipping himself around and away from the hideous thing at his feet, the deep, dark muddy hole that had swallowed his dead wife with silent glee. The whole thing was an abomination! Helen's death, the crash that had taken her, this god-awful funeral!

'Dad!'

James didn't stop. He was at the cemetery gate now, car keys in his hand, his walk now a run, even though his leg still hurt from the crash, because he couldn't get away fast enough.

'Dad! Stop!'

James hit the button on the key fob and just ahead the lights blinked on the hire car he'd been driving since the accident.

A hand grabbed at him, but he pulled away from it.

'No, I'm not stopping here!' he shouted, refusing to turn around and face whoever it was that had made chase. 'I can't and I won't, you hear? I just won't! I'm not doing this, not any of it!'

'You have to!' Ruth cried after him. 'Please, Dad! You have to! You're not being fair! It's not just about you! It's not! You can't own this! You can't own Mum's death! Please!'

At this, James jarred to a halt and whipped round, something rare broiling in his stomach, twisting his grief into a wild animal of teeth and spit.

'What did you say?'

'You can't just leave!' Ruth said, standing in front of him now. 'I know it's hard, Dad. God, it's hard for all of us, but we need you here. We all do!'

'No, you don't,' James replied 'She's gone, Ruth! That's it! And it's not like she's coming back, is it? So, what the hell is the point of any of this, can you tell me that? Can anyone? It doesn't make sense! She should be here, with me, with us, not in that . . . that awful hole in the ground over there!'

Ruth opened her mouth, but James didn't give her a chance to speak.

'I was with her, remember? When she died? Have you any idea what that was like?'

'Of course, I remember that, Dad,' Ruth said. 'It was terrible, I know it was. We all know that, which is why you need to come back, please.'

James stepped towards his daughter, his arms out in front

of him now, as though carrying something heavy, his hands splayed open.

'I held her, Ruth! Held her in these arms, and I couldn't save her! I prayed, you know that, don't you? I prayed like you wouldn't believe! I screamed at that bastard up there in the clouds to do something as my wife bled all over me! I begged him to heal her somehow, because he's God, right, and he can do that, can't he? I mean, that's the whole point of being God, isn't it? I tried to put the blood back in, to scoop it up and just get it back inside her, but it didn't work and it just kept coming and coming! Well, guess what? He didn't! He just let her die, right there in my arms!'

'You're just angry, Dad,' Ruth said. 'That's normal. How can you be anything else? It's okay, really it is.'

'Angry?' James laughed, the sound of it twisting his voice into a manic cry. 'I'm absolutely bloody livid, is what I am, Ruth! Raging inside like you wouldn't bloody believe! So, don't you go expecting me to stand over your mother's body and send prayers to Heaven! I begged for help, I begged for her life! I even offered mine in her place, did I tell you that? Well, I did, and yet here we are!'

James watched as tears rolled down the pale cheeks of his daughter's face. He turned around to climb into his vehicle, only to hear another voice join in.

'You can't just leave, Dad. It's wrong. This is Mum's funeral. It's important.'

Patricia's voice was all knives and ice, James noticed as he sat down behind the steering wheel. He made to pull the door shut behind him, but Patricia was in the way now, Ruth standing behind her.

'Best you just let me go, lass,' he said. 'Please. I don't

want an argument. I just want to go home, back to where Helen is. Where I can still feel her, that's all.'

'No, Dad,' Patricia said. 'I won't. It's like Ruth said, we need you! And even though I know you won't admit it, you bloody well need us, too! I mean, why on earth do you think Dan and I have given up our time? It's not for fun, it's to help! So you need to listen.'

James tugged at the door, but Patricia had her whole body against it now and was leaning in close. Then Ruth joined in.

'Mum loved you, Dad,' Ruth said, and James heard the tears and pain in her voice. 'And you loved her. You need to say goodbye.'

'No,' James said. 'I won't. I can't.'

'She's right,' Patricia said, backing up her sister. 'Mum loved you more than anyone ever could. But she's gone and we need to deal with that, deal with it together. So come on, out of the car, and back to where you should be. Everyone's waiting.'

James tried again with the door.

'I loved her so much,' he said. 'She was my everything. I don't know what to do. I just don't!'

'Then come back with us,' Ruth said. 'You have to, you know that, don't you? For Mum's sake, for your own?'

James turned to get out of the car, but then his eyes saw what lay behind his two daughters, the graveyard, the mourners, and all he could see then was himself falling into that grave, tumbling down into the musty, damp darkness, Helen somewhere off ahead of him, both of them falling now, and him just screaming, desperate to reach her, to bring her back, and that darkness just going on and on and on, never ending, a bleak nothingness swallowing them both whole.

Overcome with rage and grief, James slammed the car door too hard. Patricia stumbled back into Ruth, who lost her footing, then tumbled backwards and fell onto the road. She stared back up at him, confusion and hurt in her eyes, as Patricia went to her aid.

James paused, thought about helping her up, but then the grief crashed in on him once again, and the next thing he knew he was heading back down into Hawes, and on towards home, where memories waited for him in every room like ghosts.

# CHAPTER SEVENTEEN

THE FUNERAL WAS OVER AND DONE WITH, AND NOW, ON the evening of the very same day, James knew exactly what the rest of the family were thinking about him, but right there and then he simply didn't care. Not in a mean way, more that he just didn't have the space in his head right now to be dealing with it. They were all dealing with the shock of Helen's death in their own way, and this was his, wasn't it? So, the best they could do, as far as he was concerned, was to let him get on with it.

It was certainly healthier than Patricia's approach, he thought. As she had done with everything throughout her whole life, she'd simply buried whatever she was feeling good and deep, and that was where it would stay. James often wondered if at some point his eldest daughter would suffer a nervous breakdown, on account of everything she had bottled up over the years, like a bottle of fizzy pop, shaken up so much that it finally just explodes.

As for Ruth, she was probably the most normal of them all, wearing her emotions for all to see. He'd lost count of the number of times he'd found her crying. Anthony was being strong for his mum. He was sad, that was obvious, but the death of a grandparent was still a little distant, wasn't it? And looking after his mum, well, that was a good thing.

Dan, James just couldn't read. He was all concern and sincerity on the surface, but he'd never really got to know the man. That probably had little to do with him and more to do with Patricia's urge to live as far away as possible from the dales and to only visit if she really had to. And he was very interested in the house, this time, wasn't he?

'So, what happens now, then?' Patricia asked, her voice as warm as the grey ash of a long-dead fire, damp from the rain and hidden in the sweet darkness of the trees.

They were all in the lounge, sprawled out on various sofas and chairs. Anthony was lost in a game on his phone, plugged into his wireless headphones.

'We're just waiting for Beverly,' James said, looking at the clock above the fireplace. 'She's due at eight.'

'And I'm sure she'll be fashionably late,' Patricia said, 'and blame it on some nonsense like her chakras being out of alignment or something.'

'If you don't want to be here, then you don't have to be,' James said. 'I'm not forcing you to stay.'

'Oh, I'm staying alright,' Patricia said. 'I want to make sure that whatever this woman is here to do, that she doesn't get one single chance to make a fool of you, or any of us, for that matter.'

James wanted to say more but knew there was little point. Patricia was an expert at sitting in any room and absorbing all the light and warmth. It was hard to believe that she could ever have been born of someone as warm and caring as Helen. He loved her, of course, he did, he just didn't understand her, and that bothered him. And it probably always would, he thought.

A knock at the front door had everyone looking to James.

'Right on time,' he said, heading out of the lounge.

'And why does she insist on using that door?' Patricia said. 'Everyone uses the one around the back. Everyone! It's like she wants to make some kind of grand entrance, isn't it? And did you see what she was wearing? All those bangles and scarves. Ridiculous! She may as well just wear an enormous *I Talk to The Dead* badge, for goodness sake!'

James came back into the room with Beverly behind him.

'Everyone's here,' he said. 'So long as that's okay.'

'It's fine,' Beverly said, then said hello to everyone else, before walking calmly over to the windows. She stood there for a moment, staring out into the darkness, before drawing the curtains closed, shutting the night out completely. She then walked slowly across the floor back to join everyone else.

'Look, I can't say that I understand any of this,' Ruth said, walking over towards Beverly as she came back from the curtains, 'but if it helps dad deal with what happened? Then, I'll support it.'

James smiled a thank you to his daughter.

'Where do you want us?' Dan asked.

Beverly looked around the room then pointed at the coffee table in front of the fire. 'If we could pull the chairs around that, I think we'll be fine.'

'Anthony?' Ruth said, reaching over to tap her son on his head. 'You joining us?'

He pulled his earphones out and looked up at Beverly.

'Are we doing a Ouija board?' he asked. 'Awesome!'

Beverly laughed. 'Too many horror films, right?'

'No Ouija, then?'

'I'm afraid not, no,' Beverly said.

James asked for Dan to help and they shuffled and moved the chairs and sofas until they had them in a rough circle around the coffee table.

'Do you have those items I asked for?' Beverly asked.

'I do,' James said and pointed at a sideboard on the other side of the room. 'In the drawer, over there.'

'Excellent,' Beverly said. 'Now, if you could all just give me a couple of minutes alone, that would be great.'

'Alone?' Patricia said. 'Why could you possibly need to be alone in here?'

James watched as a patient smile slipped across Beverly's face.

'Don't worry,' she said, 'it's nothing to do with getting rid of negative energies and auras or anything like that. I just need a moment to myself, to collect my thoughts, so that I'm fully focused on why we're here.'

'Dad?' Patricia said. 'Are you really sure about this?'

'I am,' James said. 'So come on, let's give her a couple of minutes, shall we?'

Out in the hallway, no one said a word and James noticed how everyone was avoiding catching someone else's eyes. When Beverly called them back in, it was clear that everyone was relieved just to be getting on with it.

'Right then,' Beverly said, 'if we can all take a seat, I think we'll get started.'

James was first to sit, taking a seat closest to the fire, with his back to the window, followed by Ruth and Anthony, then Dan. Patricia stayed on her feet. He saw that the coffee table was covered in a white cotton shawl covering three items.

'Honestly, if you don't want to be here, you don't have to be,' James said. 'It really doesn't matter.'

Beverly said, 'There's nothing to be afraid of.'

At this, James watched his daughter's eyes almost pop out of her skull.

'Afraid? Why the hell would I be afraid? Are you mad?'

'Then just sit down, please,' James said. 'Or go. But decide.'

At last, Patricia sat down, thumping herself onto the sofa beside Dan.

Beverly took a seat in the last remaining chair. And it didn't escape James' notice that it was the one she had sat in earlier that day, the one Helen had so often fallen asleep in, over by the window.

'I need everyone to join hands,' Beverly said, and reached left and right, taking hold of James and Patricia's hands.

James was fairly sure that Patricia was about to snap her hand back, but he saw a nudge from Dan stop her.

Around the circle, hands were joined.

'Excellent,' Beverly said, then she released the hold she had of James and removed the shawl from the table to show the items which were hidden beneath it.

'Mum's wedding ring,' Ruth said.

'That's a great photo of Nana,' Anthony said.

The other item was the book she had taken during her previous visit.

'I asked James to provide these for this evening,' Beverly said. 'It will give us all something to focus on.'

'Now what?' Patricia asked. 'We just stare at them, do we, while you mutter some mumbo jumbo and pretend you're communing with the dead?'

'Something like that, yes,' said Beverly, 'but without the mumbo jumbo I hope.'

James was impressed with how Beverly was so totally unphased by his daughter's attempts to scupper what she was here to do. It was almost worth having her here just for that. Almost.

'I need to ask everyone to close their eyes,' Beverly said. 'I'm not going to do anything to you, and I can't anyway, because my hands are being held. It will just allow us to not be distracted.'

'But we can't see what's on the table,' Dan said.

'No, you can't,' Beverly said, 'but you know they're there, don't you? And when you close your eyes, you'll be aware of them, more so, actually. Because of what they represent, and whom.'

James closed his eyes, intent on leading by example, but then opened them again just a few moments later, to make sure everyone had followed suit. And, to his surprise, they actually had. Even Patricia.

'Now,' Beverly said, 'what I want everyone to do, is to try and empty their minds—'

'Oh, for goodness sake . . .' Patricia sighed.

'Patricia, please!' Ruth said. 'Just go with it, okay? For Dad?'

James squeezed Ruth's hand and felt a squeeze in return.

'As I said,' Beverly said again, her voice calm and soft, 'I want everyone to empty their minds, and to focus on Helen. A mother, a wife, a grandmother, a friend. Just think about what she meant to you, who she was, her voice, the times you spent together.'

James heard a sniffle at his side from Ruth.

'Good,' Beverly said. 'Now, if we can all just think about

what we would say to Helen if she were here now, how we would greet her if she came into the room to join us . . .'

James' mind wasn't empty, it was full. Bursting with memories of Helen. He could see her and feel her, and there, yes right there, wasn't that her perfume? And oh, that laugh! It was music, wasn't it? God, he missed her. How could he ever be expected to live without her? It was impossible! But these memories, they were so rich, so wonderful, that he didn't want them to stop, and the only way for that to even be, was for him to continue, wasn't it? He had to live, surely, to experience them?

'Now,' Beverly said, 'I want you all to keep your eyes closed, to keep your minds focused on Helen, and to let go of each other, and to sit back, to relax, to just sink into those memories . . .'

James let go, sat back, felt the tears warm on his cheeks.

Then came the sharp sound of something tapping at the window, and even Patricia screamed.

# CHAPTER EIGHTEEN

'WHAT THE BLOODY HELL WAS THAT?' DAN SAID, HIS voice like the sharp bark of a dog.

'Keep your eyes closed!' Beverly snapped back, and Anthony, who had said he'd join in, not just to support his mum, but because it all sounded like a bit of a laugh, something to actually talk about at school, maybe even make him a little more popular—though that wouldn't exactly be difficult, would it?—was now not too sure about any of it. He almost considered heading back to the cottage and to his room, because there was always Call of Duty to play, wasn't there? But something kept him in his seat—a mix of fear, not wanting to leave his mum, and just enough inquisitiveness to have him wondering what might happen next.

'But what was it?' Anthony asked.

'Please,' Beverly said, 'if we can all focus on Helen, that would be really helpful.'

Anthony wanted to open his eyes, not just to look at everyone else, but to also make sure that there wasn't some hideous apparition floating around the place. Though seeing that really would be something to chat about on the bus to school, wouldn't it?

The tap came again, this time not just one single knock, but a quick rat-tat-tat.

'Is that Helen?' James asked and Anthony heard the desperation in his Granddad's voice. 'Is that her? It can't be, can it? But is it? Is it really her?'

'We need to all be quiet,' Beverly said, 'so that I can hear if someone is trying to come through from the other side,' and Anthony noticed that the cheery, relaxed voice she'd entered the room with earlier, had now been replaced with something a little more on edge. And that didn't exactly make him feel good about what was happening.

For a moment, everyone was quiet and Anthony found himself focusing now on every tiny sound in the room and the house beyond. He heard creaks and taps he'd never noticed before. The wind outside was howling around a fair bit as well, and then he was thinking back to the numerous horror films he'd watched, most without his mum knowing. And if there was one thing he'd learned, other than to never go into a dark cellar to investigate a strange noise, was that séances, contacting the dead in any way at all, well, that was never a good thing in the movies, was it? Creaking floorboards, squeaking doors, taps against the window, usually all meant the same thing: someone was about to die. And horribly.

Anthony took a deep breath and tried to get his imagination back under control. But it wasn't easy.

'Helen?'

The voice was Beverly's, but there was something else about it, Anthony noticed, an echo maybe? No, that was stupid, of course, there wasn't an echo! But it didn't sound quite right, did it? It was Beverly, but also not, and that thought made no sense to him at all.

'Helen, are you there?'

Beverly's voice was back to normal now and Anthony figured he'd just been hearing things that weren't really there. Which was a relief.

'This is a safe place, Helen,' Beverly continued. 'A place of love, of family.'

Was the room getting warm? Anthony thought. Or was he making that up as well? It was entirely possible. But he did feel warmer, he was sure of it.

'Helen . . .'

Another tap, then another, and another, coming from the window, and whatever warmth Anthony had just been feeling disappeared in an instant as a raking shiver drove itself up his spine, goosebumps sending his skin into an uncanny tingle.

'I'm going to have a look,' Dan said.

'No!' Beverly shouted. 'Do not break the circle!'

'Don't you dare move!' shouted James, and Anthony noticed that desperation again in his grandad's voice for whatever it was they were doing to actually work.

Dan didn't move and Anthony was relieved that his uncle had decided to listen to his granddad. It was because of him they were doing any of this after all, wasn't it? But that was something he'd always noticed about his uncle and aunt, and that was how they really did seem to think that world revolved around them.

'It's probably just a bird,' Anthony said, attempting to help keep Dan sitting down. 'They tap at the windows some-times, eating bugs and stuff.'

'I guess so,' Dan said.

'You okay, Mum?' Anthony asked, and unable to stop himself, he quickly peeked over the table and saw her, eyes closed, face just a little white.

'Yes, I'm fine, Love,' she replied.

Anthony snapped his eyes shut again and tried to go back to focusing on Nana. It was sad, what had happened, and she had been really awesome, young, too, but he didn't feel as sad as everyone else. He wasn't really sure why. It certainly wasn't that he hadn't loved her. How could he not have? Her biscuits were amazing and she would always give him a little bit too much money for his birthday, wouldn't she, on top of what Granddad gave him?

'Oh my God, she's here . . .'

Beverly's voice sounded surprised and the words sent another shiver through Anthony. Was this for real? He'd seen more than enough TV shows about hunting ghosts to know just how much of it was total bollocks. But now that he was in the middle of what he'd seen on the screen, he wasn't so sure. It certainly felt real, didn't it? But what did that actually even mean? Weren't they all just sitting together with their eyes closed thinking about a dead person? Do that, and any sound, any sensation, would be twisted by the imagination into something it wasn't, right?

When Beverly spoke again, her voice was softer, Anthony thought, distant almost, like it was coming from outside of the room.

'Where . . . am . . . I . . .'

'Helen?'

Anthony heard the emotion in his granddad's voice as he said Nana's name.

'Helen, it's me, James. Is that you? Are you there? I miss you.'

'I've had enough of this,' Patricia said, her voice hard, and Anthony heard his aunt getting to her feet.

The next tap at the window was rapid, a rat-tat-ta-tat-tat, again and again and again, and Anthony heard Patricia scream just a little.

'Sit down!' James said, his voice loud and firm.

Beverly spoke once more, and again her voice was soft and far away.

'Bright light . . . the bright light . . .'

Hearing this, Anthony started to change his mind about what was going on. It had been a bit spooky and weird up to now, but this bright light stuff? Wasn't that what you apparently saw when you died? Yeah, it was, wasn't it? He'd seen it on a documentary about near-death experiences. There was that really cool story about someone who had watched their own body being operated on, who had then told the surgeon about the whole thing, start to finish. So, it made sense then, all of it, what this Beverly was doing; she was simply trying to help Granddad, wasn't she? Making it up, too, he had no doubt, but Granddad needed closure and if he heard that Nana was heading off to Heaven, floating off towards the light? Well, there was nothing wrong with that, was there? It was actually rather nice, he thought.

'You can go to the light, Helen,' Beverly said, her voice her own again, though Anthony thought how it sounded like she was struggling to control it, to keep it her own. 'It's safe, I promise.'

'But I don't want her to go,' James said. 'I want her to stay. To be here, with me!'

'This was the before,' Beverly said, speaking in that hauntingly faint voice once more. 'Not the now . . . a bright light . . . blinding . . .'

Tapping at the window again, but this time it wouldn't stop, as though not just one bird but half a dozen were out there, tap-tap-tapping at the glass. And then Beverly's voice was no longer faint, but a droning moan, as though of someone at the bottom of a well, calling out, but without words.

'Mum . . .' Anthony said, almost without thinking, unable to disguise the fear in his voice.

'It's okay, Love,' Ruth said.

But Anthony wasn't so sure that it was, because the tapping was still going on, and Beverly's moaning was twisting into something else, a scream scratching at the back of it.

Tap-tap-tap! Tap-tap-tap!

Anthony heard a sharp movement then the eeriness in the room was ripped apart by a wrenching howl that heaved itself out from Beverly's throat.

'Right, that's it!' Dan shouted.

Anthony opened his eyes to see Beverly on her feet and it looked to him like she had just had an electric shock, standing there as she was, stiff as a board, eyes wide, mouth pulled open, arms by her side, her fingers splayed outwards. Uncle Dan was at the window, had snapped the curtains open.

'Right, you bastards!' he shouted. 'Think you're funny, do you? Well, you're not!'

Then Aunty Patricia was up out of her chair as well and she was raging, jabbing a pointed finger at Beverly, screaming at her, right in her face, spittle on her lips.

'How dare you come into our house and do this and play cheap tricks on us! How dare you! And whoever that is out there throwing stones at the glass? Friends of yours, are they? Thought you could come over here and have some cheap fun, am I right? Well, it's over! This is over! You are over, you mad bitch!'

Anthony couldn't believe what he was seeing, what he was hearing.

Dan was back from the windows now and Patricia was still screaming.

'I'm going outside,' Dan said. 'I tell you, if I had a shotgun, I'd send a couple of barrels off just to scare the crap out of whoever that is out there! That would teach them a lesson!'

Dan marched out and Anthony watched his aunt chase after him. A moment later, a torch beam sliced through the night outside. Then Anthony looked over at his mum and his granddad. They were both quiet, tears in their eyes.

'It was her, I know it,' James said, still holding Ruth's hand. 'I want her back. I just want her back . . .'

Anthony looked up at Beverly. She had relaxed a little, but that wasn't saying much, he thought, because right now she just looked plain terrified, her face drained of colour and clammy.

'Are you okay?' he asked.

Beverly didn't respond straight away, but when she did, she turned wide eyes to look down at him, and Anthony was sure that in them he saw real fear.

'What was that?' he asked. 'You did something with your voice. And the tapping at the window. How?'

Beverly was still staring, and Anthony didn't like it at all. It was freaking him out.

'Look, I get it,' he said, 'all of this, the weird creepiness, but you can stop, okay?'

Beverly shook her head as though trying to dislodge something.

'I . . . I . . .'

Anthony stood up. 'I'll show you out.'

'This wasn't supposed to happen,' Beverly said. 'I'm so sorry.'

Beverly pushed herself to her feet and walked over to the window where the tapping had sounded from. Anthony watched her reach up to the latch then she dropped her hand and rested her head against the glass, wringing her hands together in front of her stomach.

Dan and Patricia stormed back into the room, crashing through the door, slamming it into the wall. A picture crashed to the floor, the glass bursting from its frame in deadly slivers.

Beverly turned to face them.

'I'm so sorry,' she said. 'I . . . this isn't . . .'

'Sorry?' Patricia said, cutting in with a mean laugh crisping up the edge of her voice. 'You're sorry? Look at my dad! Look at him! He's a blubbering mess, because of you! Why the hell any of us agreed to this, I just don't know! But it's done! It's over!'

'We'll be reporting this,' Dan said. 'You have my word on that, you bloody charlatan!'

Beverly glanced down at Anthony, then across to Ruth and James.

'I don't know what that was, that voice,' she said. 'Really, I don't. What did I say? What happened?'

'Right, enough of this tosh,' Dan said, then pointed at the lounge door. 'Out! Now! Before I kick you out!'

Beverly stepped out of the circle of chairs, stumbling a little and Anthony followed.

'Yes, that's it, Anthony,' Patricia said. 'Make sure she is off our property!'

In the hall, Anthony followed Beverly along the hall and to the door. He jogged past her and opened it. Beverly stepped out into the cold night air.

'You said something about a bright light,' Anthony said.

'What?'

Beverly looked round at Anthony and he saw in her eyes that fear again.

'Back then, before . . . You asked what you said. And what you said, well, it was something about a bright light. So, I'm guessing that was Heaven, right? That's what you were talking about, to help Granddad? Make him think Nana is there now?'

Beverly stared at Anthony.

'This has never happened before.'

'It doesn't matter if it was fake,' Anthony said. 'I don't know how you did it, the tapping, the voice, but I get why you did it, why you do this. To help people deal with stuff.'

'But the light,' Beverly said. 'The knocking, yes, I know about that, but what I said . . . the voice . . . I don't under-stand! It wasn't . . .'

'It was Heaven, right?' Anthony said. 'That's why you said it, so that Grandad would think Nana was in Heaven now.'

From behind him in the house, a shout chased along the hallway, the voice of his aunt as cold as steel.

'That mad bitch had better not still be here, Anthony! I want her out!'

Beverly turned to leave, but stopped, and looked back at Anthony.

'It wasn't Heaven,' Beverly said then. 'The light, that's

not what I saw. It's not what I was being shown, it was something else. Helen was showing me another light . . .'

Anthony was confused now. What the hell was this woman saying?

'What?' he said. 'But you said you saw a bright light and I've seen this stuff on TV. And it's Heaven! It's always Heaven, isn't it? And then the spirit or soul or whatever it is, drifts off down this tunnel of light and at the end of it there are relatives waiting to welcome you—'

'It was a bright light, yes,' Beverly said, interrupting. 'But that's not all it was.'

'Then what was it?' Anthony asked. 'What was it you saw? What were you talking about?'

Beverly stared at him then and Anthony couldn't help but shiver a little under her gaze.

'It was a bright light, yes,' she said. 'But it wasn't Heaven or a tunnel of light. It was just this bright light shining out onto an empty road. And I couldn't see. That's what I saw.'

Then she turned and was gone. And the chill Anthony had felt earlier came at him once again and for a moment he really wasn't sure which was worse: walking back into a house of ghosts, or back to his bedroom somewhere out there beyond the dark. He decided to go with heading back to the lounge, at least then he would be with his mum.

'Is that mad bitch gone?' Patricia asked, looking over to Anthony who watched as she handed large glasses of whisky to his granddad and uncle.

'Yes,' Anthony said.

'Please, don't use that kind of language around my son,' Ruth said, and Anthony saw the look his mum sent at his aunt bullet-quick as she came to stand next to him. 'We're going now. We'll see you all tomorrow.'

'Sorry it all got a bit strange,' James said.

'No, it was fine,' said Ruth and Anthony nodded in agreement.

'Think I might head out to the shed for a while,' James said and stood up, walking over to pick up the whisky bottle Patricia had poured the drinks from.

'Don't stay out there too long,' Ruth said.

Dan yawned. 'Well, I'm going to bed.'

'I'll come with you,' said Patricia.

Anthony felt his mum's hand on his arm. 'Shall we go?'

'Yeah, Mum,' Anthony said.

Outside the house and walking back to the cottage, Anthony thought back to everything that had happened. 'Mum,' he said, 'do you think that was Nana? I mean, the tapping, the weird voices?'

'I don't know what it was,' Ruth replied. 'I just know that I need to get to bed and get to sleep. It's been a very strange day and I'm exhausted.'

Anthony agreed and followed his mum home. Later, when he was lying in his bed, staring into the darkness, all he could think about was what Beverly had said to him before she'd left. If the light she'd apparently seen hadn't been Heaven, then what?

# CHAPTER NINETEEN

HARRY WOKE IN DARKNESS, HIS GROGGY BRAIN BEING attacked by a thin, metallic shrill sound, as though somewhere in the flat, Ben had decided that the middle of the night was a really good time to put up a shelf. Rubbing his eyes, he reached for his phone, which seemed to delight in informing him that it was just coming up to one-thirty.

'What . . . I mean, Grimm,' he said, his voice cracked with tiredness.

'It's Liz,' came the reply. 'We've got a fire.'

'Who's on duty?'

'Just me,' Liz said. 'Jadyn's around, but he's been called off to something else down dale with Gordy.'

Harry yawned and stretched with all the aches and grumbles of a bear waking from hibernation.

'Where is it?'

'Other side of Appersett,' Liz said. 'I've called Matt and he's on his way over. Told me to call you.'

'What about Jim and Jen?' Harry said, then, 'Actually, scrap that. We'll be fine with the three of us. Then those two can be all fresh for tomorrow if needs be. Where are you?'

'Just heading back from a reported break-in up in Gayle, which turned out to be nowt,' Liz said.

'What, nothing at all?'

'Owner's dog,' Liz said. 'It had got out and was trying to get back in. Mad little bugger it was.'

'I'll meet you outside the community office, then,' Harry said.

'On my way,' Liz said.

Harry went to kill the call, but something hooked him back, something Liz had said about where the fire was.

'Did you say beyond Appersett?'

'Yes,' Liz said. 'Couple of miles out the other side.'

'Where, exactly?' Harry asked. 'Black Moss House?'

'Yeah,' Liz said. 'How—?'

'A hunch,' Harry said, and closed the call.

After somehow managing to dress himself without tripping too often over his tired legs, Harry headed off through the flat.

'Something up, Harry?'

Ben was at his bedroom door.

'The joy of police work,' Harry said. 'High stress, no sleep, early death.'

'No change there, then,' Ben replied, then looked at his watch. 'It's not even two in the morning!'

'No consideration, some people,' Harry said and let himself out.

Outside, Harry found Hawes to be a place of almost serene quiet, the kind he had only ever really found in cathedrals. Not that he made a habit of visiting places of worship, but it had always amazed him the places where police work had taken him. And what had that one been? he thought, trying to recall a long-ago case, eventually giving up and instead just settling back to taking in the bright, icy air.

As he walked down towards where one of the response cars was parked, windows stared back at him from shops and pubs, hotel rooms and cafes, their glass eyes impenetrable pools of deep black. On the wind, he heard the hoot of an owl, and behind that the far off, almost haunting bleat of sheep on the fell.

Ahead, movement caught his eye, then he saw light shine out from a car door being opened.

'Away then,' Liz called out. 'I'll drive.'

Harry didn't argue and dropped himself down into the passenger seat.

Liz climbed in next to him and said, 'So, have your hunches always been uncannily accurate?'

'Sadly, no.'

'Then how did you know?'

'Things clearly aren't right up there, are they, after the accident? And you were there at the funeral with Matt and me, so you saw what happened. I just put two and two together, as they say.'

'If I do that, I usually end up with five,' Liz said, starting the car then kicking them forward with a sharp tap on the accelerator. 'And how was your afternoon?'

'My what?' Harry replied.

'After the funeral,' Liz said. 'You had to head off. In a bit of a rush, you were, too.'

'Oh, that,' Harry said, thinking back to the job interview which, after another push from Firbank, he'd finally gone for. He was keeping it a secret that he was going for the DCI job, and it would be staying as such until his success or not was confirmed. 'It was fine.'

'Important, was it?'

'A little.'

Leaving Hawes, Appersett was soon rushing towards them.

'What is it we're actually dealing with?' Harry said, rubbing sleep from his eyes and keen to not talk about the interview. 'Who called it in?'

'We'll find out soon enough,' Liz said, as she swept them over the bridge on the other side of the village.

Harry glanced over at the speedometer and found himself agreeing and reaching up for the handle above the door at the same time. What was it, he thought, with people in the dales driving like complete nutters?

He saw the orange flickering light in the darkness first, as Liz hammered along the main road, then the house came into view through the trees. Harry was relieved to see that neither it nor the cottage beside it, were on fire. And yet tongues of flame were licking at the darkness at the back of the main house, thick plumes of grey smoke chucking themselves high into the sky.

'So, what's actually on fire, then?' Liz asked, slowing down to turn off the main road.

As they bounced up the lane to the rear of the house, Harry saw that the Fire Service had already arrived and were dealing with the fire, which he could now see was coming from the rather expensive cabin James Fletcher had laughingly referred to as a shed. As Liz parked up, Harry heard sirens, then saw more emergency lights as an ambulance tore its way up the lane.

Outside the car, Harry had Liz head over to liaise with

the other two emergency services, while he turned himself towards the house and the small gathering of people huddled together at the back door. The roar of the fire was a terrifying thing, Harry thought, snatching a look at the flames, the heat of it forcing him to turn his walk into a quick jog.

At the house, where the heat was just about bearable, he saw the family was standing together and staring at the flames. Patricia was standing in front of her husband, Dan, and Ruth was huddled up close to her son, Anthony. But where was James?

'Mrs Hurst,' Harry said, realising that as yet none of them had noticed his approach.

When Patricia turned to face him, Harry saw a face riven with horror, eyes ringed black from tears and lack of sleep. The other three faces turned and none of them looked any better, Harry thought, which was when the hunch kicked in again, and he knew that here, right now, something was very, very, wrong indeed.

'It's Dad,' Patricia said. 'He's . . . Oh, God . . .'

Harry was helpless to do anything as Patricia who, when he had last met her, had seemed to have a hardness to her that even a diamond wouldn't scratch, broke down, sweeping herself round into the arms of her husband, whose face was a reflection of darkness and horror. Ruth and her son Anthony looked all out of tears, their faces lost to an impossible pain neither one could fathom.

'I think it would be better if we all moved inside,' Harry said. 'Then you can tell me what exactly happened here. When you're ready to, that is.'

No one moved, the four of them held as though hypnotised by the blaze at the rear of the house.

'Please,' Harry said, this time his voice loud enough to get their attention, which was no small feat above the sound of the fire. Four sets of dead eyes turned towards him and he gestured at the house behind, deciding in the end to take the lead himself, dodging behind them and pushing open the door. 'It's better that you all stay inside,' he said. 'And we'll be able to talk a little easier, too.'

As they moved into the house, away from the hellish heat, Harry wanted to ask where James was because his absence was so obvious, so stark, but he also knew that he didn't need to. Because the answer was behind him, scorching his jacket into his back.

# CHAPTER TWENTY

HARRY HAD THE WHOLE TEAM GATHERED IN FRONT OF him, including Fly, who was hiding under Jim's chair. Everyone had a fresh mug of tea, Matt had done a quick stop off at Cockett's for some bacon butties, and now all that was left was to get on with the job in hand. The trouble was, Harry was having a time of it trying to find the words which would get the proceedings started. He knew what he had to say, what task the team was now on with, but his voice was stuck in his throat, refusing to budge.

With the soft mumble of voices in front of him, as the team chatted quietly waiting for him to start, Harry stared out through the window into the day beyond. His mind had plenty rushing around in it, from having Ben living with him and wondering what their dad was up to now and if they'd ever hear from him again, to having to wait now to hear about how the job interview went, and if he got it, if he was given the role, if he actually wanted it, and now this.

And, of course, there was the sheep rustling thing, and he hadn't even had a chance to talk with the team about the hours they'd spent up at the auction mart, even though it was only a couple of days ago, but with the funeral the day before, and the fact that he'd been out of the office at the interview, well, there hadn't really been much time. Not that they'd found much, Harry thought. Nothing, actually, was closer to the truth. Though it wasn't for lack of trying, and Jim's mate, Neil, he'd been particularly enthusiastic about the whole thing, clearly feeling guilty about having kept Jim away from the farm when the theft had happened. Once they were done and back to the office, Jadyn had revealed that he'd collected quite a few cigarette butts just in case. Harry had once again been impressed with the constable's keenness, though as longshots went, it was right up there.

Harry's mind snagged for a moment on the interview, and his stomach twisted just a little. If he was successful, if he got the job, then it would be the biggest change in his life since he'd left the Paras and joined the police. He wondered how Ben would react. He'd put off telling him, mainly because he was positive that he wouldn't get the job anyway, but now, having been to the interview, he wasn't so sure. Tonight, then, he decided. That's when he'd tell Ben. Then they could worry about it together. A problem shared and all that, he thought.

'Right, then,' Harry said at long last, glancing at his watch, his voice rolling from his mouth like a sour gobstopper, 'best we get started, then.'

'I've sorted a new board,' Jadyn said, pointing to the wall behind Harry. 'I forgot to mention it, but I found one going spare over at the Leyburn station and, well, I sort of apprehended it.'

'Did you now?' Harry said. 'Had it been a particularly

naughty board, then, Constable? Going around causing trouble, was it, that kind of thing? Bit of vandalism, perhaps?'

'I think you mean commandeer,' Gordy said, and Harry heard the laugh just tickling the back of her voice. 'Not unless the board was doing something criminal.'

Jadyn looked up at Harry then turned to face Gordy, a flicker of confusion on his face, then light broke through and he smiled. 'Yes, that's what I mean. I think.'

Harry looked at the shiny new board on the wall behind him. It was bigger than the other one, which was now resting on a table and leaning against the wall.

'So, who's going to be in charge of getting the details down, then?' he asked.

Jadyn was out of his chair before anyone had a chance to stop him.

'Me, Boss,' he said, grabbing the packet of pens from beneath it. Then he looked around at the rest of the team. 'Unless someone else wants to, I mean.'

'Jen?' Harry asked, knowing she was usually all over it. Not only that, when she did it, there was a sense of order to what she was writing on, or pinning to, the board. With Jadyn, it was a little more haphazard. The details were always there, yes, but finding them was sometimes a problem.

'No, I'm good,' Jen said. 'I'll jump in if I'm needed, but Constable Okri can do just as good a job, I'm sure.'

Harry witnessed Jadyn's face break into the world's largest smile as he opened up the pens and got ready to write.

'Best we get started then,' Harry began, only to be interrupted by Jadyn.

'What shall I call it?'

'Pardon?'

'It needs a title, doesn't it?' Jadyn said. He then pointed

at the other board. 'That one's Sheep Theft, isn't it? So, what shall I call this one?'

'It doesn't really matter,' Harry said. 'Just use your imagination.'

'Oh, now that's just asking for trouble,' said Matt, shaking his head then hiding his eyes behind his hand. 'Jadyn's imagination. The world isn't ready for it.'

'What about house fire?' Jadyn asked. 'No, wait, we need the place as well, don't we, otherwise, we won't know what it's referring to. So, what about Fire at Black Moss House?'

'Sounds like the kind of novel you find for a quid in the discount bin in a bookshop.' Liz laughed.

'You know, that's what Hawes is missing,' Gordy said. 'A decent little bookshop of its own. I know there's that second-hand one in the market hall, but it's not the same, is it?'

'One that sells coffee and has events on,' Liz agreed. 'Yeah, that would be lovely, wouldn't it? You should head over to Sedbergh, there's some good ones over there.'

Harry held up a hand. 'Exciting though this is, to discuss our views on the literary needs of the local community, I think it best if we get back to what we're all here to actually do, by which I mean, some police work!'

'Black Moss Fire!' Jadyn exclaimed. 'Perfect!'

Harry watched Jadyn write the words at the top of the board.

'Brilliant.' Matt sighed, shaking his head. 'Sounds like a movie on Netflix.'

'So,' Harry said, 'this is what we know so far. At some point last night, a fire broke out in the cabin over at Black Moss House. Emergency services were called. Liz and I arrived just after the fire service and just before the ambulance. While the fire was being dealt with, I took the family inside to find out what had happened, Liz joined me soon after, having liaised with the other two emergency services.'

'Which was when we were informed that James was missing,' Liz said.

'And tragically,' Harry said, 'it was then later confirmed that a body was found in the remains of the burned-out cabin. It's currently with forensics and I'm hoping we will hear later today, just to confirm identity, really.'

'But it can't really be anyone else, can it?' Jim said.

'No, it can't,' Harry agreed. 'Fire investigators are over at the scene this morning to identify how the fire started. We should hear from them later as well.'

'Who made the call?' Matt asked.

'That was Ruth, James' youngest daughter,' Liz said. 'She only noticed it because she'd gone outside to get some more wood for her fire. But Pat, James' other daughter, and her husband, they were up by then as well.'

'Yeah, it was a cold night,' Jim said.

'And what time was that?' asked Gordy.

'About eleven forty-five,' Liz said.

Harry caught Gordy flash a look up at him.

'Late to be adding more fuel to a fire,' she said.

It was, Harry thought, but it was a little early in the day to start being suspicious. All they really knew was that James Fletcher had been killed in a fire. The reason for the meeting this morning was to get down all the information that they could so that they could respond accordingly when they heard from forensics and the fire investigators. For all they knew, James had suffered a heart attack, a spark had jumped from the stove in the shed, something had caught fire, and by the time anyone noticed it was just too late to do anything about it. It was sad, but it was the kind of thing that happened.

'Ruth's having trouble sleeping, I think,' Liz said. 'Can't blame her, to be honest, with the weirdness that's been going on over there since she lost her mum. And I think something's up with her son, Anthony, as well.'

'How do you mean?' Harry asked.

'Not sure really,' Liz said. 'He was off school with a migraine when Jen and I were over there, but I think there's something else going on.'

'School stuff probably,' said Jadyn.

'Yeah, I reckon,' Liz agreed.

Harry said, 'Perhaps it's best if we have a quick run-through of what's going on, with the family I mean, what happened last week, what we've been called out there for. Just so we're all aware.'

'But we all know, don't we?' Jadyn said.

'I know we all know,' Harry nodded, 'and that's because we're a small team that actually communicates, which is rarer than you'd believe, trust me, but it's still best to make sure we all have the facts straight, I think.'

'You reckon it all might be relevant, then?' Matt asked.

'Everything's relevant right now,' Harry said. 'Even if it doesn't look like it is at the moment. And there's no denying that it's all been a bit odd.'

'So, where do you want to start then?'

'With you,' Harry replied, nodding at Matt. 'If that's okay? You attended the accident. And although it's not directly linked to the fire, it does give the background to how James was and how the family is, I think.'

Matt relayed what they knew from the accident, that James and Helen had been returning from Kendal, Helen driving, when a bright light, most likely from an oncoming car, had caused Helen to lose control of the car. 'It was pretty awful, if I'm honest,' Matt said. 'Nothing ever prepares you for something like that, you know? Nothing at all.'

'Ruth said something about her mum not liking to drive in the dark,' Liz added. 'But I think it was just James trying to blame himself for what happened.'

'How do you mean?' Harry asked.

'She drove because she wanted him to have a drink on his birthday, and apparently, she would really only ever drive at night if it was a special occasion.'

'Maybe she just didn't like driving,' Jadyn said. 'My Gran's like that. Gets a brand new car every year, never drives the thing though. Just has it sitting in the drive.'

Next, Gordy spoke about when she had visited the family in the morning and the very apparent trauma they were suffering in light of the event. 'There was a real, palpable sadness to the house,' she said. 'I sat with them for a good while, talked things through, advised them on what support was available. They'd already been in touch with the Methodist minister, and James' eldest daughter was turning up the next day. So there was a support structure in place.'

'Then we had the intruder,' Matt said, and went on to quickly relay what he and Harry had dealt with when they had gone over.

'James was convinced he'd seen his wife,' Harry said. 'Which clearly he hadn't. There was no evidence of an intruder, and we checked with the rest of the family, and none of them had been out where James had apparently seen this woman who he claimed was his wife.'

'Poor bloke,' Jadyn said, pausing for a moment from writing on the board. Harry glanced at it and wished that he hadn't, because right now all it seemed to be was a sea of squiggles and lines, and he felt then that if he stared at it too long he would end up being hypnotised.

'Then Jen and I were out there again,' Liz said, 'and I think it had only gotten worse, to be honest.'

Liz then told everyone how Ruth had told her about the visit by the medium, Beverly Sanford. 'James wasn't just convinced he'd seen his wife, he wanted to communicate with her, have proof that she was still around. It was a bit weird, if I'm honest. His daughter, Ruth, she was clearly exhausted by it.'

'I had a look around the property again, like you did, Matt,' said Jen, 'and like you, found nowt.'

'You've seen how similar they all are though, right?' Liz said. 'Ruth and Patricia, even Ruth's son, Anthony. They all look like each other, like Helen. It's uncanny.'

'So, you think it was just a case of James seeing them, and considering his state of mind, turning it into something else?' Gordy asked.

'It's the only answer that makes sense,' Liz said, holding her hands up. 'Again, none of the family was where he said he'd seen Helen, but the way he was acting, I'm not sure it really mattered. And there's that weirdness with Ruth and Anthony.'

'Then we have the episode at the funeral,' Harry said, 'and now this fire, which has taken the life of James.'

'Actually, that's not everything,' Liz said.

The team all turned to stare at Liz.

'There's something else?' Harry asked. 'How can there be? You were out there with me last night and I don't recall anything else being mentioned.'

'It only came through to me this morning,' Liz said. 'I got

a call from Patricia. She was still very upset and kept apologising for not mentioning it last night, but anyway, you know that medium who James had out to see him?'

'Yes,' Harry said. 'What about her?'

'Turns out that she was there last night, before the fire.'

'What?' Harry said. 'Why?'

'They held a séance,' Liz said. 'And apparently, it all went just a little too well.'

# CHAPTER TWENTY-ONE

Harry was outside, grabbing some fresh air to clear his head. He was sure he could still smell the fire from the night before on his skin, despite scrubbing himself raw in the shower when he'd got back and throwing his clothes in the wash. What was worse, though, was that his brain was telling him there was another smell beneath it, even though there wasn't, and that was a smell he could remember from being back in the Paras, seeing burned-out vehicles, broken tanks, their shells burning, and their human contents blackened husks inside. That was so long ago now, another lifetime, but still, the memories had a way of crawling their way back to the surface again, like creatures that lived on the bottom of the deepest and muddiest of ponds, desperate for a glimpse of the sun.

'You okay, Boss?'

Harry gave a nod, though he didn't turn to look at his detective sergeant.

'You nod a yes, I see a no, though,' Matt said. 'What's bothering you?'

190 DAVID J. GATWARD

'What isn't?' Harry said.

'I know, it does all seem a bit odd,' Matt said, 'but my guess is it's all just a bit tragic really. That's the way life is, sometimes, isn't it? Horrible, I know, but we'll deal with it and help the family as best as we can.'

Harry wanted to agree with Matt, he really did, but he just couldn't.

'You're right, I know,' he said, 'but there's something niggling about all this, just at the back of it all.'

'Is that a hunch rearing its ugly head?' Matt asked.

'Not yet. Well, not exactly, no,' Harry said. 'But it just strikes me as a rather odd collection of events, when they're all stacked up alongside each other, that's all. They all seem to make sense, with one thing leading to another, but still . . .'

Harry's voice faded, because he just couldn't explain what his thoughts were doing right at that moment, other than busying themselves with getting in the way of each other.

'Is there anything else?' Matt asked.

'There's the sheep thing,' Harry said. 'I mean, it was all very educational going around the mart, but what did we get from it? Bugger all, is what.'

'It was good of Jim's mate, Neil, to join in,' Matt said. 'But you're right, we didn't get anything from it.'

'Except a nice pile of little evidence bags filled with cigarette butts courtesy of Constable Okri,' Harry said.

Matt laughed. 'It's impossible to dislike the lad, isn't it?'

'I have to say it's all eating at me a bit, if I'm honest,' Harry said, his voice dropping low enough to grind itself into the tarmac at their feet. 'The thought that somewhere, whoever did it, well, they know that they got away with it, don't they? And that's not right. Not only that, they're probably planning to do exactly the same again, somewhere else.'

'Our presence might have done something though, right?' Matt suggested. 'Seeing us around and that, it might have spooked them, if they were there, made them think again about having a go at another farm.'

Harry's response was a low rumbling growl.

'You're right about all of that,' Matt said, 'but there's something else bothering you, isn't there? I'm sure of it. I'm right, aren't I?'

'No, there's nothing else,' Harry said.

'Bollocks, there's nothing else,' Matt said, then he caught himself and apologised. 'Shit, sorry, Boss, I didn't mean to be—'

'It's alright,' Harry said. 'No offence taken. Just speaking your mind, and I appreciate that.'

'Then what is it?' Matt asked. 'I've known you long enough now, so don't go thinking you can pull the wool over my eyes, because you can't. And you'd best be out with it before I get Fly out here to lick it out of you. Or worse, I'll call Jadyn out here and I'll tell him that you've a secret and that it's down to him to find out what it is. Reckon you can handle that? All the questions? The relentless enthusiasm? He won't stop either, you know that, don't you? He'll be on at you all day.'

Harry couldn't help himself and laughed. 'God no, anything but that.'

'Well, then?' Matt pressed again. 'What is it?'

Harry breathed deep. 'It's about the job.'

'What job?' Matt asked, cutting Harry off before he could say any more. 'Your job? What about it? Swift giving you hassle, is he? That's not on, not by a long shot. You're brilliant. You've fitted in right well with the team, too. And—'

'No, it's not that,' Harry said. 'But I have been speaking to Swift and Firbank, my DSup down in Bristol. And you know I was away, after the funeral, right? Well, you see—'

Harry was about to tell Matt about the interview, about how it did or didn't go, because really he wasn't sure, and he had been told that he wouldn't hear for a few days anyway, when Jadyn crashed out of the community centre doors.

'Good grief, lad!' Matt said. 'Are you trying to break the door off at the hinges?'

'There's a call in,' Jadyn said. 'For Harry, I mean Grimm, I mean, there's a call for you, Boss. Inside. On the phone. Because that's where calls come from, isn't it? Phones?'

Jadyn stopped talking as much to his own relief as Harry and Matt's.

'He's good at the details, I'll give him that.' Matt laughed. 'But don't think you've escaped, Boss. I want to know, right? Whatever it is. That's how things work round here, just in case you were wondering.'

Harry followed Jadyn back into the office and picked up the phone.

'Grimm.'

'It's Rebecca Sowerby,' said the voice at the other end. 'How are things in Wensleydale?'

'A bit strange, if I'm honest,' Harry said, never really sure as to how best to speak to the pathologist. When they'd first met, they'd not exactly got on, but over the months initial loathing had thawed into something that resembled mutual respect and toleration. 'And I'm hoping that what you're about to tell me puts an end to it and wraps everything up nice and neatly.'

'Oh,' said Rebecca.

'That's not a good start now, is it?' Harry sighed. 'Come on then, best get this told so that we can deal with it accordingly. What have you got?'

'I suggest you sit down.'

'I already am,' Harry said, pulling out a chair and slumping down into it. As he did so, Fly slinked over and ducked his head against Harry's thigh. Harry reached out and scratched the dog's head. He glanced up to see the rest of the team staring at him, expectation in their eyes. He then pulled out his notebook and a pencil. 'Go on then, what have we got?'

'Well, I've been in touch with the fire investigators,' Rebecca said. 'I needed to have a good understanding of what had happened, what they'd found, that kind of thing. They're putting a report together anyway and that will be to you in just a few minutes I suspect.'

'And?' Harry said.

'And it looks as though the fire was started deliberately.'

'That's not exactly what I wanted to hear,' Harry said, jotting down notes as Rebecca spoke.

'It's not exactly what anyone wants to hear, I'm sure,' Rebecca replied.

'So, what do they think happened?' Harry asked.

'Well, it all ties in with what I've found,' Rebecca said. 'Obviously, the body was in a very poor state after the fire, but I can confirm that the deceased was James Fletcher.'

'That's something, anyway,' Harry said. 'And the fire or the smoke I'm assuming killed him?'

'Yes,' Rebecca said, 'but only because he was unconscious at the time. There's was an awful lot of alcohol in his system.'

'Drowning his sorrows, I should think, the poor sod,' Harry said. 'And who can blame him?'

'There wasn't enough to have him so unconscious that he wouldn't wake up in a fire, though,' Rebecca said.

'So, what was it, then?' Harry asked.

'A sleeping agent of some kind,' Rebecca said. 'Not sure what specific drug as yet, but I'll let you know as soon as I can, assuming that I can, obviously.'

'So, he mixed sleeping tablets and alcohol,' Harry said.

'Yes, and also no,' Rebecca replied. 'We've found nothing to suggest that he actually swallowed tablets.'

'But you just said—' Harry began, but Rebecca cut him off.

'I said sleeping agent, not tablet. If there are tablets, then they were most likely crushed first and mixed with the alcohol he was drinking.'

This immediately had Harry worried. He'd met James and although he was clearly suffering from the stress of losing his wife and dealing with it in a way that hadn't struck Harry as entirely normal, the man hadn't come across as the kind of person who would go to the trouble of what Rebecca was suggesting. It all seemed very much out of character.

'So, he's somehow unconscious,' Harry said, 'and then his shed burns down. How?'

'Investigators found the stove door open,' Rebecca said. 'A spark or a piece of burning wood could have fallen out onto the floor. As we both know, domestic fires start very easily. It doesn't take much. They think he was in a chair by the stove when the fire started.'

'But what you're suggesting is that he took his own life,' Harry said.

'I'm not actually suggesting anything at all,' Rebecca said, and Harry heard the bristles in her voice for the first time since she'd called. 'I'm simply giving you the facts. The stove door was open. A fire started. But they believe an accelerant was used. As do I.'

Harry could feel the world around him crushing in, as the information he was now taking onboard served only to turn the day dark.

'You mean petrol?'

'Not this time,' Rebecca said. 'The fire started at the stove, with its open door. It spread rapidly across the body of the deceased, who is believed to have been sitting in front of it.'

'It was where his wife used to go and sit,' Harry said, remembering what James had said about the chair by the stove.

'The fire is centred around the stove and the body and the chair the deceased was sitting in at the time,' Rebecca continued. 'It looks as though the body and the area around it were soaked in something and then set alight.'

'And by having it near the stove, it would all look like an unfortunate accident,' Harry said.

'We've found alcohol residue in the remains of the clothing he was wearing,' Rebecca said.

Harry rubbed his eyes till he saw sparks. 'It could all still be an accident though, couldn't it?' Harry said. 'None of this actually points to something more deliberate.'

'I've given you the facts,' Rebecca said. 'James Fletcher was unconscious, through a mix of alcohol and drugs. The fire started at the stove, the door open. James Fletcher was, for whatever reason, unconscious in front of said fire, his clothes soaked in alcohol. I can only assume that a rather large log fell out of the stove and was still alight, because trying to get clothes to burn, even with a good dousing of alcohol, is not easy at all.'

'God Almighty.' Harry sighed, rubbing his eyes again, this time even harder, like he was trying to push them out of the back of his skull.

'Anyway, I'd best be going,' Rebecca said. 'I'll send my report through now.'

Harry said his goodbyes and put down the phone.

'Well?' Matt said.

'Well indeed,' Harry said, and looked at the rest of his team, wondering if he was already developing a headache from what he'd just learned. 'I'm assuming you all got the gist of all of that, what the pathologist was saying, am I right?'

Everyone nodded.

'So, did he kill himself or not?' Jadyn asked.

'That's a good question, Constable,' Harry said. 'A very good question.' He then handed Jadyn his notebook.

'For the board?' Jadyn asked.

'Yes,' Harry said, 'though you might want to tidy it up a bit.'

Jadyn's face fell.

'By which I mean,' Harry said, not wanting to dent his enthusiasm, 'you've got a lot of information on there, which is great, but I think you might just need to step back a bit and have a look at it and maybe work out a way to present it more clearly.'

Jadyn did exactly as Harry had suggested.

'It's a right mess, isn't it, Boss?'

'It is,' Harry said.

'Looks like alphabetti spaghetti.'

With Jadyn now occupied with redoing everything he'd just done, Harry looked back to the rest of his team.

'Right now,' he said, 'I'm thinking we've a proper mess to be dealing with. And the only way to clear up any mess, it to just get stuck in and started on it, otherwise it'll still be a mess tomorrow.'

'So, where do we start?' Jim asked.

Harry thought for a moment, thinking back over the last couple of weeks, running through what had happened and what he'd just been told.

'It's not just where, it's how,' Harry said. 'Matt?'

'Boss?'

'Time to get that Action Book out.'

# CHAPTER TWENTY-TWO

As Harry had driven back up the lane to Black Moss House, he'd noticed how the fells behind the place had taken on a more foreboding air than when he'd last seen them. The weather was coming in now, and it was bringing with it the first breath of winter, icy cold, and rolling in front of it was a fearsome storm, pushing it down the hills towards the house.

As Harry climbed out of his car, the storm hit, whipping rain at him like chains on a wheel, but it wasn't enough to rid the air completely of the acrid stench from the burned-out cabin.

Harry took a moment to have a look around the remains, pulling up his collar against the rain. It was a ruined thing now, grey with ash, with black bones of burned wood sticking out. And it was where James Fletcher had died. Harry knew the man had been unconscious, but he still wondered if James had known what was happening, if the agony his body would have felt as the flames took hold had somehow reached down into his subconscious, tried to wake him, and failed.

Turning back to the house, Harry walked over to where Matt was standing with Jen and Jadyn, at the back door of the house, waiting for him.

'It's properly coming in now, isn't it?' Matt said. 'Reckon it's settling in for the day as well.'

'More likely the whole week,' Jadyn said.

'Then let's get ourselves inside,' Harry said and knocked at the door, which opened soon after.

Ruth Fletcher stood staring at them and Harry wondered what she looked like when she wasn't exhausted and burned out from the sorrow and the tears.

'Yes?' Ruth said.

'Can we come in, please?' Harry said. 'There's something we need to discuss.'

'Is there?' Ruth said, and Harry saw not just the pain in the woman's eyes and the exhaustion, but confusion, too. 'What? And why are there so many of you? What's this about? What's going on?'

'Please,' Harry said. 'If it's okay? I know this is a really difficult time, but this is important.'

Ruth stepped back from the door and Harry followed Matt inside, with Jen and then Jadyn coming in behind. Ruth closed the door and Harry was struck for a moment by the sudden soft quietness of the house, the wind and rain silenced by the thick wood and walls now between them and the storm.

'Through here,' Ruth said, and she led Harry and the others down the hallway and into the lounge.

'Is the rest of the family here?' Harry asked as they

stepped into the room. It was a cold space, and gloomy, but there was the faint sweet smell of an open fire in the air.

'Yes,' Ruth said. 'Well, Pat and Dan are. Anthony's at school today. I said he should stay home, after what had happened, but he insisted on going. I think he just wanted to keep busy, you know? Rather than just sit around and dwell on it all.'

'That makes sense,' Harry said. 'If you could fetch Pat and Dan, though, that would be very helpful. But we will need to speak to your son as well, after school.'

'You've not said why you're here yet, though,' Ruth said. 'Or why there's four of you.'

Harry saw the worry in Ruth's eyes, but he didn't want to say anything until they were all together. He hadn't called to announce their arrival for the same reason, not with what it was they now had to discuss.

'Please, if you could just get Pat and Dan, that would be great,' Matt said.

Ruth left the room, confusion and worry sketching lines into her already weary face. A moment or two later, Patricia entered the room and Harry was put in mind of a sleek, grey racing yacht, shoving its way through to the front. Dan, her husband, followed after.

'I can't say that it's good to see you,' Dan said. 'And I've a horrible feeling that whatever this is about, it's certainly not going to be anything to make me change that view, is it?'

'It's probably best if everyone sits down,' Matt said, and he gestured at the sofas and chairs which Harry then noticed were all pulled into a circle around a coffee table.

Patricia said nothing and immediately set about rearranging the chairs.

'Well, come on, Dan,' she said. 'We can't have them like this, can we? Not after last night!'

As Dan helped, Ruth entered the room carrying a tray of tea and biscuits, which she set down on the table.

Once Patricia had finished, Harry took a seat and the others followed his lead. Ruth poured out the drinks and passed around the biscuits.

'Can we just get on with this, please?' Patricia said. 'It's not like today isn't bad enough already without all of this, too. Not that we know what all of this actually is.'

Dan said, 'I'm sure that whatever the police are here about, it's important.'

'It is,' Harry said. 'And it's about James, your father.'

At this, Harry saw three pairs of eyes all sweep around to stare at him, wide and fearful. The eyes of his officers were all sat in faces impassive and professionally expectant, because they knew why they were here and what was to come next.

'What?' Ruth asked. 'What about Dad? What now? How could there be anything else?'

Harry explained then that he had spoken with the pathologist and that they had received an initial report from the fire scene investigators.

'We know how he died and why,' Patricia said. 'Dad was upset, and I think that bloody séance just pushed him over the edge. God knows why we agreed to it. But he wasn't right after it, none of us were. And he must have just headed out to that shed of his, drunk too much, and never woken up. That's all there is to it. Smoke, I would assume, then the fire. It's terrible, but that's it.'

'He burned to death!' Ruth spat, turning on her sister. 'Dad burned to death! That's what happened, Pat! How can you be so, so *you* about it all? So bloody cold and matter of fact?'

'I'm not being anything about it!' Pat said. 'I'm just saying what happened! Dad did a stupid thing and we have to sort everything out now, don't we? Have you thought about that? Have you? This house? The will? Everything!'

Harry watched as Dan rested a hand on his wife's knee, but she knocked it off.

'And don't you go thinking that helps!' she snapped, glaring at Dan.

Harry had seen exactly these reactions before, relatives unable to deal with the grief they were feeling, confronted by more terrible news. The brain just wasn't designed to take it all in and people lashed out.

Dan edged away just a little from Patricia.

'I think it's best if we all just calm down for a moment,' Harry said. 'What I've got to tell you, well, it's not easy to deal with I'm afraid. And we will need to speak to you all separately about it, just so that we can all be clear about a few things.'

'What do you mean?' Patricia said. 'You're starting to make it sound like this already truly awful thing that happened is actually much worse.'

That's because it is, Harry thought, and after a long, slow breath in and out, said, 'Your father died in the fire. That much you know. And we really are truly sorry for your loss. Particularly after the loss of your mum. You've all had a rough time of it and we really don't want to add to what you're going through. However—'

'However?' Patricia said. 'You say all of that and finish with *however*? Just get to the point will you!'

Harry glanced at Matt, who was sitting opposite him,

hands together, then said, 'Although we're unable to give you the exact details, for obvious reasons, we now have reason to believe that James', your father's death, was suspicious.'

'And just what does that mean?' Dan asked. 'Suspicious? How can a man dying in a fire be suspicious? What's suspicious about it?'

Harry knew he had to be careful now, because under these circumstances, with what had happened to James, he wasn't just sharing this news with relatives, but with suspects. And if he gave too much away, then there was always a chance that he was going to give whoever was responsible a way to cover their tracks.

'All we can say is that we now need to investigate the death further,' Harry said. 'Which is why we're here today, to talk to you all individually about what happened last night.'

'You're serious, aren't you?' Ruth said.

'He's rarely anything else, to be honest,' Matt said.

'But what do you mean by suspicious?' Dan asked. 'That's a bit vague, isn't it?'

'It means,' Harry said, doing his best to explain, 'that although we know the cause of death, how the victim, I mean James, died, we have reason to believe that it may not have been an accident.'

At this, the room erupted and Harry sat back as everyone started speaking at once.

'Not an accident?' Ruth said. 'Then what? What else was it? What are you saying you think dad did, kill himself? He'd never do that, ever! He just wouldn't!'

Patricia spoke, backing up her sister. 'Absolutely ridiculous! Why would dad kill himself? Yes, he was upset, but I agree with Ruth, he just wouldn't do that! This is nonsense! Who's your superior? I want to speak to them, immediately!'

Dan then stood up and Harry watched as the man tried to calm everything down.

'Perhaps it's best if we just give the police a chance to do their job?' he said. 'Clearly, we all know that there's no way that anything suspicious happened, and it just needs clarifying or something, and I'm sure it will all work out fine. Isn't that right, Detective?'

Harry said nothing at that moment because really there was nothing to say.

'I just don't see how it could be suspicious,' Ruth said, and Harry heard real confusion and not a little anger in her voice. 'Dad would never kill himself, would he?'

Dan, Harry noticed, was still looking at him, brow furrowed deep.

'Wait a minute,' he said, taking his eyes from Harry, 'it's not that they think it was suicide at all.'

'Then what?' Patricia demanded. 'What else could it be?'

It was then that the chatter finally died to nothing.

Harry decided to speak before anyone else did, this time working to give his voice a harder, clearer edge, not aggressive as such, but commanding, demanding attention. 'As I've said, we are here now to speak to you all individually about what happened last night. This will enable us to clarify certain facts about what actually happened and how that relates to the evidence so far collected.'

'You think he was murdered,' Patricia said, and her words sent a chill through the room, a ripple of doom that swept out to touch everyone.

'Murdered?' Ruth said, her voice a bark of shock and disbelief. 'Dad? But . . . I mean, by who? Who would do that? Why? He can't have been murdered! That's, well, it's just insane!'

'But what about that intruder he'd been seeing?' Dan asked.

'He was just seeing things that weren't there!' Ruth said. 'It wasn't a real person, we all know that, don't we? It was grief and exhaustion, and that's all it was.'

'But what if it wasn't?' Dan asked. 'What if it was someone and he disturbed them and they killed him?'

'Please,' Patricia sighed, looking at her husband, a finger raised to shush him, 'shut up.'

Patricia's words brought a moment of calm to the scene and Harry cast an eye back over his team before addressing the family again. 'The sooner we get on with this, the sooner it's done, and we can leave you all in peace.'

'Agreed,' Patricia said. 'I'll go and put the kettle on. We're going to need more tea.'

# CHAPTER TWENTY-THREE

Harry was in the kitchen sitting at the large table opposite Patricia, with Jadyn beside him. Matt was with Jen and Ruth in James' study, and Dan was on his own in the lounge. Jadyn had just confirmed Patricia's details, her name, her telephone number, and was now waiting, pencil poised to start taking notes.

'So, what is this, exactly?' Patricia asked. 'An interrogation? Surely I need to speak to my solicitor first, wouldn't you agree?'

'No, this isn't an interrogation,' Harry said. 'Right now, we're just here to ask you all a few questions, that's all. Obviously, I can't stop you calling your solicitor, but that will take time, and like I said, this is just us trying to establish what happened last night in the run-up to your father's death.'

'So, you're not accusing me of anything?'

'No,' Harry said, shaking his head. 'I am most definitely not accusing anyone, at this moment, of anything at all. This is just a few questions, a little chat, that's all.'

'But you think one of us killed Dad, don't you?' Patricia

asked. 'I can see it in your eyes, it's in your voice. Otherwise, why would you be here at all?'

'Like I said,' Harry reiterated deciding to avoid Patricia's questions, 'we're just going to run through a few details, that's all for now. If we need to question anyone further, then that will happen in due course.'

Patricia stared at Harry for a moment then switched her glare to Jadyn.

'He means later on,' Jadyn said. 'As in another time, like, you know, not right now?'

Harry had to wonder if Jadyn's brain was incapable of stopping his mouth from talking or was simply happy to spend its life lazing about in the passenger seat.

'I know what he means,' Patricia said, her voice seething through her teeth, 'but how much later? We've got so much to be getting on with now, as I'm sure you'll understand. I don't think any of us have time for this. And really, how much more do you think we can handle? You've seen Ruth, haven't you? She's a mess! We all are.'

'I know, and I completely understand,' Harry said.

'Do you, though?' Patricia snapped back. 'Experienced many murdered family members yourself, have you?'

*Yes, actually, I have*, Harry thought, but he said, 'I understand you came up last week?'

'Yes,' Patricia nodded. 'We're both self-employed so we can be flexible.'

'And what is it you do?' Harry asked.

'Finance,' Patricia said. 'I'm setting up a new consultancy, advising companies on accounting, investments, tax, that kind of thing. I've a lot of experience in those areas, you see. Best way to make money is to work with money, you know?'

Harry really wasn't interested, but asked for a few more details for Jadyn to write down, then said, 'Can you just run through what happened last night?'

'What else is there to say, other than what you already know?' Patricia replied. 'Dad burned to death!'

Harry breathed deep.

Jadyn leant across the table and said, 'Would you like a glass of water?'

'Pardon?' Patricia said.

'A glass of water,' Jadyn repeated. 'Sometimes helps, you know, with the questions I mean.'

'Does it?'

'Yes, it does,' Jadyn said.

'Well then, yes I will, thank you,' Patricia said, and Jadyn got out of his chair and fetched her a drink.

'Look, I'm sorry,' Patricia said, taking a sip of water, her voice calm for the first time. 'This is all just rather a shock, you know? What with the car accident, Mum's death, Dad's behaviour, and now this? It's just too much, for all of us.'

'Perhaps you can tell us about what happened earlier in the evening then,' Harry suggested. 'Just run through the events as they happened.'

'You mean the séance?' Patricia said, a laugh at the back of her throat. 'Really? You want to know about that?'

Harry said nothing, just nodded, and noticed that Jadyn was already scribbling away.

'Well,' Patricia began, 'this woman, this medium or psychic or whatever the hell she says she is, she turns up last weekend, invited over here by Dad.'

'Why?' Harry asked.

'Because ever since the accident Dad was acting off, wasn't he? Which is fair enough for most people, but Dad wasn't most people, was he? He was a military man, good at keeping himself together.'

'I was in the Paras myself,' Harry said. 'And I've seen how death can affect everyone differently.'

'Yes, but this was different, wasn't it?' Patricia said.

'You mean about how he thought he was seeing—'

'Mum?' Patricia said, finishing Harry's sentence. 'Yes, exactly that. The accident was horrible, but I think it affected him in ways none of us will ever really understand. Anyway, that's why he invited this Beverly, this medium over, because he wanted to contact Mum. By which I mean talk to her, communicate with her spirit, I suppose. See? That's just not normal.'

'And how did you all feel about that?' Jadyn asked.

'Sad, more than anything, actually,' Patricia said. 'Mum is dead and we were all having to deal with it, with that loss, and yet there's Dad, talking about it all like he would see her again or had seen her or was going to speak to her. It was mad.'

'So, this behaviour wasn't entirely normal, then?' Harry asked.

'Good God, no!' Patricia replied. 'Military man, remember? But he'd been blaming himself for what happened, the accident I mean, and then he was seeing things, wasn't he? A woman he thought was Mum, which was clearly the most ridiculous thing ever.'

'And do you know why he blamed himself?' Harry asked. 'Did he say anything to you about it?'

'I have no idea at all why,' Patricia said. 'Just guilt I think.'

Harry remembered then what Ruth had said about Helen not being too happy about driving at night. 'So, he never said anything specific?'

Patricia shook her head, then said, 'Oh, you mean about Mum and her not being able to see in the dark thing? That?'

Harry said nothing, just waited for Patricia to keep talking.

'She just didn't like driving at night, that was all. It was her funny little secret.'

'Secret?' Jadyn said.

'She didn't think that we knew about it, but of course, we all did. And Dad did all the driving anyway, well, most of it. So, I guess that's what was playing on his mind.'

Harry decided to move the conversation back to the night before, the hours before James died. 'So, this séance,' he said.

'Dad had never been into anything that weird before,' Patricia said. 'Not at all. I think he found out about that woman on the internet or something. But anyway, she comes over for a visit, and the next thing we know she's back over again, after the funeral. Can you imagine? I mean, we'd just buried Mum, and there she was! What the hell Dad was thinking, I don't know, but it was all about him right then. Very selfish.'

'Do you have her details?' Harry asked.

'Absolutely,' Patricia said then reached over and took Jadyn's notebook and pencil before he could do anything to stop her. 'There,' she said, handing it back. 'I've a mind for numbers, you see.'

Harry was about to ask Patricia about the séance when she started speaking again.

'Of course, she just flounces in here like having a séance is completely normal, something that everyone does all the time, but it isn't, is it? I mean, this isn't the 1890s, is it? We're not all running off to some spooky gathering at a Victorian mansion to discuss faeries and ectoplasm!'

'Are you saying Mr Fletcher said he saw faeries as well?' Jadyn asked.

The look Harry and Patricia both gave him made him slump just a little further down into his chair.

'In she comes,' Patricia said, 'this medium, and she asks to be left in the room alone for a few minutes, and we're stood outside in the hall, and that was all a bit awkward, I can tell you.'

'She was in the room alone?' Harry asked.

'Yes,' Patricia nodded. 'To add to the theatre of it all, I'm sure, you know? Perhaps even to creep us out a bit?'

'And then you went back in,' Jadyn prompted.

'Yes,' Patricia said. 'We all sat around the coffee table and there was a photo of Mum on the table, next to her wedding ring and a favourite book of hers, and then, well, it all got very strange indeed, didn't it?'

'Strange how?' Harry asked. 'What actually happened?'

Patricia explained then about the tapping at the window, the strange voices Beverly had used, and how it had all finally come to a somewhat inglorious end.

'We threw her out straight away!' she said. 'Honestly, it was horrendous! Everyone was so jumpy! Dad was really upset. It was a total nightmare. We really shouldn't have gone ahead with it, but Dad was pretty insistent.'

'And you all heard this tapping at the window?' Harry asked. 'But there was no one outside?'

'Well, there must have been, I'm sure of it,' Patricia said. 'How else would she have done it? And it certainly scared us all, but Dan went and looked out the window and saw nothing so they'd obviously disappeared by that point.'

'Did you go outside?'

'What was the point?' Patricia said. 'It was a horribly dark night, and whoever it was out there, whoever that woman had brought along with her to help, I doubt we would have been able to see or find them. Dan did, though. I think he decided to be all manly for a moment. Very unlike him.'

'So, there's this medium doing her thing,' Jadyn said, 'and then we've someone throwing stones at the window.'

'That's what it sounded like,' Patricia said. 'Tap-tap-tap, against the glass. And if you ask me, this Beverly woman, she was just there to make a name for herself or something.'

'How so?' Harry asked.

'You know the stories about the house, right?' Patricia said. 'About how it's apparently haunted. Not that anyone's ever seen anything. But she said she knew about the house when she arrived, so I reckon that's what all this was about, not Dad at all.'

'Did you have to pay her?' asked Jadyn.

'No,' Patricia said. 'And we wouldn't have anyway, not after what happened. Honestly, it was awful. And I wouldn't be at all surprised that if we hadn't allowed it to happen, then Dad would still be here. I'm sure of it, actually.'

Harry decided not to follow that line of thought. It was more than a little tenuous. Then his mind cast a line back to what Patricia had said a few moments ago. 'The stones against the window, they actually sounded like that did they? Tap-tap-tap?'

'Isn't that how stones sound on a window?' Patricia asked.

'No, what I mean is,' Harry explained, 'you said tap-tap-tap, like there was a rhythm to it, and that doesn't sound like someone throwing something at the window, does it?'

'No, I suppose it doesn't,' Patricia said.

Harry made a mental note about the sound at the window, then said, 'So, later on, after the séance, did anything happen before the fire?'

'No,' Patricia said, shaking her head. 'We all went to bed. Dad went off to his cabin. After a day like we'd all had, we were exhausted.'

'On that,' Harry said, remembering what the pathologist had said about the drugs found in James' body, 'can I ask if you ever take anything to help you sleep?'

'No, never,' Patricia said. 'but I wish I had done last night, I was so exhausted, by the stress of everything, you know? And today I just don't feel like I've slept at all. I should've had one of Dan's, but they don't agree with me.'

'Dan takes sleeping tablets?' Harry asked.

Patricia nodded. 'Not all the time, just when he really needs to.'

'What about everyone else?' Harry asked. 'They all went straight to bed as well?'

'Ruth and Anthony headed back to their house, the cottage. Dad went to the shed or cabin or whatever it is you want to call it. Dan and I went to bed.'

'So, if you were in bed,' Harry said, 'how did you know about the fire?'

'It was the smell that woke me,' Patricia said. 'Woke us all I think. The smoke. Dan and I rushed outside and there was Dad's cabin, just this huge inferno, you couldn't go near it. And we couldn't find Dad anywhere.'

'And then you called the emergency services?' Jadyn asked.

'Immediately,' Patricia said. 'Well, Ruth did, didn't she? And we all kept looking for Dad all around the place, checked every room, the garden. We none of us thought for a minute that he was in there, you know, in the fire. It didn't even cross our minds.'

'Is there anything else that you can remember?' Harry asked.

'Nothing,' Patricia said. 'We had the séance, we all went to bed, the smell from the fire woke me up, and now here we are.' She sighed, then added, 'It's bloody horrific, isn't it?'

Harry said nothing for a moment, then asked, 'Is there anything else you can think of, anything that seemed odd or out of place or strange?'

'In what way?'

'In any way at all,' Harry said.

Patricia shook her head and leaned back in her chair. 'Everything that's happened has been odd,' she said. 'None of this is normal.'

Harry had to agree with her, and after he thanked her for her time, Patricia stood up and left the room.

'So, what do you think so far?' Harry asked, looking across at Jadyn.

Constable Okri checked his notes, then looked up at Harry, shaking his head. 'To be honest, Boss, I haven't got a sodding clue.'

'No,' Harry said. 'Neither have I.'

# CHAPTER TWENTY-FOUR

DAN GLANCED ACROSS THE TABLE INTO THE STONY FACE of Detective Chief Inspector Harry Grimm and couldn't help but feel guilty. It wasn't just the detective's eyes that did it, though they were things of hard, cold stone, he thought. No. And it wasn't the scarring either, though that really was something to behold, the man's skin cracked like the surface of a lava flow. It was what lay beneath all of it, he realised, an invisible and altogether frightening presence which seemed to seep from the man like fog, to wrap around him and choke him. He'd seen Patricia briefly in passing, as he'd been called in by the constable for a chat, and she had certainly looked drained. And Ruth had looked just the same as well. So, now it was his turn, and that feeling of guilt just wasn't shifting. And that wasn't good, was it?

'Probably best if you just tell us what happened in your own words,' the detective said.

'How do you mean?' Dan asked. 'Tell you about what exactly? So much has been going on, hasn't it? What with

Helen's death, James seeing things, that thing last night, the fire.'

Dan was sure that he could see cogs moving behind the detective's eyes.

'You came over here last week, is that right?' the detective asked.

'Yes,' Dan said. 'As soon as we could. I was away on business, you see.'

'Doing what?' the constable asked and Dan noticed how the young man was busy jotting notes down as they spoke.

'Property development,' Dan said. 'But it's not always the money-spinner everyone thinks it is.'

'So, you flip houses?' the constable asked.

'Not just houses,' Dan answered. 'Property in general. It's been a bit tough lately, with a few large projects not exactly going to plan, cashflow issues, that kind of thing, but that's business, right?'

God, what was he saying! They don't want to know about any of that! And he absolutely didn't want to be telling them any of it, or indeed anyone else, did he? Even Patricia didn't know! Cashflow issues? Now that was a massive understatement, wasn't it? And Patricia thought she had problems from when her last venture had gone wrong! She hadn't the faintest idea, which was probably for the best. Yes, there was probably a very good argument for them sharing more with each other, being honest, but that just wasn't them, was it? They were private people, even with each other, and he'd been away because he'd had to try and sort things out.

'So, you're both self-employed,' the detective stated.

'Yes,' Dan said. 'It comes with its own challenges, and it's certainly risky, as I'm sure Patricia told you, but better that than working for someone else and putting money in their pocket instead of my own.'

The detective then asked about how James had seemed to him since the accident.

'Not great,' Dan said. 'But that's not a surprise really, is it? The accident was terrible. It's no wonder he was a bit off.'

'What do you mean by a bit off?'

'Well, all that stuff about seeing Helen around the place. I think it was just emotional exhaustion or something, his mind showing him what he wanted to see, which was Helen around the place, that's all.'

'So, you don't think there was an intruder?'

'No, of course, I don't,' Dan said, and then something just popped into his head. 'I think a big part of it is that Ruth and Patricia, even Anthony, well they all look so similar, like Helen, don't they? You must have noticed. And I reckon he just saw them around the place and his mind was turning them into Helen. That's it. That's all it was.'

'And what about the séance?' the detective asked.

Dan shook his head and laughed, then realised just how wrong it sounded, how it was the most inappropriate thing to do, the sound cold and broken like a glass smashed on concrete, and he quickly shut it down.

'It was ridiculous,' he said, forcing his voice back to being serious. 'A séance? I mean, have you ever heard of anything so completely stupid in your life, contacting the dead?'

The detective didn't answer and instead asked, 'Can you tell us what happened?'

Dan thought back to the evening before, to when that medium, that Beverly Sanford woman had turned up, and what had happened after.

'It was all going fine,' Dan said, 'and it was a bit of fun I suppose, not that I was taking it seriously, but I was happy to support James if that's what he wanted to do, not that Patricia approved though. But then the tapping at the window started.'

'And what did that sound like?' the detective asked.

'Like something tapping at the window,' Dan said with a shrug. 'How else would it sound?'

'Can you describe it?'

Dan knew he was pulling a face at the detective, one that said *why, what's the point?*

'Was it a regular tap-tap-tap,' the detective clarified, 'or was it more irregular?'

'Oh, it was a tap-tap-tap,' Dan said, then tapped his finger on the table. 'Yeah, like that. And then the woman, she started speaking in a really weird voice, which was very creepy. Then there was more tapping and by that point, everyone was getting a bit jumpy, to say the least, and I'd certainly had enough, so I went to the window to see who was out there and—'

'Did you see anyone?'

'Not a soul,' Dan replied. 'I even went outside to check. Took my torch as well, and it didn't pick anything out at all, and that thing can pick out a fly on a cow's arse a mile away, I'm sure. So, whoever was out there, they must've run off sharpish. Good job, too, because if I'd gotten my hands on them . . .'

Dan felt an adrenaline surge as he spoke, but knew that actually, deep down, he was pleased he hadn't found anyone outside, because what would he have done, really? Nothing at all most likely.

'What about the fire?' the constable asked.

'Pat woke me,' Dan said. 'I was absolutely out for the

count. Anyway, she shakes me awake and I can smell the smoke. And, well, you know the rest.'

'Did you see James go to the cabin?' the detective asked.

'No,' Dan said. 'I went to bed. Took my tablets and that was me out.'

'Tablets?' the constable asked.

'Statins and aspirin,' Dan said. 'I'm young for them, I know, but heart disease runs in the family so it's a precautionary thing. Took a while to get the right ones. Some give you the worst headaches.'

'What about sleeping tablets?' the detective asked.

'What about them?'

'Do you take them?'

'I used to,' Dan said, immediately wondering then why he was being asked about something no one knew about. 'I still do now and again, it depends. Why?'

'So, you have them with you?' the detective said.

'That's correct,' Dan replied. 'Started in my teens with bouts of insomnia. Continued through college and out the other side. Then I met Pat and for whatever reason, it got a little bit better. Love, right? So now, it's only now and again.'

'And you carry them with you?' the constable asked.

'Always have them to hand,' Dan said.

'What are they called?'

Dan had blurted out the name of the tablets before he'd even wondered why they were so interested in them.

For a moment, the detective and the constable sat in silence, each checking through the notes the constable had taken.

'Right then,' the detective said, rising to his feet, 'would you be able to show me where you heard this knocking sound at the window?'

'Of course,' Dan said, and with that, he stood up and led the detective and the constable through to the lounge.

'SO, WHICH WINDOW WAS IT?' Harry asked, now standing in the lounge. 'The one you heard the knocking at?'

Harry had never had to investigate the possible source of supposed ghostly rappings, so this was a first. Though the house suited it, he thought, and he found himself easily imagining the stories being told about the place over the decades, of strange noises from the attic, odd shadows seen on gloomy evenings, whisperings in the dark. But how any of that, of what Matt had told him, tied into what had happened, he hadn't the faintest idea at all, but it was his job to investigate, so that's what he was going to do.

'That one,' Dan said, pointing, and Harry followed over to stand at the window.

Beyond the glass, Harry stared out onto a well-manicured lawn, a silent army of trees beyond it, and further still, the distant hills of the dales, and he couldn't escape the feeling that he was being watched. Not necessarily by a person, but by the very landscape itself, like it knew something that he didn't about what had gone on, and other things, too, darker events, held hidden by the silence and darkness of time.

'Something definitely tapped against the window,' Dan said. 'I mean, it could've been a bird I suppose, but that just seems like too much of a coincidence, doesn't it?'

'And you didn't see anyone at all out there?' Harry asked. 'Not a movement or anything? Something that you thought looked a bit strange?'

'Nope, not a thing,' Dan replied. 'It was dark, so there

was no chance anyway, but I still went outside for a look. Seemed the sensible thing to do.'

Harry understood people's urge to go and look for an intruder when they heard a noise, that urge to protect what was theirs, their property, their family. But it didn't always end up well for those involved, did it?

'Right, best I go have a look outside then,' Harry said, and he left the room and headed through the house and round to the door leading out to the front. Outside, in the grey light of day, with the wind bringing with it a chill both dry and sharp, Harry marched across the lawn, the house on his left. The road was at the bottom of the property, trees were in front of him. If there had been someone here, then it wasn't just a question of where they went, but how did they get here in the first place? He supposed that the medium could have dropped them off to hide in the woods on the way, but that was showing just a little too much dedication to the art of faking it, he thought. Because it had been a cold night, and hiding out in the dark woods, waiting to sneak over to tap a window? In his time, Harry had done more than his fair share of sneaking around in the dark, and he knew just how miserable it could be.

Walking over to the house, Harry came up to the window and stared in, seeing Dan and Jadyn on the other side. The constable, on seeing Harry, smiled and waved. Ignoring him, Harry had a look around beneath the window for some sign that someone had been there the night before. But there were no footprints, no damaged plants, nothing. So just what had caused the tapping?

Harry sighed and strode back into the house, making sure to wipe his shoes clean of any dirt first.

222 DAVID J. GATWARD

'Did you see anything?' Dan asked as Harry entered the lounge.

Harry shook his head and went back to the windows once more. 'And you're sure it was from this window you heard the knocking?' he asked.

'Yes,' Dan said. 'But I've no idea what it was. It really spooked us all, that's for sure.'

Harry shook his head, doing his best to try and dislodge anything in his mind which might be of help. But with nothing coming loose, he turned away from the window, except as he did so he caught sight of something. At first, he thought it was little more than the thin thread of a spider's web, and he was about to ignore it, when something scratched at the back of his mind and he leaned in for a closer look.

'You found something, Boss?' Jadyn asked.

Harry didn't answer as his face came to a stop just millimetres from the latch holding the windows closed. Whatever it was, it certainly wasn't a spider's thread, he realised, not unless spiders had grown particularly clever and taken to tying knots.

Harry dipped a hand into a pocket and pulled out an evidence bag.

'Constable, would you mind just nipping through to the kitchen to fetch a pair of scissors for me, please? I'm sure there's a pair in a drawer somewhere.'

'What have you found?' Dan asked as Jadyn jogged out of the room, but Harry ignored him and dropped his eyes, which was when something else caught his eye, sitting in the thick pile carpet beneath the window. He dropped to his knees and lowered his face to the floor.

'Everything okay, Boss? I mean, I'm sure praying on the

job is fine, but I'll be honest, I'm surprised to find you doing it.'

Harry heard his detective sergeant's voice. 'You got a pair of tweezers or a penknife handy?' he asked.

'Always,' Matt said and Harry heard the man walk over, then saw a hand appear beside his face, a Swiss Army knife clutched in its fingers.

Harry took the knife and removed the tweezers from the handle as Jadyn entered the room and came over with the scissors. The thing in the carpet Harry was able to tease free, clamping it in the tweezers and then slipping it into the evidence bag. Then he was on his feet and back at the window.

'What do you think this is?' he asked, handing the evidence bag to Matt, and taking the scissors from Constable Okri while pulling another evidence bag from his pocket and turning back to the window. He then snipped the thread, which was tied around the window latch and hanging down about six inches against the glass, and dropped it into the second bag. 'And this,' he said, handing it to Matt.

Matt stared at both bags and Jadyn leaned in for a closer look.

'This one,' Matt said, holding up the first bag, 'is a fishing weight. And I know that because of a childhood spent trying to clip the fiddly little buggers to my line, fishing on various becks, and catching nowt. I'm not a very good fisherman, you see. I mean, I'm a patient man, like, but fishing? Drove me mad!'

'And that's fishing line,' Jadyn said, looking at the other bag. 'Dad's a fisherman. A good one, too.'

'Excuse me, Mr Hurst?'

'Yes?' Dan said, coming over to join Harry, Matt, and Jadyn.

'Do you recognise either of these items?'

Dan leaned in. 'No,' he said. 'What are they anyway?'

'You didn't see them last night?'

'Should I have?'

Harry took the bags from Matt then scratched his head, turning around to hold the bags up to the light coming in through the window, only as he did so, they knocked against the glass.

'What was that?' Dan asked.

'What was what?' Harry asked.

'That sound,' Dan said. 'Just then. That tap. It wasn't just me that heard it, was it?'

Harry looked from Dan to the bags in his hand then swung them gently against the window. A tap sounded, dulled by the plastic bag a little. 'You mean that sound?'

'Yes, exactly that,' Dan explained. 'That tap. It's the same as the one last night. The one we all heard at the séance.'

Harry stared at the bags in his hand, up at the window again, then thought about everything he'd heard that morning.

'Matt?'

'Yes, Boss?'

'How do you fancy us both going to have a little chat with a spiritualist medium, then?'

# CHAPTER TWENTY-FIVE

It was now the afternoon and Matt had driven Harry out to the small market town of Sedbergh. He had the rest of the team set to various other tasks, to try and pick apart as much as they could about not only what had happened, but about the only possible suspects that they had, those being James' daughters, Ruth and Patricia, and Patricia's husband, Dan. And that would involve finding out more about their backgrounds, their work, anything that might be of help.

Harry had also sent a message to Rebecca Sowerby with the name of the tablets that Dan mentioned. As yet, he'd heard nothing back. And Jim was going to be having a chat with Ruth's son, Anthony, once he returned from school. And of course, there was also the whole sheep rustling thing and to avoid it being lost in the work being done on the death of James Fletcher, Harry had the ever-keen Jadyn working on it, doing another drive around various farms, and even though it was a desperate move, checking up on the small collection of cigarette butts from the auction mart they'd sent off to forensics.

A couple of miles further, after they'd crossed over a river, he'd taken a right down a thin lane until they'd passed an old railway viaduct. A mile or so further, and a small cottage had come into view and Matt had pulled them through the open gate and onto a small gravel drive. The house, Harry noted, was a small farm cottage, with a slate roof, and a garden not so much overgrown as allowed to run wild, but within reason, as though the owner did just enough to keep it in check, but not enough to make it look controlled. This was the garden of someone who clearly relished freedom though, but what that told Harry about the woman they were about to meet he wasn't exactly sure.

'Nice little place,' Matt said, leaning over the steering wheel to glance up at the cottage. 'Converted barn by the looks of things.'

Harry climbed out of the car, hunching his coat up against the cold. 'Looks a bit quiet, doesn't it?'

'It does that,' Matt agreed.

'And we're sure Jadyn called ahead?'

'I was there when he did it,' Matt said. 'Very polite he was and didn't give anything away.'

'So, as far as she's concerned, we're visiting about booking her,' Harry said. 'I just don't like turning up at quiet houses. Always makes me think something's not quite right.'

'A naturally suspicious nature.'

'Something like that, yes.'

Harry stepped away from the car and walked over to the front door of the cottage. There was no electric buzzer that he could see so he rapped his knuckle against the wood. The sound echoed inside the house.

'Shall I go check round the back?' Matt asked.

'Might be a good idea,' Harry said, knocking again, but as Matt set off to head through a side gate, there was a sound of a chain being rattled on the other side of the door.

Harry stepped back so as to avoid being completely in the face of the owner.

The door opened and Harry found himself staring down into the face of a woman he guessed to be at least eighty years old, with bright, piercing eyes and a warm smile.

'Hello,' Harry said, a little confused, as whoever this was, she didn't match the description of the woman that they'd been given by Dan, Pat, and Ruth.

'You've come about a possible booking, yes?' the woman said. 'Do come in!'

Harry hesitated. 'Can I ask your name, please?'

Harry saw a flicker of distrust in the woman's eyes.

'We're police,' Harry said, and showed her his identification.

The woman leaned in, eyes squinting, as she said, 'Oh, well, so you are. I'm Mrs Sanford. Is something the matter?'

Matt appeared by Harry's side, saw the woman, and frowned. 'Oh,' he said. 'Well, this can't be right, can it, Boss?'

Harry didn't answer, his focus still on the woman in front of him.

'What can't be right?' the woman asked. 'If you're a little nervous, that's okay, you know. People do find what I do a little bit strange to begin with. I don't think I've ever done a consultation with the police. How exciting! Is it a crime? Is that what you need help with? I saw a programme on television once, it was American I think, where the police had a psychic consultant. It was fascinating! And I promise to be as helpful as I can!'

'And what is it that you do exactly?' Harry asked.

'Why, I'm a medium,' the woman said, and Harry heard the surprise in her voice at being asked. 'But you know that already, don't you? Would you like some tea?'

'And your name is Sanford?' Matt asked.

'Yes, that's what I said,' the woman replied. 'Grace Sanford.'

'Grace?' Harry said now beginning to wonder just what the hell was going on. 'Are you sure?'

A look of sharp indignation cut across Grace's kindly face. 'Of course I'm sure!' she said. 'It's my name, isn't it? I may be eighty-five, but I'm not about to forget that, am I? Named after my own aunt. And she had the gift, too, you know.'

'Then who's Beverly when she's at home?' Matt asked, looking to Harry.

'Beverly?' Grace said. 'You mean my granddaughter?'

'Do I?' Harry asked.

'What has that girl done now, may I ask?'

'We thought you were her,' Matt said.

'Well, as you can see, I'm not!' Grace replied. 'Is she in some kind of trouble?'

Harry said, 'You just asked what she'd done now, implying that she's been in trouble with the law before.'

Grace folded her arms, rolled her eyes. 'She has the gift, like me,' she said, 'but she's a little too keen to get some recognition for it. I think she just gets a bit carried away, you know, but it's not the best way to do things, is it?'

'Do you know where she is?' Matt asked. 'We were supposed to be meeting her here.'

'Well, she was here until a few minutes ago,' Grace replied. 'She's been a bit odd today. All started when we were watching the local news and there was something about a fire I think, over Hawes way. Anyway, she had jobs to do, around the house, and she was obviously in a rush to get off when she eventually left. Flew off out of here at goodness knows what speed. Honestly, she'll get herself killed driving like that!'

'What car was she in?'

'Mine actually,' Grace said. 'Hers is in the garage, on account of it being an old Mini and not very happy about the cold weather. But will she get a new one? Of course not! So stubborn!'

Harry held up a hand in an attempt to stop Grace from talking so much. 'Can you give us your car's details, please, Mrs Sanford?'

'Of course I can,' Grace replied. 'She's probably back at her own place, you know. She said she had a few things to check on.'

'Address?' Harry asked.

Grace told them the address and Matt punched it into his phone, Harry then taking down Grace's car details.

'It's back in Sedbergh,' he said.

'Then that's where we're heading,' Harry said. 'Come on!'

With a swift goodbye, they were back in the car and Matt was racing them out of the drive and back down the road, towards Sedbergh. Pulling out of the lane onto the main road, a car zipped past just fast enough to catch Harry's attention long enough for him to see it and do a double-take.

'Bloody hell, that was her!' he said.

'You sure?' Matt said.

'Of course, I'm sure! Floor it!'

Instead of heading left to Sedbergh, Matt swung right,

chasing after the speeding car. 'Doesn't hang about, does she?'

'Don't chase too hard though,' Harry said. 'If she's making a run for it, then she's flighty enough as it is.'

Matt eased off.

'Where's this lead to?' Harry asked.

'Straight on and you'll be to Kendal and on to the Lake District,' Matt said. 'But before that, you can jump on the M6.'

A couple of minutes later, Harry saw the car ahead indicate left. Matt followed and rolled them onto the motorway.

'Right, time for some blues and twos,' Harry said.

Matt did the honours and the car erupted into a parade of sound and light.

'She's slowing down,' Matt said.

'Sensible,' Harry said, watching as the car in front of them eased back, indicating left, onto the hard shoulder.

With Matt parked up, Harry was out and at the driver's door of the other car in a heartbeat. He leant down at the window to see a woman matching the description they'd been given of Beverly Sanford, sitting in the driving seat, her head in her hands.

Harry knocked a knuckle against the window.

The woman looked up, her face riven with panic as she dropped the window.

'Beverly Sanford?' Harry asked.

The woman nodded.

'Just wondering if you had time for a little chat?'

# CHAPTER TWENTY-SIX

'I'M SORRY,' BEVERLY SAID, AND HARRY COULD TELL SHE meant it. 'I just panicked. I didn't know what to do. I wasn't thinking straight. Am I under arrest? Am I going to prison?'

Harry was sitting opposite Beverly in the room given over to interviews, back at the offices in the Community Centre in Hawes. Matt was with him and on the table was a ubiquitous tray of tea and biscuits. There was also the new recording device which Harry had been able to persuade Detective Superintendent Swift to have provided. Though the offices they used in Hawes weren't exactly your normal, everyday police station, Harry believed it was important for them to be treated as such. And having to drive any suspect all the way to Harrogate for questioning had struck him as not just a huge waste of time and resources, but also really annoying. The words 'saving money' had been enough to convince Swift though. They didn't have any cells, that was true, and so questioning someone who was actually under arrest would therefore still have to take place away from their base of operations, but it did mean they could do things not just a little more efficiently and effectively, but also professionally.

'We just need to ask you a few questions,' Harry said.

'But why do we have to do that here?' Beverly asked. 'Why am I here? And how am I going to get home? I had nothing to do with what happened, with the fire! I didn't, I promise!'

'Your car is outside,' Harry explained. 'We had a couple of our team head out to fetch it for you. And you're here because, although not under arrest, running away from the police doesn't exactly demonstrate a willingness to cooperate. And after what happened, you can understand why we need to talk to you.'

'I said I'm sorry,' Beverly said, her hands twisting her mug around on the table, the sound of it a faint grinding squeak. 'I didn't mean to drive off.'

'Still,' Harry said, 'I'm sure you can understand our need to be cautious. For now.'

Beverly gave a shallow nod then sipped her tea.

'Firstly,' Harry said, 'and in light of your attempt to avoid talking to us—'

'I've said I'm sorry!' Beverly said.

'We do need to caution you,' Harry continued, ignoring Beverly's interruption. 'You do not have to say anything. But it may harm your defence if you do not mention when questioned something which you later rely on in court. Anything you do say may be given in evidence.'

'So, I *am* under arrest then!' Beverly said. 'But I didn't do anything!'

Harry sat back in his chair and did his best to look relaxed and approachable. Judging from the look on Beverly's face, it had the opposite effect.

'Can you take us back to when James Fletcher contacted you, please?'

'It was just through my website,' Beverly said. 'It's not a very good one, I know, but I don't want it to look too slick, if you know what I mean, like it cost a lot? Because otherwise people will think I'm into this for the money, and I'm not. I'm really not!'

'Into what?' Matt asked.

'Being a medium,' Beverly said.

'And can you explain what that means?'

'It means that I mediate—thus the name medium—communication between the dead and the living.'

'And how do you do that?'

Beverly shrugged. 'I'm not really sure. I just do.'

Harry said, 'And that's why James contacted you, yes?'

'He wanted me to help him contact his wife. And I agreed to help. I mean, why wouldn't I? Like I said, I don't do this for the money. If you saw my car, you'd see just how true that was!'

'So, you visited the family house,' Harry said.

'I always do an initial visit, a consultation I suppose, to see what I'm dealing with, if it's legit or not. I've lost count of the number of times I've been asked to visit someone only to find that it was just a few idiots wanting to take the piss.'

'And what did you find during the first visit?'

'A family in mourning,' Beverly said. 'It was awful what had happened, to James' wife. And I really wanted to help, you have to believe that! But I nearly didn't go, when I realised, you know, which house it was.'

'What about the house?' Matt asked.

'The stories,' Beverly said. 'Everyone knows them. I mean, there's not much on the Internet about it, but there are enough rumours about it for some of it to be true. And I wasn't really sure about mixing up the two, something for the family, which is really personal, but in a house like that. I mean, it had a part of it knocked down because it was so haunted! That's something you can't ignore, not doing what I do.'

Harry was having trouble taking Beverly seriously, but there was no doubt in his mind that she fully believed every-thing she was saying.

'So, you had this consultation and then you visited once again.'

'Yes,' Beverly nodded. 'For the séance.'

'You've done a lot of these, yes?' Harry asked.

'Quite a few,' Beverly said. 'Gran's been doing them all her life.'

'Grace?' Matt said.

'Yeah, she's amazing!' Beverly said, her eyes lighting up. 'It was her who said I had the gift and helped me explore it.'

'And how did this séance go?' Harry asked. 'The one at the house?'

'It was okay, to begin with,' Beverly said. 'There's always some resistance to what I do, but they all seemed okay with it. But then it all went a bit, well, wrong, I suppose.'

'How do you mean?' Harry asked. 'And you'll forgive me here, because I know nothing about what a séance involves.'

Beverly then explained what had happened, how she had arrived at the house, set the room up, then had everyone sitting around the table.

'This knocking you mention,' Harry said. 'Is that normal?'

'It depends,' Beverly said. 'On how strong the spiritual energies are, that kind of thing.'

'So, how did it go wrong?'

Harry saw that at this question, Beverly looked uneasy.

'There was a feeling to the place,' she said, shifting in her chair. 'I can't really explain it. I've done this enough times before to know if someone's trying to get through, from the other side, but nothing like this.'

'How do you mean?' Matt asked.

Beverly went to speak, then fell quiet.

'Just take your time,' Harry said.

'There was something else in that room, that house,' Beverly said.

'Another person?' Harry asked.

Beverly nodded. 'Yes and no. Helen came through, I could feel it, feel her, but there was something else, too, something or someone trying to take control.'

'You'll have to explain it a little more,' Harry said.

Beverly took a slow deep breath, then exhaled.

'We were in the circle,' she said. 'There was the knocking, we all heard it. Then I could feel Helen coming through, but she was finding it difficult, I think. I don't know. Maybe that doesn't make sense. But it's like a door, you see? And sometimes doors are too heavy or they get stuck and you need help to open them. I think that's what this was like.'

'Someone helped Helen?' Harry asked, trying to ignore that he was now questioning someone about communicating with ghosts.

'Yes,' Beverly said. 'Another presence, older, it helped Helen, because she seemed weak, I think because she had only just crossed over, so she probably doesn't know what she was doing, might even have been a little scared. But then there she was, but there were two of them, this other one helping Helen, channelling her through me, and then there was that voice, and it was my voice, but it wasn't, and there was this bright light—'

'What bright light?' Matt asked.

'I saw it,' Beverly said. 'It blinded me, but I think it's because Helen was showing me, what happened to her I mean, in the accident? At least, that's all I can think it was. I couldn't see! It was just this light, and a road, and then the sound of a crash and—'

Beverly stopped talking and a choked cry broke from her mouth.

Harry pulled out a couple of evidence bags from his pocket and placed them on the table between himself and Beverly.

'Do you recognise these?'

Harry watched as the colour drained from Beverly's face, her voice visibly stuck in her throat.

'Well?'

'Yes,' Beverly said. 'Yes, I do.'

'And can you tell me why?'

Beverly was quiet again.

'These were found in the room where you conducted the séance,' Harry said.

'I know,' Beverly replied.

'And why would that be?'

'Because I put them there.' Beverly sighed, slumping forward, her head in her hands.

'I think I know why,' Harry said, 'but perhaps you would be so kind as to explain.'

Beverly dropped her hands to the table then looked up at Harry.

'First time I did it,' Beverly said, 'I was nine-years-old . . .'

# CHAPTER TWENTY-SEVEN

'I don't know where I got the idea from,' Beverly said, her voice clear and firm for the first time since Harry and Matt had pulled her over on the M6. 'I probably read it in a book or a comic I think, but then maybe I came up with it myself.'

'Came up with what, exactly?' Harry asked.

'Dad's always fished,' Beverly explained. 'Still does. So getting hold of the materials was easy, you see? Just a length of fishing wire and two or three small fishing weights, the little round ones which just snap onto the line.'

'So, what is it that you did, then?' Matt asked, and Harry could see the confusion in the DS's face because he hadn't told him how he suspected the wire and weights had been used.

'I went up to bed,' Beverly said. 'Read for a bit, just to make sure that Mum and Dad were all settled downstairs and not about to come up and check on me. Then I pulled out this spool of fishing line I'd taken, and the weights, and went across the landing to their bedroom.'

'Then what?' Harry asked.

'I tied the end to the latch on the window,' Beverly explained. 'Then a few inches down, I attached some of the weights. And then I strung the line down from the window to the floor, across the bedroom floor, out across the landing, and into my own room. And then I just waited.'

'For what?' Matt asked.

'Mum and Dad went to bed at half ten, so I'd had to force myself to stay up. Wasn't that difficult, if I'm honest, as I was so excited about what I was about to do.'

'And your parents went to bed?' Harry said.

'They did,' said Beverly, 'and they didn't see the fishing line. Why would they? It's basically invisible if you lay it on the carpet. I waited for them to turn out the light, gave it a few more minutes, you know, until the house was really, really quiet, and then, in my own bed, pretending to be asleep, I just gave a little tug on the fishing line.'

'What happened?' Matt asked.

'I didn't expect it to work at all!' Beverly said. 'But there was this sound of tapping from the window in my parents' bedroom!'

'And they heard it?' Harry asked.

'Not right away, no,' Beverly said. 'I tapped again, waited a minute, then again, and then I heard Mum say to Dad that she could hear something tapping against the window.'

'And I bet you got a right old bollocking!' Matt said, shaking his head.

'Dad got up, went over to the window, and I thought I'd had it, but all I heard him say was that he couldn't see anything outside, then he pulled the curtains shut again and went back to bed!'

'You got away with it?' Matt said.

'I did,' said Beverly. 'So, I waited, and did it again.'

Harry was amazed. 'And what happened then?'

'Mum was in a right panic,' Beverly said. 'Started telling dad someone was outside throwing stones at the window. Then the lights were on and Dad was up and grumbling as he went to the window, and he's looking out and saying that there's nothing out there, that no one's throwing anything, and then he finds the fishing line!'

'You must have been grounded for months!' Matt said.

'I threw the end of the line out onto the landing,' Beverly said. 'Dad was following it but pulling it in so by the time he was outside the bedroom he had the end of it in his hand, so he had no idea who had done it, me or my sister.'

'Didn't he check?'

'I think he was just too tired,' Beverly said. 'And they never said anything in the morning either. I've never asked why. Sometimes I wonder if they just forgot, or maybe they were just amazed that one of their own kids could do such a well thought out trick. It was amazing how it worked, it really was!'

'And that's what you did at the Fletcher's, wasn't it?' Harry asked.

'I'm not proud of it,' Beverly said. 'I asked to be left alone, fixed up the line and weights, then had everyone back into the room. I've done it before and it's always worked.'

'So, you fake séances, then,' Matt said. 'Why would you do that?'

'No, I don't,' Beverly said. 'I don't fake them. I just add to the atmosphere a little. And it usually helps. It's like if you're watching a horror film and how it's always better if you turn the lights out, right? So, if you have something unexplained happen while you're doing a séance, then people are more open to it all and proper things happen, real experiences and phenomena. If they can accept a knocking at the window, then they can accept that perhaps the dead can and do want to communicate with us.'

'Sounds a bit dodgy, if you ask me,' Matt said.

'And what about the voices?' Harry asked. 'We've spoken to the family and they've all said about how you did something to sound different when you spoke.'

'That wasn't me,' Beverly said, her expression now firm and serious. 'I promise you that. Absolutely bloody terrified me.'

'But you've just told us that you faked the tapping at the window,' Matt said.

'I did,' Beverly said, 'but not the voice. That was new. It's never happened before. Like I said, it was bloody terrifying!'

'I think,' Harry said, 'I need to remind you that you are under caution.'

'I'm not lying!' Beverly snapped back. 'I know I'm under caution and I told you I faked the tapping! I've admitted that, haven't I? That fishing line, the weights, they're mine! Ask my parents how I did it as a kid if you don't believe me! I thought I'd picked it all up, but obviously not, because there it is. But it doesn't mean I faked the whole thing. I wouldn't know how! I had nothing to do with the fire!'

'I need to ask if you've ever been to the house before,' Harry said.

'Before when?' Beverly asked.

'Before your first visit,' Harry said. 'The family reported the sighting of an intruder on the property in the time between Helen's accident and last night.'

'What, and you think I was out there, do you, scouting around the place? Why would I do that?'

'Why would you fake a séance?' Matt asked.

Harry asked the question again, detailing the sightings that he and Matt, and Jen and Liz had responded to.

'It wasn't me,' Beverly said.

'And you can prove that?' Matt asked. 'Are you able to prove where you were at those times?'

'Do I have to?'

'If you can show you were somewhere else at the time, then it will be fairly obvious that you weren't on the property,' Harry said.

'Well, the second date I was at work,' Beverly said. 'I work at the private school in Sedbergh. The first, I'll have to double-check.'

Harry checked his watch. 'Then I'll leave you to do that with DS Dinsdale,' he said, bringing the interview to its official end he turned off the recorder and rose to his feet.

'So, I'm not under arrest?' Beverly said.

'No,' Harry said. 'However, we may have other questions to ask you, in light of the information you've provided, and if anything else comes to our attention.'

Harry left the room only to find Matt chasing after him.

'Everything alright, Boss?'

'No, it bloody well isn't!' Harry said, trying to rub the tiredness away from his eyes, and failing. 'What is any of this other than a complete mess that makes no sense to anyone? We're investigating a suspicious death by interviewing someone who reckons she can talk to the dead but at the same time admits to basically faking it! And we can't really arrest her on that, because she's not defrauding people out of money, and I doubt there's any link between her and the family other than James contacting her to do what she did!

So, where are we? No, don't answer, because I'll tell you. Nowhere at all, that's where!'

Harry took in a heavy breath through his nose, exhaling with the sound of an angry bull.

'Maybe it was suicide,' Matt suggested. 'I mean, it could've been, couldn't it?'

'No, I'm not buying that,' Harry said. 'Someone wants us to believe that, I'm sure, and all this stuff with James seeing things and the séance, well I think that's just given whoever it was a nice smokescreen to hide behind. But it's not enough. Something here just doesn't smell right, not right at all. In fact, it absolutely bloody stinks.'

'What, though?' Matt asked.

'Every last bit of it,' Harry said, and turned away, leaving DS Dinsdale alone in the corridor as PCSO Jim Metcalf entered the building.

'You got a minute, Boss?' Jim asked.

'No,' Harry said.

'Didn't think so,' Jim said. 'But I've just got back from chatting with Anthony.'

'Ruth's son?'

'Yeah,' Jim said.

'And?'

'And I think I've found our intruder.'

# CHAPTER TWENTY-EIGHT

Harry leaned back in his chair and stared at the ceiling.

'And you're sure about this?'

'He told me himself,' Jim said.

'So why didn't he or his mum admit it earlier, then?' Harry asked.

'A mix of things I think,' Jim said. 'Ruth was definitely very embarrassed, and to be honest, I don't think she connected the dots. You know, her dad thinking he'd seen her mum, and her son, Anthony, disappearing into the woods.'

Harry was getting a headache. And he didn't do headaches. 'Run me through it again,' he said, leaning forward to scratch Fly's head, the dog sitting between himself and Jim. 'Just so I'm clear.'

'Anthony's been having trouble at school,' Jim said. 'I think he's just found the whole teenage thing a bit much to cope with, like some do, you know? And he's drifted a bit from friends, bit of a loner I'm guessing.'

'So, he's been having time off school,' Harry said.

'Yes,' Jim said. 'Ruth's been covering for him, giving excuses. Sometimes he's up in his bedroom, other times he's out in the woods.'

'And you said he's got a little den out there or something?'

'It's some of his granddad's old military kit,' Jim explained. 'It's pretty cool actually. He's got a shelter, with a fire nearby, a little woodpile, some mess tins. I think he just goes out there to clear his head. It's not like he creeps around the house to get there. He just heads out if he needs to. Only Ruth knows about it. And I spoke with her and she said that her dad and her mum had no idea about it either, mainly because she didn't want them worrying about Anthony.'

'Still seems a stretch to me,' Harry said.

'She thinks she's the black sheep of the family,' Jim said. 'You know, the one with the divorce, the one still living with her parents, while her sister and husband are out there being all successful. Proud, I think. Wants to deal with things herself.'

'So, there's no intruder then,' Harry said. 'It was Anthony all along.'

'Well, yes and no,' Jim said. 'It was definitely him the second time, that's for sure, you know, when Liz and Jen went out to the house? But the first time, Anthony swears it wasn't him and that he was in his room the whole time.'

'And was he?'

'Can't prove it either way,' Jim said, 'but I can't see why he'd lie about it when it's already clear that the other time was definitely him. And he's nothing to gain from lying either, has he?'

'No,' Harry said, a grumbling rumble in his voice, 'I suppose not. What did he have to say about the séance?'

'Well, he's confirmed everything we know so far about it, the knocking at the window and whatnot. He actually saw her out of the house once it was all done.'

'And he went to bed right after, like everyone else,' Harry said.

Jim looked down at his notebook to check his notes. 'He saw his uncle and his granddad having a whisky together and then he went home with his mum.'

'And now, here we are,' Harry said.

'Oh, and he repeated what everyone else had said about the medium talking about the bright light, and he said that bit was the weirdest part of the whole evening.'

'How so?' Harry asked.

Again, Jim checked his notes and read from them. 'What Anthony actually said was, "*She said she saw a bright light on an empty road and it blinded her.*"'

'An empty road?' Harry said, remembering what Beverly had told him and Matt. 'He said that?'

'Yes,' Jim said, shaking his head. 'That's what she said to him apparently, just before she left.'

Harry had had enough and pushed himself up onto his feet. 'Well, thanks for going out to chat with him,' he said. 'And at least the whole intruder thing is cleared up.'

'What about the first time, though?' Jim asked.

'Could've been anything,' Harry said. 'I think James was under massive strain. You doing anything this evening, then?'

'Meeting up with Neil,' Jim said. 'He's coming over. You know, he's been over to visit my dad at least three times since it all happened.'

246 DAVID J. GATWARD

'That's good of him,' Harry said and made his way over to the door. 'You have a good evening then and send my regards to your dad. Tell him we're doing everything we can.'

'I will,' Jim said.

Outside, and walking back to his flat, Harry wished, not for the first time in his life, that doing everything he could came with results, because he was beginning to feel with the sheep rustling, and with what had happened out at Black Moss House, that they were getting nowhere at all.


THE FOLLOWING morning welcomed Harry with all the warmth and love of a ravenous wolf on the scent of an easy kill, and he sorely wished he could just stay in bed and find some of the sleep which had evaded him for most of the night. Ben was already off to work by the time he rose, and a breakfast of cereal and toast tasted like dust as he washed it down with strong coffee. The walk down through the marketplace was a thing of grey cold, as the wind seemed to howl at him out of every alleyway to snap at his heels and scratch at his bones. If this was a sign of the day to come, Harry thought, then it really didn't bode well at all.

Walking into the office, Harry was greeted with his huge mug, the one Matt had presented him with a few months ago, filled almost to the brim with steaming tea.

'Looks like you need it,' Matt said, as Harry took the mug from him.

'I need sleep more,' Harry said, sipping the liquid and burning his lip.

'Bad night?'

'The worst.'

'There's a lot going on,' Matt said. 'Oh, and just to add to your joy, Swift's been in touch and is on his way over.'

It really wasn't the news Harry wanted to hear. 'And when's he going to be here, exactly?'

'No idea,' Matt shrugged. 'He was delightfully vague about that bit. But he said it was important to speak to you, in person, I mean, rather than on the phone.'

Harry knew what it was about and was pretty sure it had nothing at all to do with the investigations the team were currently involved in. With the interview done, this had to be Swift driving over to tell him the news. And if he was looking to do it in person, then Harry couldn't help thinking that the news was bad.

'So, what have we got?' Harry asked, deciding it was best to just not think about Swift's impending visit. Instead, he looked around the office at the rest of the team, who were all more than a little busy, but who, at the sound of his voice, all stopped what they were doing and swivelled round to face him.

'This a morning briefing?' Jadyn asked. 'Because, if it is, I need to be over by the board.'

'No, it's okay,' Harry began, but he was already too late, Jadyn moving from his chair to the board in a single bound.

'Let's start with the thing over at Jim's farm,' Harry said.

'We're still waiting on the results from the cigarette butts I sent through,' Jadyn said. 'I'm pretty hopeful that'll turn something up.'

'Well, I'm glad one of us is,' Harry said.

'And that's about it,' Jim said. 'We're no further on with it. Dad's okay now, though, so that's something, and we've got the insurance company sorting through things. But it's not really about the money, not for dad.'

'Well, you never know,' Harry said. 'Hopefully, something will come from what Jadyn sent through.'

With nothing else to say on the matter, Harry moved things on to the death of James Fletcher.

'We now know that the intruder seen by James was actually Anthony, his grandson,' he explained. 'So, that clears that up. And we've interviewed under caution Beverly Sanford, the woman who led the séance. Not that we gathered much from that, other than to confirm what everyone else has said happened that evening.'

'So, is she still a suspect, then?' Liz asked.

'They all are,' Harry said. 'But not only have we no real idea of what happened, we're also lacking in motive.'

'I can't see why any of them would want to kill James,' Jen said. 'He's Ruth and Pat's dad, and Dan's father-in-law.'

'Agreed,' Harry said. 'And as far as we can ascertain, the first time Beverly and he made contact was when he called her to come over about doing the séance. So, let's just chat through everything from yesterday, and see if anything stands out.'

'Well, I don't see how it can be Anthony,' Jadyn said. 'He's only a kid, right?'

'Kids can kill,' said Matt.

'I know,' Jadyn replied, 'but I'm just not feeling it.'

'Feelings don't make good evidence,' Harry said. 'And remember, we've now identified that it was him that James saw. What if he was doing it on purpose?'

'And why would he do that?' Liz asked.

'Maybe he blamed his grandad for what happened to Helen,' Gordy said.

'Maybe they all did,' Jen said then looked at Liz. 'What was that thing with her eyes?'

'What, that she couldn't see well in the dark?'

'Yes, that,' Jen said.

'A whole family getting together to kill the father seems more like the stuff of Hollywood than Wensleydale, though, don't you think?' Harry said.

'It was Ruth that mentioned it though,' Liz said. 'The eyes thing. I'm not saying she said she blamed her dad for what happened, like, but . . .'

Harry picked up on Liz's pause. 'But what, Liz?'

Liz pulled out her notebook and flicked back through the pages. 'It was when I was talking to her, after we'd chatted to her dad,' she said. 'We were in the kitchen and she said about how her mum would generally only drive at night if it was a special occasion.'

'Which it was,' Harry said. 'It was James' birthday.'

'And she said,' Liz continued, 'that her mum would be alive if her dad had been driving.'

The room fell quiet for a moment as Liz's words floated in front of them all, demanding attention.

'She actually said that?' Jim asked.

'She did,' Liz said, 'but it's hardly an admission of guilt, is it? She felt awful for saying it, said that, too, actually.'

'Best jot it down,' Harry said to Jadyn, only to see that he already had. 'So, that leaves us with Pat, Dan, and the medium, Beverly.'

'What motive is there for Beverly?' Gordy asked. 'Like you said, the first contact she had with the family was when James contacted her. And her background hasn't thrown up anything weird, well, nothing other than the fact that she does what she does, but each to their own, right?'

'Maybe he figured out that she'd faked the whole thing,'

Jim suggested. 'What if he confronted her so she came back and—'

'Drugged him and burned him to death,' Matt said, finishing Jim's sentence. 'Bit of a stretch I think, but we can't ignore it as a very, very remote possibility.'

'That leaves us with Pat and Dan,' Harry said. 'So, what have we got on them?'

'They're backgrounds check out,' Matt said. 'Their businesses are on Companies House. I don't think they're worth as much as they would like everyone else to think they are, but most folk are like that, aren't they?'

'I'm not,' Harry said, looking over to Matt as his phone buzzed in his pocket.

'And there was me thinking you drove that old Rav4 of yours to show off.' Matt smiled.

Harry pulled out his phone and said, 'So, no motives there, either, then?'

'What if James actually did do it himself?' Jim asked.

Harry wasn't listening.

'Boss?' Matt said.

Harry was staring at his phone screen.

'Jim,' Harry said, 'didn't you say Anthony saw James and Dan having a whisky together?'

'Yes,' Jim said. 'That's what he said. Why?'

'Text from the pathologist,' Harry said. 'Those tablets of Dan's? They contain the same drug that was found in James' body.'

'But I thought she said they found no evidence that he'd taken any tablets,' Jadyn said.

'They didn't,' Harry said. 'But she also said that if the sleeping agent that knocked him out was from tablets—'

'Then they would've been crushed up first and mixed with the alcohol he was drinking,' Gordy said.

'Like a whisky, for example,' said Matt.

'Exactly like a whisky,' Harry said, and was up and out of the door before anyone could stop him, Matt chasing after him.

# CHAPTER TWENTY-NINE

'I know you don't want to meet up with Swift,' Matt said, as Harry swung the car over the bridge out of Appersett and on towards Black Moss House. 'Who does? But do you really need to drive like Jen to make sure of it?'

'There's nowt wrong with my driving,' Harry said.

'There's another for the tally,' Matt said.

The road was slick with water from a shower that had shot through the valley and Harry knew that he was pushing it as the tyres slipped a little.

'How many am I up to?'

'Well,' Matt said, 'you're about halfway between *Oh, I say* and *Ee ba gum.*'

'Was that you attempting to do a southern accent?' Harry asked.

'There's nowt wrong with my Queen's English,' Matt said.

'No, there isn't,' Harry said, 'but I'm from Bristol, remember? Somerset? I'm about as likely to say *Oh, I say* as I am to order caviar and champagne next time we go to the pub!'

'I thought everyone was posh down south,' Matt said.

'Trust me,' Harry said, 'if you come from a place where you ask directions with the words *where's that to, then?* I can assure you that the very last thing everyone is, is posh.'

Matt pointed ahead. 'There it is, Black Moss House.'

Harry saw that clouds were gathering on the hills behind the house, a thick gloom of grey and black, and beneath it the wispy ropes of rain thrashing against the earth below. He indicated off the main road and onto the lane leading up behind the house.

'You know, I've spent my whole life wondering what this house was like inside,' Matt said, as Harry pulled the car to a stop, 'and now, all I can think of is that I hope I'll never have to see inside it ever again.'

'It's quite a place, though,' Harry said, climbing out of the car and smelling the rain in the air.

'It is,' Matt agreed, 'but a bit too grand for the likes of us, I think.'

'And what do you mean by that?' Harry asked.

'No, you're right,' Matt said. 'If there's one thing about you I've noticed since you arrived here, it's that what you really hanker for is a massive house with a dozen bedrooms. Probably because it's all you talk about.'

'Yeah, sorry about that,' Harry said, then nodded at the huge sweep of fells behind Matt. 'Best we get in before that hits.'

The rain was falling unbothered by wind, just thick planks of the stuff falling to the ground, and Harry could see it approaching, marching almost, across the fields.

'Weird when it's like that, isn't it?' Matt said. 'I mean, what's that, probably no more than a couple of hundred metres away, is it? And it's pouring down. And yet here we are, over here, bone dry.'

'We won't be in about thirty seconds,' Harry said. 'Come on.'

At the back door, Matt stepped forward to knock. 'What approach are we going for?' he asked.

'This is further questioning,' Harry said. 'But I want him back at the interview room in Hawes.'

'Fair enough,' Matt said. 'And you're sure you don't want to arrest him?'

'Not enough to go on,' Harry said. 'Not yet, anyway. Which is why we need him over in Hawes.'

Matt knocked at the door as Harry's phone rang.

'Should've left it in the car,' Matt said.

'And I should've left it on silent and vibrate,' Harry said, and held up the screen for Matt to see.

'You'd best answer that,' he said.

Harry walked away from the door and lifted the phone to his ear. 'Good morning, sir,' he said.

'Grimm,' Swift said, 'did you not get my message that I was on my way over?'

'I did, yes,' Grimm said, 'but something rather urgent came up.'

'More urgent than your future?'

Harry didn't really know what to say to that, so went with, 'Are you at the office now, sir?'

'I am,' Swift said. 'And as you know, I'm not a fan of wasting my time. How long will you be?'

'Hopefully not too long,' Harry said. 'Just bringing someone in for questioning.'

'Then I'll stay here and wait for you.'

'You don't have to, sir,' Grimm said. 'Can you not just tell me what this is about now?'

'Well, it's probably best that we talk face-to-face and in private,' Swift said. 'That is why I've driven over here in the first place, after all.'

'I'll be as quick as I can,' Harry said.

'I'm very sure that you will,' Swift replied and hung up.

Harry made it back over to Matt just in time for the rain to hit, the door to swing open, and in its place, Dan standing and staring at them.

'Quick, get yourselves inside,' Dan said, as the rain fell against the side of the house, the huge drops thundering down to kick up crowns of dirt.

Harry followed Matt into the house and Dan closed the door behind them.

'That's come in pretty suddenly,' Dan said. 'Didn't think it was even forecast till later. But that's the dales for you, right? The only consistent thing about the weather is that it's inconsistent!'

Dan laughed then and Harry wasn't really sure what to do with his face, so he just left it as it was, not that it really helped.

'So, how can I help?' Dan asked. 'Pat's just nipped round to check up on Ruth. She was very upset yesterday. But everyone is, aren't they? I think everything just came crashing down on her, you know? Pat's worried it's a nervous breakdown. And she told us about Anthony as well, how he's been skipping school? Poor lad. He's gone today, though, so that's good, isn't it?'

'We'd like you to accompany us to the station,' Harry said, if only to stop the man from rambling on anymore, though referring to the rooms they used at the community centre in Hawes as a station was pushing it a bit, he thought.

'What, all of us?' Dan asked. 'I'll go and get Pat and Ruth.'

As Dan made to move, Harry held up a hand to stop him.

'No, just you, if you wouldn't mind?' he said.

Dan stopped dead.

'I'm sorry, what?'

'Just need to ask you a few more questions,' Matt said. 'So, if you could come with us now, it would be very much appreciated.'

Listening to Matt, it struck Harry then, just how strangely polite the police often were when dealing with crime of almost any kind. He'd lost count of the number of people he'd arrested more through polite discourse than persuasive action. Though, on a lot of those occasions he was sure that he would have felt considerably better using actions rather than words.

'Are you arresting me?' Dan asked. 'I thought I'd answered all your questions! What's this about? I don't understand!'

'It'll be easier for us to explain things over in Hawes,' Harry said.

'Why?' Dan asked. 'Why do we have to go there? You're arresting me, aren't you?'

'Please, Mr Hurst,' Matt said. 'It really is best for everyone if you just come along with us now.'

Dan started to back away.

'Mr Hurst,' Harry said. 'Dan . . . Please don't make this difficult.'

'I'm not going anywhere until you tell me what this is about.'

'There's really no need for this,' Harry said.

'You're absolutely right, there isn't!' Dan replied, taking another step away from Harry and Matt. 'I've done nothing wrong!'

'If that's the case, then this really won't take long at all,' Matt said. 'Now, come on, Mr Hurst. No more of this nonsense.'

For a moment, Dan stared at Harry and Matt, and Harry was almost hopeful that they were going to get him into the car with no more bother. Then the man spun on his heels and bolted.

'Bollocks!' Harry shouted and with Matt on his heels, chased after Dan down the hallway, only to see the man slip on the floor as a rug went from under him and sent him flying through a door with a painful yell.

Harry leapt after him only to land in the space where Dan had been and see the door slam shut, cracking him hard on the head.

Harry roared in pain as Matt reached down and pulled him to his feet.

'You okay, Boss?' Matt asked.

'No, I'm bloody well not!' Harry hissed through gritted teeth, rubbing his head.

'That looked sore.'

'Felt it, too,' Harry said. 'And it looks like we'll be changing our plan and arresting him after all,' he added. 'For assaulting a police officer!'

Matt thumped his hand against the door.

'Mr Hurst? You need to stop this now. Just open this door and come with us back to Hawes. You don't want to make it any worse for yourself.'

From the other side of the door, Harry heard furniture

being dragged across the floor. He pushed against the door and felt it give a little everywhere other than right at the top.

'Nowt like running away to make the police suspicious,' Matt said.

Harry looked up at the top of the door. 'Must be a latch or a bolt up there.'

'Really?' Matt said. 'Why?'

'Old house,' Harry said. 'Rooms change use over the years. Maybe it was a private study at some point.'

'Never thought of that,' Matt said.

'Only just thought of it myself.' Harry shrugged and pushed against the door again.

'You thinking what I think you're thinking?' Matt asked.

'We need to get in there now,' Harry said. 'He can't actually go anywhere, because the only way out other than this door are the windows out to the front, but I don't want him doing himself a mischief. He's in a panic and the last thing we need right now is our key suspect hurting himself.'

Matt leaned into the door. 'A good shove, then?'

Harry leaned in next to the detective sergeant. 'After three?'

When Harry shouted, 'Now!' both men heaved against the door. Harry felt enough resistance to make him think that the door was going to hold, only to have it then give way, the latch above them snapping in half, sending them both sprawling into the lounge. And there, standing on the other side of the room, panic scratched into his face, was Dan, armed with a bottle of whisky.

# CHAPTER THIRTY

'Probably best you don't do anything stupid, Mr Hurst,' Matt said.

'Bit late for that,' Harry muttered, then said, 'Whatever you're thinking of doing with that bottle of whisky, I suggest you unthink it, and quickly.'

'I'll throw it!' Dan said. 'I will!'

'And you'll miss,' Harry said. 'But go ahead, be my guest.'

Harry saw Matt turn to stare at him, confusion on his face.

'He won't throw it,' Harry said. 'He's not a complete idiot.'

The bottle flew between them and Harry was too surprised to say anything as it hammered into the wall and shattered.

'I stand corrected,' Harry said, then turned to face Dan. 'Mr Hurst,' he roared, 'you are now under arrest for assaulting a police officer, resisting arrest, and throwing a bottle of good whisky at a wall!'

'I'm not sure that last one's actually a crime, Boss,' Matt said.

'Well, it is now!' Harry said, and started to march over towards Dan, who had now backed himself into a corner.

'Pat's going to kill me,' he whimpered, as Harry drew close.

'I'll be honest with you,' Harry said, 'I think that right now you've got other things to be more concerned with, don't you?'

'It was a bottle she brought with us, for her dad,' Dan said. 'An expensive one as well. Tasted wonderful. And I only had one glass.'

'And now it's all gone,' Matt said, coming to stand beside Harry and pulling out a pair of handcuffs. 'Which is a shame, I have to say. Now, on to more pressing matters, Mr Hurst. Which means, I'm afraid, that I'm going to have to read you your rights.'

Harry stepped back as Matt did as he had said, noticing the tang of the spilled whisky in the air.

'I'm sorry,' Dan said, as Matt secured the cuffs on the man's wrists. 'I . . . I just panicked. I didn't mean to run. And I'm sorry about throwing the bottle. I'm a terrible shot anyway. I didn't mean to. I don't know what I was thinking.'

Harry wasn't listening. He was staring at the smashed bottle of whisky.

'Come on then,' Matt said to Dan. 'Best we get you into the car. Boss?'

Harry didn't answer. He was staring at the whisky bottle and the weary matter in his head was churning now, trying to bring far too many things together at once.

'Boss?' Matt said again. 'You okay?'

Harry turned away from the whisky and looked at Dan. 'What was it you just said about this whisky?'

'That it is, or was, a good one,' Dan replied.

'No, not that,' Harry said. 'You brought it for James, yes?'

'Pat did, yes,' Dan said. 'She's never bought me one that good.'

'And where's Pat now?' Harry asked.

'Next door, with Ruth,' Dan said. 'I'm surprised she's not back, to be honest. Perhaps Ruth is in a bad way still.'

Harry turned and strode out of the lounge.

'Boss?' Matt called out.

'You stay with Dan,' Harry called back, breaking into a run back down the corridor. At the back door, he realised that he should've gone the other way, taken the front door, because it was more direct, and he skidded to a halt, knocking into a small shelf at the side of the door. Something fell off and clunked down onto the floor. It was Dan's torch and instinctively Harry reached down to pick it up, switching it on, just to check that it still worked. The beam from the torch blasted out into his face and Harry dropped the torch, momentarily blinded.

Swearing, and rubbing his eyes to clear them of the blotches now floating in front of them, Harry stumbled outside and into the rain, to make his way around to the cottage Ruth lived in with Anthony. It wasn't exactly easy for him to see, either, with the rain still coming down, and the near blindness he was now temporarily suffering from thanks to the torch. And then, as he reached the front door of Ruth's house, he remembered what Beverly had said about what she had seen the night of the séance, what she had said to Anthony as she'd left the house that night, about a bright light and the empty road.

Harry crashed through the front door of the cottage.

'Ruth? Pat?'

No answer.

Harry swept around downstairs, checking the lounge, the dining room, the kitchen, all empty.

'Ruth?' Harry cried again. 'It's DCI Grimm! Pat? We need to talk!'

Harry moved to the stairs and started to climb. They were narrow and steep and forced him to lean a little to the right, sliding his shoulder along the wall.

As he climbed, he thought back through everything, trying to sift through it, to make sense of it somehow, but it wasn't easy, not by a long shot. But what had happened with Dan, with the whisky, that had set his synapses aflame, and his thoughts came at him burning hot.

At the top of the stairs, Harry was faced with a small landing and four doors. The first door was open, leading into what was very obviously a bathroom. It was empty, he was sure, but he still checked, just in case. Then he moved on to the next room.

'Ruth? Pat?' Harry called again, and pushed open the door into another empty room. Two doors to go . . .

Harry stood between the remaining doors. He knew that whichever one he chose, it was going to be the wrong one. That was just the way of things, wasn't it? So, he wasted no time, didn't even call out, and kicked open the door to his left.

The door burst open, hammering into the wall. Ruth was lying curled up on a double bed. At her side was a glass of water, half empty. Harry dashed over to her, checked for a pulse. It was faint, but it was there.

'Ruth? Ruth! It's Harry!'

There was no response.

'Ruth!'

Harry pulled out his phone, punched in a call. 'DCI Grimm! I need an ambulance here quick! Looks like an overdose!' He then gave the address and hung up.

'Ruth?' he said, trying again. 'It's okay, there's an ambulance on its way. You just hang on, okay? Don't you go doing something stupid like dying!'

A sound from the other bedroom, the one he hadn't yet checked, caught Harry's attention. He quickly put Ruth into the recovery position on the bed and was on his feet and out of the door just in time to see the shadow of a figure sweeping down the stairs. Harry reached over the bannister from the landing but caught only a snick of cloth.

'Pat! Stop!' he shouted, hauling himself around and down the stairs after the figure. 'Just bloody well stop, will you? Stop!'

At the bottom of the stairs Harry saw that the front door was swinging open and he charged through it, out into the rain once again. Only it was worse now, thick and heavy, and a wind had come along and was twisting it into tumbling waves, which crashed into Harry, making it difficult to see.

Harry looked across the lawn, saw nothing, then a raw yell hacked its way through the storm and he snapped his head left, to the darkness between the two buildings, to the sunken courtyard. The rain stabbed at his face, stinging his eyes as he raced towards what he had heard, a sound of stark, violent fear. Then the sunken courtyard was in front of him and there, lying in its embrace, was the body of Patricia Fletcher, her face staring up at him, a thick pool of red spreading out from the back of her head, the rain already washing it away.

Harry dropped down into the courtyard, fell at Patricia's

side, knew that there was no life in those eyes, but still checked, just to make sure, because that's what you did. But there was no pulse and Patricia was gone, and Harry slumped back against the wall of the courtyard, cold and wet to the skin, as Patricia's blood made its slow way towards him, steaming a little in the cold.

# CHAPTER THIRTY-ONE

HARRY WAS SITTING IN THE PUBLIC BAR OF THE Fountain Hotel in Hawes. The first time he'd been there had been with Liz and Matt a few weeks ago to discuss a case, play darts, and drink beer. This time, darts was definitely not on the menu, of that he was certain.

'You didn't need to drive all this way just to speak to me,' Harry said, staring across the table over the top of his pint. 'A phone call would've been fine, I'm sure.'

'I disagree,' said Detective Superintendent Alice Firbank, taking a sip from her gin and tonic. 'And I needed an excuse to get away for the weekend, so here I am!'

'But I'm fine,' Harry said.

'Yes, but are you, though?' Firbank said. 'You've had rather a lot on of late, wouldn't you agree?'

'I would, yes,' Harry said, 'but that's just life, isn't it? I'm not saying I don't appreciate the visit, I do, it's just that I'm not one for fuss, as I'm sure you know.'

'I do,' Firbank said, 'but this isn't a fuss, it's a professional courtesy that I've taken full advantage of.'

Harry knew there was no arguing with Firbank so he took a deep gulp of his beer, a pint of Butter Tubs, the same as the last time he'd been there, and said, 'Well, thank you, Ma'am. It's appreciated.'

'Good,' Firbank said. 'It's never easy when an investigation ends up as messy as the one you and your team have just had to deal with.'

'No, you're not wrong,' Harry agreed.

'And there's nothing you could have done. You know that, don't you?'

'I do,' Harry said.

'You don't sound very convincing.'

Harry slumped back a little on his stool. 'If I'd checked that other room first, then Patricia, she would be alive, wouldn't she? That's a tough one to swallow, that's all.'

'You don't know that,' Firbank said. 'Patricia made her own choices.'

'And I made mine and now she's dead,' Harry said.

'But her sister isn't,' Firbank pointed out. 'If you'd gone into that other room first, for all you know Ruth might not have made it.'

Harry's response was a low, rumbling grumble.

'How is she, by the way? And the rest of the family?'

'She's back home,' Harry said, 'with Anthony.'

'And Patricia's husband?'

'He's staying around for a while, I think,' Harry said. 'The poor bloke, having to deal with all of that.'

'And he had no idea at all?'

'Apparently not,' Harry said. 'They didn't really share anything it seems, you know, like a normal couple. He had no idea just how badly her last business had gone south. And it had taken a load of her investments with it.'

'Desperate times, desperate measures,' Firbank said.

'I don't think she was close to her dad,' Harry said. 'And I'm guessing she couldn't see another way out. She knew they were heading out on his birthday, Dan was away, so she drove up and waited for them to head home.'

'Inheritance does funny things to people,' sighed Firbank. 'And she was on the phone to her dad when the crash happened?'

Harry gave a shallow nod. 'That was the one thing I couldn't work out, how she'd know exactly where they'd be and when. Amazing what you can find when you check someone's phone records, isn't it? And she didn't mention it when we interviewed her, which is hardly a surprise, is it?'

'Not really, no,' Firbank said.

'I'm not even sure that she was actually trying to kill them,' Harry said. 'Maybe she was just trying to cause an accident, force their hand into selling up and sharing out the money. But that torch really did a number on her mum and instead of a small crash, well, the worst happened, didn't it?'

'Then, it sounds like it just became a case of in for a penny, in for a pound,' said Firbank.

'She saw an opportunity and took it, I guess,' Harry said. 'Drugged her husband with the same stuff she'd used on her dad, Dan's own sleeping tablets, so that she could sneak out, I'm assuming to ply her dad with even more whisky, before setting the place on fire. As evil plans go, it wasn't a bad one. Ruth was lucky to survive her supposed suicide.'

'I understand that it doesn't feel right though,' Firbank said. 'Sort of unfinished, because there's no arrest, no trial, nothing. Just a broken family.'

Harry nodded, had nothing to say, took another mouthful of his beer. 'Where are you staying?' he asked.

'At The Herriot,' Firbank said. 'You spoke so highly of it, so I thought, why not?'

'Watch the breakfasts though,' Harry said. 'They're terrifying.'

Firbank pulled something from a bag she had resting to one side on the floor.

'Here,' she said, sliding a plain brown envelope across the table towards Harry. 'Various bits and bobs to sign, to make it all official. Assuming you're still decided, that is?'

'I am,' Harry said, reaching out for the envelope.

'And Ben?'

'He's fine about it,' Harry said. 'Happier, I think, now that the decision is made. Bit of stability, you know?'

'Everyone needs it,' Firbank said, then she reached for her gin and tonic and finished what was left, before getting to her feet.

'For what it's worth,' she said, looking down at Harry, 'I think this is possibly one of the best decisions you've ever made.'

'You're only saying that because you'll miss me.'

'I will, Harry,' Firbank said, 'but not necessarily for all the right reasons.'

Harry wasn't exactly sure what the DSup meant by that.

'Any plans for the weekend?' Firbank asked, picking up her bag.

'Matt's taking Ben caving,' Harry said. 'So, I'll be waiting for them in the car with a good book and a flask of something hot and sweet.'

Firbank laughed. 'A book? What has happened to you, Grimm?'

'Wensleydale,' Harry said with a smile.

Then Firbank was gone and Harry was alone with his beer.

For the next few minutes, as he finished his drink, Harry did his best to avoid thinking about everything that had happened over at Black Moss House, but it wasn't easy. It had all ended up just too messy, really, but then it had been a strange one from the off, hadn't it? And he was fairly sure that from this point forward, if there was any hint of an investigation involving anything supernatural, he'd be doing his best to convince Detective Superintendent Swift to take it on instead.

Standing up, Harry finished his pint and made his way over to the door, pushing his way out into the Friday evening air. The day was finishing off cold, with ice in the wind, and Harry turned into it to head home. As he did so, his phone buzzed in his pocket, as he'd put it on silent while chatting to his soon to be ex Detective Superintendent. He answered it without looking at the number.

'Grimm?'

'Harry, it's Jim.'

'It's Friday evening,' Harry said. 'You do know that, don't you? You're not even on duty!'

'I know,' Jim said, 'but I didn't know who else to call.'

Harry heard then the worry in the PCSO's voice. 'Jim?' he said. 'What's up? What's happened?'

'It's Neil,' Jim said.

'Neil?' Harry said. 'What about him? What's happened?'

'He's dead.'

And Harry's Friday night swirled about him as, at the end of the line, he heard Jim start to cry.

HARRY and his team return in the thrillingly dark *Death's Requiem*

---

## JOIN THE VIP CLUB!

SIGN up for my newsletter today (at davidjgatward.com) and be first to hear about the next DCI Harry Grimm crime thriller. You'll receive regular updates on the series, plus VIP access to a photo gallery of locations from the books and the chance to win amazing free stuff in some fantastic competitions.

You can also connect with other fans of DCI Grimm and his team on Facebook by joining The Official DCI Harry Grimm Reader Group.

---

### Enjoyed this book? Then please tell others!

The best thing about reviews is they help people like you: other readers. So, if you can spare a few seconds and leave a review, that would be fantastic. I love hearing what readers think about my books, so you can also email me the link to your review at dciharrygrimm@hotmail.com.

## AUTHOR'S NOTE

The dales are hauntingly beautiful and will stay with you long after you leave. Even now, over thirty years later, I can still walk the same paths and lanes in my mind, and the fresh, crisp air of an April morning will easily send me back to the footpath that leads through the fields from Hawes to Gayle, which I would tread every Sunday afternoon with my brother, as we walked to Sunday School.

So, why a ghost story? Well, I saw my first ghost when I was fifteen. I was doing my Saturday job of mowing the lawn at The Old Rectory in Epworth, a house famous for its own haunting in the 1700s. The day was bright and warm and I was plugged into my headphones listening to the KISS album, Crazy Nights. As I mowed long strips into the huge lawn I looked up to see, standing under an enormous tree, a figure in a black suit and black hat, hands crossed in front of his body, looking at me. I looked up again, the figure was gone. I turned the mower off, leaving it in the middle of the lawn, and went home, returning later that day to finish it. But

I was always wary of the place afterwards. I saw my second ghost when I worked at Marrick Priory, over in Swaledale. I was 18, living in a static caravan on site. I woke up one night to find the caravan lit with light and standing inside was a woman in a corseted dress, hair pulled up behind her head. I've had other similar experiences, too, but as to an explanation? That I cannot provide.

The story here is from one I remembered from living in the dales (and I even checked up on it with an old friend to make sure!) I didn't want it to be just a ghost story, but more an exploration of what grief and stress can do to the mind and how we react to it. Whether I've achieved that is for you to decide, but I certainly had a lot of fun writing it.

The house exists, under a different name, and once again I wanted the dales to be as much a character in the story as the people you get to meet in these pages. Cotter Force is a sight to behold, and well worth the walk, and when you happen upon it, it is hard to believe that such a place can exist and is not so famous as to have a ticket booth and a car park! But then, that's the beauty of it, I think, that it is a hidden gem and requires a modicum of effort to go and find.

The small village of Burtersett is a beautiful little place, and Jim's family farm is one a friend of mine lived in when we were children (I dedicated book one, Grimm Up North, to him and another old school friend). I remember visiting it, wandering around the fields, the farm. And the auction mart, which I'm sure will feature again, was a mainstay of my own father's life when we lived there. It really is worth a visit. You may feel a little out of place, wandering around the pens, surrounded by animals and farmers, but you will be walking through the very essence of the dales, I promise you. And when you leave, I have no doubt that a little piece of the dales will go with you, and those memories, like ghosts, will haunt you, and you will sure to want to go back.

# ABOUT DAVID J. GATWARD

David had his first book published when he was 18 and has written extensively for children and young adults. *Restless Dead* is his fifth crime novel.

Visit David's website to find out more about him and the DCI Harry Grimm books.

f facebook.com/davidjgatwardauthor

ALSO BY DAVID J. GATWARD

THE DCI HARRY GRIMM SERIES

Grimm Up North

Best Served Cold

Corpse Road

Shooting Season

Death's Requiem

Blood Sport

Cold Sanctuary

One Bad Turn

Blood Trail

Fair Game

Unquiet Bones

Made in the USA
Monee, IL
25 July 2023

39889618R00157